Henry James's
Permanent Adolescence

John R. Bradley

PS
2127
.P8
B7
2000

First published 2000 by
PALGRAVE
Houndmills, Basingstoke, Hampshire RG21 6XS and
175 Fifth Avenue, New York, N.Y. 10010
Companies and representatives throughout the world

PALGRAVE is the new global academic imprint of
St. Martin's Press LLC Scholarly and Reference Division and
Palgrave Publishers Ltd (formerly Macmillan Press Ltd).

ISBN 0–333–91874–6 hardback

This book is printed on paper suitable for recycling and
made from fully managed and sustained forest sources.

A catalogue record for this book is available
from the British Library.

Library of Congress Cataloging-in-Publication Data
Bradley, John R., 1970–
    Henry James's permanent adolescence / John R. Bradley.
        p. cm.
    Includes bibliographical references and index.
    ISBN 0–333–91874–6
    1. James, Henry, 1843–1916—Knowledge—Psychology.
    2. Homosexuality and literature—United States—History.
    3. Psychological fiction, American—History and criticism. 4. James,
    Henry, 1843–1916—Characters—Men. 5. James, Henry, 1843–1916–
    –Psychology. 6. Adolescence in literature. 7. Narcissism in literature. 8.
    Young men in literature. 9. Desire in literature. 10. Boys in literature. 11.
    Sex in literature. I. Title.
    PS2127.P8 B7 2000
    813'.4—dc21
                                                        00–033338

10   9   8   7   6   5   4   3   2   1
09   08   07   06   05   04   03   02   01   00

Printed and bound in Great Britain by
Antony Rowe Ltd, Chippenham, Wiltshire

For
Kelvin

Contents

Textual Note

Since this book traces the chronological development of the stylistic and structural treatment of a particular theme in James's fiction, quotations are from the first published magazine or book versions rather than from the often heavily revised *New York Edition of the Novels and Tales* (1907–9). The exception is *The Ambassadors*. The New York Edition of the novel now in print has the benefit of having the chapters in the correct order, and with this late novel the question of chronology is less of an issue anyway: it was published during the same decade in which it was revised, and the revisions to the sentences (as opposed to the arrangement of chapters) were not extensive.

List of Abbreviations

The following abbreviations refer to works by Henry James, which are cited parenthetically in the text. Full references to the editions used are given in the bibliography.

A	*The Ambassadors*
AB	'The Author of *Beltraffio*'
AC	*The Art of Criticism*
AM	*The American*
AP	'The Aspern Papers'
AUT	*Autobiography*
BJ	'The Beast in the Jungle'
C	*Confidence*
DL	'The Death of the Lion'
DM	'Daisy Miller'
DMF	'The Diary of a Man of Fifty'
GGP	'The Great Good Place'
HJG	*Letters of Henry James to Edmund Gosse*
HJL	*Henry James Letters*
HJLL	*Henry James: A Life in Letters*
IC	'In the Cage'
LM	'A Light Man'
TP	'The Pupil'
PL	*The Portrait of a Lady*
RH	*Roderick Hudson*
TOS	'The Turn of the Screw'
TM	*The Tragic Muse*

1
Critical Hostility

Henry James famously did not believe that there was a need to include the explicitly erotic in fiction. Concentrating on sex in isolation, he wrote, led to a failure to convey the way intercourse in the bedroom is related to diverse events, and the broad motivations behind them, in the wider social world:

> That sexual passion from which [D'Annunzio] extracts with admirable detached pictures insists on remaining for him *only* the act of the moment, beginning and ending in itself and disowning any representative character. From the moment it depends on itself alone for its beauty it endangers extremely its distinction, so precarious at the best. For what it represents, precisely, it is poetically interesting; it finds its extension and consummation only in the rest of life. Shut out from the rest of life, shut out from all fruition and assimilation, it has no more dignity than – to use a homely image – the boots and shoes that we see, in the corridors of promiscuous hotels, standing, often in pairs, at the doors of rooms. Detached and associated these clusters of objects present, however obtruded, no importance.[1]

This commentary has been taken by unsympathetic readers of James – most conspicuously Max Beerbohm, who parodied James's comments on D'Annunzio in a cartoon[2] and wrote elsewhere of how James 'does not deal with raw humanity, primitive emotions'[3] – as symptomatic of an imagined voyeurism and prurience; but James clearly did not criticise the depiction of sex acts merely

1

because of sexual inhibition. He considered a sole focus on the 'detached pictures' of 'sexual passion' to be an *imaginative* failure. What it 'represents' is indeed 'poetically interesting', but only what it represents, because it 'finds its extension and consummation only in the rest of life'. This is theoretically consistent with James's best-known remark on the craft of novel-writing in 'The Art of Fiction' (1884), written 20 years before the essay on D'Annunzio appeared: 'I cannot imagine composition existing in a series of blocks, nor conceive, in any novel worth discussing at all, of a passage of description that is not in its intention narrative, a passage of dialogue that is not in its intention descriptive, a touch of truth of any sort that does not partake of the nature of incident, or an incident that derives its interest from any other source of the success of a work of art – that of being illustrative' (AC, 174).

Unsurprisingly, James found distasteful the idea that his own personality could be summed up with the deprecating label 'homosexual' – by his being categorised as a male, that is to say, who wished to engage in sexual acts solely with other males. As if, one can easily imagine him thinking, *that* could be taken as a 'beginning and ending in itself and disowning [of] any representative character'. And in pointing out the lack of conceptual justification for a sole focus on sexual acts, he still does not necessarily seem eccentric or prudish, as there are writers in our age of 'gay rights' – such as Gore Vidal – who refuse to use the word 'homosexual' as a noun rather than strictly as an adjective.[4]

Recently, however, and largely as a result of biographical speculation by Sheldon M. Novick, critics have been probing the extent to which James may in fact have engaged in homosexual sexual activity. Novick himself is of the opinion that James had a sexual relationship, whilst still a young man at Cambridge, with his close friend (and later Supreme Court Judge) Oliver Wendell Holmes. He quotes one of James's late reminiscences as evidence:

> The point for me (for fatal, for impossible, expansion) is that I knew there, had there, in the ghostly old C. that I sit and write of here by the strange Pacific on the other side of the continent, *l'initiation première* (the divine, the unique), there and in Ashburton Place ... Ah, the 'epoch-making' weeks of the spring of 1865.[5]

Jamesians have reacted to Novick's hypothesis with characteristic guardedness. Millicent Bell's review of the biography argued the standard line that the experience recalled James's elation at having received his first payment as a writer. Her implication is that Novick's scholarship is bad, and that James moreover is done a disservice by the homosexual insinuation.[6] In a reply, Novick pointed out that Bell acted 'as if she were the defence counsel for James, insisting that every particular of an indictment of sexual misconduct be proven beyond a reasonable doubt, and darkly hinting at the prosecutor's malfeasance'. He also remarked that James's homosexuality has been 'an open secret' for at least a century, and he asked why, if the reference was about a sum of money James had received, the incident had remained, even 50 years later, 'impossible' to reveal because of unspecifiable 'fatal' consequences.[7] Novick's interpretation is plausible, but it is not of course indisputable: despite the thoroughly researched biographical context, he may have read into the passage too much significance, as it is stylistically self-indulgent in a way typical of late James. The hostility Novick's biography generated can itself, however, be taken as symptomatic of the defensive or dismissive tone often adopted by Jamesians when they are presented with criticism exploring homo-erotic undercurrents in James's life and writing.

Philip Horne has attacked 'queer theorists' – particularly Eve Kosofsky Sedgwick and her imitators[8] – for what he terms 'the abuse of speculation', which he summarises as follows: '(1) James writes about the unnameable; (2) homosexuality has often been spoken of as unnameable; (3) James therefore means homosexuality when he refers to something unnameable.'[9] Lyndall Gordon unreservedly endorsed Horne's essay by writing in her own biography of James of how there have 'been "closet" readings of *The Aspern Papers*, "The Pupil" and "The Beast in the Jungle", but Philip Horne has demolished scaffolds of supposition constructed without one firm fact'.[10] 'Demolished' is antagonistic, and is more importantly unjustified: Horne does not even discuss *The Aspern Papers* (1888) or, in any detail, 'The Beast in the Jungle' (1903), and I have argued elsewhere in an essay listed by Gordon but ignored in the main body of her text[11] that Horne's approach raised at least as many questions about biographical speculation as it endeavoured to answer, and at times bordered unpleasantly on the homophobic – as when he asks, for example, what we should do, 'as literary critics, with biographical homosexuality even when established'. Surely the question is what one should do with *any* kind of biographical sexuality? Why single out homosexuality for special consideration and rules? Horne himself attempts to answer this question by musing on the fact that 'there's a good deal of confusion about what it means to be "homosexual", what homoerotic means, etc'; but with that ominously vague 'etc', this sentence seems more concerned with creating further confusion and barriers than with attempting to establish a useful definition. Nor does Horne acknowledge that, within gay studies, there is considerable debate about the quality and worth of Sedgwick's work. The most striking and eloquent example is an essay by David Van Leer, which calls into question the validity of Sedgwick's very methodology and accuses her of (amongst other things) unconscious homophobia, having difficulty in dealing with anything but homosexual stereotypes, and effectively reducing 'gay self-knowledge to a camp'.[12]

The refusal by Bell, Horne and Gordon to engage with gay criticism in anything other than a discouraging manner leaves them vulnerable to charges of double standards. For instance, Gordon's insistence on the need for 'firm facts' whenever James's homosexuality is discussed is exposed as rather dubious when she paradoxically states in the first chapter of her own biography that 'James's awareness of buried possibilities, the gifts of the obscure, and gaps between the facts, invites the infinite challenge of his own life ...'[13] This is the rationale behind the methodology underpinning Gordon's subsequent speculation about James's relationships with Mary Temple and Constance Fenimore Woolson, the chief subject of her biography; and she writes unambiguously about how she will approach James's life 'at precisely the points he screened' it.[14] Elsewhere, with reference to Novick's belief that James was meaningfully homosexual, Gordon again bullishly asserts that no 'formal proof has so far come to life' and adds that Novick unsuccessfully tries 'to prove that HJ was an active homosexual from the mid-1860s ...' The argument, she writes, 'is not based on provable evidence but on a tissue of supposition ... Informed scholars will know that he wrote also in ardent tones to women ... We cannot safely demarcate his sexuality; those who try to do so have a predetermined political or critical agenda which, I believe, will soon date.'[15] One is reminded of Novick's comment about Bell acting as James's 'defence counsel' by insisting that 'every particular of an indictment of sexual misconduct be proven beyond a reasonable doubt'.

For Gordon, there are more clearly two kinds of rule. The first, strict one applies to those who discuss James's homosexuality and requires 'firm facts', 'formal proof' and 'provable evidence'. The second, looser rule applies to those who, like Gordon, Bell and Horne, discuss exclusively James's entanglements with females. Then the only requirement is the mere 'awareness of buried possibilities, the gifts of the obscure, and gaps between the facts'. The reference by Gordon to 'informed scholars' is simple offensive and obstinate; but more significant is that it is followed by a bizarre claim that all critics attempting to 'demarcate' James's sexuality (this presumably refers principally to his probable homosexuality) have 'a predetermined political or critical agenda'. Novick, for one, has no such agenda, and in a recent essay[16] – where, incidentally, his discussion of how 'facts' and 'proof' relate to the biographer's art is strikingly similar to Gordon's own[17] – he writes that it is unfortunate that James should have been dragged into the culture wars. Equally unfounded is Gordon's assertion that all essays on James's homosexuality 'will soon date'. Incisive, unrelated articles have been appearing since the 1960s, and although Gordon seems blissfully unaware of this body of critical work, it has collectively suffered no more or less from the passage of time than have essays on any other aspect of James's fiction.[18]

Novick has written about how a supposed 'absence of passion and jealousy' in James's life 'has been treated as a vacuum and filled in all sorts of ways' to avoid dealing with the evidence of his homosexuality.[19] Gordon's theories about the need not to explore James's homosexuality are perhaps the most extraordinarily resourceful yet to appear, and certainly the most flawed:

> An undisguised attraction to young men declared itself later in James's life. How early he felt this is not known; nor is there proof of commitment. The ease of his expressiveness to men in an age when deviance (as it was seen) was punishable by law, suggests that, for James, there was a significant difference between imaginative desire – extending to hugs and kisses – and consummation ... To label him would be reductive; suffice to say

he aimed to use the full human endowment, displacing the distorted manhood his father had imposed on his fighter sons.[20]

There is an awkward shift away from 'undisguised attraction' to young men towards the dogmatic reference to an assumed lack of 'proof of commitment'. We might ask what precisely could constitute 'proof of commitment' in a time when open cohabitation was not a realistic option for male lovers who were sensitive, as James always remained, to the possibility of public exposure. If we accept as an acceptable working definition of 'proof of commitment' a 'deep emotional reciprocation, the sustained and expressed desire to be in one another's company, and a documented desire to embrace', then there is undoubtedly greater evidence of 'commitment' in James's letters to younger men later in his life than there is in the extant ones between James and Gordon's principal female subjects, Temple and Cooper. The double standards which earlier characterised Gordon's arguments about 'evidence' are found again when a need for 'proof' is casually abandoned in favour of psychological waffle grounded entirely (as much as it is grounded in anything) on 'suggestion'. 'The ease of his expressiveness to men in an age when deviance (as it was seen) was punishable by law,' Gordon claims, 'suggests that, for James, there was a significant difference between imaginative desire – extending to hugs and kisses – and consummation ...' Has there ever been a person for whom there was not a 'significant difference between imaginative desire ... and consummation'? Gordon is flatly contradicted, in any event, by James's own commentary on the relationship between sexual acts and the creative imagination, in his essay quoted above on D'Annunzio. There, in a truthful inversion of Gordon's theory, James links the social with the sexual by stating that 'a sole focus' on the 'detached pictures' of 'sexual passion' is an imaginative failure *precisely* because what it 'represents' is 'poetically interesting' when it 'finds its extension and consummation only in the rest of life'. Gordon's other distinction, between 'hugs and kisses' and 'consummation' (presumably anal intercourse), serves no purpose other than to distance James arbitrarily from what Gordon does not want him to be associated with. The idea that a person is to be judged as having or not having had homosexual inclinations and emotional attachments *purely* on the basis of whether he buggered or was buggered (or for that matter engaged in any kind of sexual activity) is absurd. Again, Novick is in agreement that James probably disapproved of buggery.[21]

By trying to avoid the obvious, Gordon gets herself into yet more difficulties. The polarity she establishes between James's physical behaviour in the company of young men and what was condemned 'by law' as 'deviance (as it was seen)' is incontestably erroneous: by the time James began the friendships with younger men to which Gordon alludes two laws had been passed by Parliament. The Criminal Law Amendment Act of 1885 had extended legal prohibition of the act of sodomy to virtually all male homosexual activity or speech, whether in public or private; and the Vagrancy Act of 1898 had made even homosexual soliciting illegal.[22] Hugs and kisses would therefore have provided sufficient evidence for James to have been prosecuted as 'a homosexual', and since James followed closely the trials of Oscar Wilde[23] – who was initially charged, it will be remembered, merely with 'posing' as a sodomite, and who was eventually prosecuted under the Criminal Law Amendment Act of 1885 – he would have known that his own private acts could have been used against him in a court of law. To a neutral observer, then as now, James's behaviour would have 'suggested' his homosexual propensity, so the 'evidence' cited by Gordon reveals him to have been someone determined to indulge his homosexual propensity *despite* the intrusiveness of anti-homosexual laws into the private sphere.

To label James, Gordon concludes, 'would be reductive'. It must 'suffice to say' that 'he aimed to use the full human endowment, displacing the distorted manhood his father had imposed on his fighter sons'. That sentence lacks common sense if related to James's (or indeed anyone's) libido, and is at best tenuous (and at worst baffling) if related to his broader personal and social life. James's attachments to young men in his later years cannot be approached through his (unprovable, by Gordon's earlier criteria) 'displacing the distorted manhood his father had imposed on his fighter sons', whatever that means, because it is the kind of biographical reductionism Horne would rightly have referred to in another context as the 'abuse of speculation'.

When viewed alongside her unyielding critical stance and general tone of animosity, these arguments by Gordon, like those of Horne and Bell before her, warrant by way of response the accusation that she is (perhaps unconsciously) homophobic. As far as 'facts' are concerned, it is irrefutably the case that she stubbornly adopts double standards. The cause of her hostility, however, is likely to have been ignorance, rather than prejudice. This is revealed by the fact that she underpins almost every statement she makes on the subject with citations to the essay by the hostile Horne, and even his newspaper reviews. Horne, Bell and Gordon's attempt to prevent serious discussion of James's homosexuality, in any case, is as misguided as any attempt to claim James as a representative homosexual would be, because unearthing a concern with homo-sexuality in James's life and writings should not be viewed as an attempt to invalidate all other lines of inquiry, and *vice versa*. A failure to recognise this fact is the mistake made by Lee Siegel in an otherwise penetrating essay which echoed Horne's more valid concerns about (as Siegel puts it) the negative influence of 'Sedgwick, the mother of queer theory, and her chief disciple Michael Moon' on literary criticism in general and James studies in particular. Much of queer theory, writes Siegel, 'is partly about the more militant gay-liberationist goals of the 1960s "passing" into the tortured sexual readings of the 1980s and 1990s', and both Sedgwick and Moon are said to offer ludicrous and critically inept readings of James's fiction.[24] Siegel's essay has been cited by critics sympathetic to the need for a greater understanding of James's gay-inflected life and writing as being part of a backlash against all gay readings of James;[25] but there is little if anything in the following extract from it that could be objected to in terms of homophobia or the general trivialisation of gay studies:

> Why am I being so hard, so mean? Because the result of Sedgwick's inestimable influence has been, among her followers – all of whom either are college teachers or will some day be college teachers – a deadness, not just to beauty and fineness of perception and fragile inner life, but also to human suffering. [Michael] Moon's new book, *A Small Boy and Others*, is interesting only as an illustration of this.
>
> Of the seven chapters in Moon's book, three are concerned with Henry James. (*A Small Boy and Others*, in fact, is the title of one of James's autobiographies.) In James's wonderful story 'The

Pupil', the touching and fairly uncomplicated relationship between a tutor and a young boy named Morgan in his care reveals, in Moon's expert hands, each one's sexual desire for the other. The story is not about what James seemed to have meant it to be about: two injured souls supporting each other amidst the shabby genteel Moreens' cruel manipulations of both the tutor and their son. And it is the boy's mother, Moon has discovered, who has extended to the tutor the 'invitation to desire Morgan'. This, Moon tells us, is because the mother herself has probably been engaging in incest with her eleven-year-old boy.

Moon works up this last point by patiently and calmly explaining that the *'gants de Suède'* that Mrs Moreen draws through her hands are made in material that is described as 'undressed kid' in 'English-language guides to proper dress from midcentury forward'. And 'kid', Moon discloses, also means 'child'. (Impressive references to William Morris and the Earl of Shaftesbury drive home this point.) 'Undressed kid, therefore, means 'undressed child'. Get it?

It follows from this that, in having Mrs Moreen draw her gloves through her hands, James wants us to understand that she is unconsciously reenacting sex with her son. What role incest plays in this story, though, Moon never tells us. He merely 'recuperates' it in this one isolated moment. And he never returns to it, which is not surprising, since a work of art can no more be split up into atomized particles than pleasure can be isolated from emotion, meaning, and value.

Having fattened Moon up for the kill, Seigel proceeds to carry out the execution:

As if to acknowledge this technical obstacle, Moon goes on to draw a helpful conclusion from the story. With a kind of eerie remoteness, he writes:

Like little Morgan and his tutor and the other 'small boys' and young men that figure in these texts, we all often find ourselves possessing what seems to be both more knowledge than we can use and less than we need when we try to think

about such difficult issues as our own relations to children
and young adults, especially our students ...

Comparing James's 'The Pupil' to the film *Blue Velvet*, Moon
describes Dennis Hopper's brutal beating of Kyle Maclachan as
representing 'the two men's desire for each other that the newly
discovered sadomasochistic bond that unites them induces them
to feel'. How the Master would have loved that scene! Midnight
Cowboy, moreover, is not about the shelter of intimacy that the
physically crippled Dustin Hoffman and the physically wounded
Jon Voight find with each other away from economic and sexual
confusions; it is, says Moon, 'about how two men can have a
meaningful S-M relationship without admitting to being
homosexuals' ...

   In *A Small Boy and Others*, the seventy-year-old James writes
about how, as a young boy visiting the Louvre, he 'felt myself
most happily cross that bridge over to Style constituted by the
wondrous Galerie d'Apollon ... a prodigious tube or tunnel
through which I inhaled little by little, that is again and again, a
general sense of the glory'. Professor Moon has an orals question
about this passage: ' What's large enough for one to walk
through but small enough to take into one's mouth?' And so the
young James and his tutor are having sex. And the older James
goes to a Yiddish play on the Lower East Side perhaps because he
wants to have sex with the famous Yiddish actor Boris
Thomashefsky. And on, and on, and on, and on.[26]

The point that Siegel misses is that one could convincingly argue
that gay readings of James's stories and novels are valid *without*
producing this sort of nonsense, or indeed while agreeing with
everything Siegel writes. *Henry James's Permanent Adolescence*
demonstrates how, by focusing on character, plot, structure, style,
historical context and sensible biographical speculation, and authorial intention we can achieve not only valuable gay readings of
some of James's most important novels and tales (including, incidentally, 'The Pupil'), but also reveal that they cannot intelligently
be appreciated without such an emphasis. While not blindly antagonistic to queer theory and gay studies, this book approaches the
relationship between James's sense of manhood in his early years

and his affection for men throughout his later life by way of an exploration of what we can say we understand James to have known about same-sex attraction, and how his social environment and his personality – or, more precisely, his *ever-changing* social reality and personal identity – were mirrored in the stylistic treatment of the theme in his fiction.

There is a great deal of historical and biographical evidence that reveals James as having been confidently aware of his homosexuality from his adolescence. There is textual evidence that shows he consistently dealt with the subject in his fiction. The intention in the chapters that follow is to enter into James's homosexual consciousness. There is no wish to deal with the unrelated and, for me, largely irrelevant issue of whether James was or was not sexually active, a subject on which there is indeed no clear evidence. What follows is not a bland assertion that 'because James wrote about the unnameable he therefore wrote about homosexuality', but an inquiry into a documentable and central aspect of James's life and writing.

2
Defining James's Homosexuality

One evening around the turn of the nineteenth century, in the garden of Lamb House, Henry James revealed to Edmund Gosse what the latter assumed to be one of the novelist's most intimate secrets. 'As twilight deepened and we walked together,' Gosse was later to recall,

> I suddenly found that in profuse and enigmatic language [James] was recounting for me an experience, something that had happened, not something repeated or imagined. He spoke of standing on a pavement of a city, in the dusk, and of gazing upwards across the misty street, watching, watching for the lighting of a lamp in the window on the third storey. And the lamp blazed out, and through bursting tears he strained to see what was behind it, the unapproachable face. And for hours he stood there, wet with the rain, brushed by the phantom hurrying figures of the scene, and never from behind the lamp for one moment was visible the face. The mysterious and poignant revelation closed, and one could make no comment, ask no question, being throttled oneself by an overpowering emotion. And for a long time Henry shuffled beside me in the darkness, shaking the dew off the laurels, and still there was no sound at all in the garden but what our heels made crunching the gravel, nor was the silence broken when suddenly we entered the house and he disappeared for an hour.[1]

Hugh Walpole was also famously confided in, some years after Gosse, when James fleetingly explained to him that, sexually, he had 'suffered some frustration'. 'What that frustration was I never knew,' Walpole later wrote, 'but I remember him telling me how he had once in his youth in a foreign town watched a whole night in pouring rain for a figure at a window. "That was the end," he said, and broke off ...'[2] By offering a meaningful account of an event of significance only teasingly to break off before giving the crucial details, James was treating himself as if he were a protagonist in one of his late novels. Walpole, too, may have been being disingenuous, for what he did or did not know about James's 'sexual frustration' is open to debate. He told Stephen Spender, for example, how on another evening at Rye he had offered himself to James, to be refused with the words: 'I can't! I can't!'[3] James also wrote to Walpole more abstractly about his feeling of having in some sense when he was young given up on living fully. 'I think I don't regret a single "excess" of my responsive youth,' he said. 'I only regret in my chilled age, certain occasions and possibilities I *didn't* embrace.'[4] And in a letter to Merton Fullerton late in 1900, he was more specific in stating that his loneliness had always been, from his own point of view, the 'deepest thing' about himself:

> The port from which I was set out was, I think, that of *the essential loneliness of my life* – and it seems to be the port also, in sooth, to which my course again finally directs itself! This loneliness (since I mention it) – what is it still but the deepest thing about one? Deeper, about *me*, at any rate, than anything else; deeper than my 'genius', deeper than my 'discipline', deeper than my pride, deeper, above all, than the deep counterminglings of art.[5]

James's memoirs reveal that, up to the very end of his life, he cultivated a sense that, to quote F.W. Dupee, 'his present self [was] continuous with his past self' (AUT, xiv). His secretary, Theodora Bosanquet, wrote that no 'preliminary work was needed' before James began dictating his life-story; that it was 'extra-easy for him to recover the past'.[6] The first volume, *A Small Boy and Others* (1913), was originally intended as a series of recollections about his recently deceased elder brother, William, but instead became an account of James's own early years to the extent that his brother was narratively marginalised and does not appear in his own right as an objectively portrayed individual. James was enraptured by a sense of his own past. This is more apparent in *The Middle Years* (1917), in which he describes having to 'wrench' himself 'with violence from memories and images, stages and phases and branching arms, that catch and hold me as I pass by' (AUT, 551). In the opening chapters, the subject often moves away from the actual details of James's past to how James understands such experiences to be retrospectively transformed through memory, and how this process has invested that lived reality for him with an imaginative and almost mystical power:

> I foresee moreover how little I shall be able to resist, throughout these Notes, the force of persuasion expressed in the individual *vivid* image of the past whenever encountered, these images having always such terms of their own, such subtle secrets and insidious arts for keeping us in relation with them, for bribing us by the beauty, the authority, the wonder of their saved intensity. They have saved it, they seem to say to us, from such a welter of death and darkness and ruin that this alone makes a value and a light and a dignity for them, something indeed of an argument that our story, since we attempt to tell one, has lapses and gaps without them. (AUT, 511)

The contrast is between a present memory of certain moments of epiphany in the past and an otherwise general regret for a 'welter of death and darkness and ruin', and in *A Small Boy and Others* James acknowledges that his vocation as a writer resulted in his going 'without many things, ever so many – as all persons do in whom contemplation takes so much the place of action ...' (AUT, 476). As with T.S. Eliot,[7] there is a general impression that, when he reached his final years, James felt ambiguously about sacrifices made for his art. This is perhaps best summed up in the piece of advice the protagonist of *The Ambassadors* (1903) famously gives to Little Bilham – it 'doesn't so much matter what you do in particular, so long as you have your life. If you haven't had that, what *have* you had?' (A, 153). James had more reason, in one respect, than did Eliot for gloominess, because he failed both commercially and financially to achieve the kind of success his dedication to his art had warranted.[8]

The contrast between contemplation and action is compounded by the fact that towards the end of his life James spent much of his time actively revising and commenting on the writing that had resulted from his past years of inactivity. Between 1905 and 1907 he revised much of his fiction for inclusion in the *New York Edition of the Complete Tales and Novels* (1907–9), and in composing his prefaces and rewriting his earlier sentences James was obviously immersing himself in his creative memory in as intimate a way as could have been possible. Sedgwick has located a narcissistic, homo-erotic consciousness this process related to:

> The James of the prefaces revels in the same startling metaphor that animates the present-day literature of the 'inner child': the metaphor that presents one's relation to one's own past as a relation*ship*, intersubjective as it is intergenerational. And, it might be added, almost by definition homoerotic. Often the younger author is present in these prefaces as a figure in himself, but even more frequently the fictions themselves, or characters in them, are given his form ... James certainly displays no desire whatever to become once again the young and mystified author of his early productions. To the contrary, the very distance of these inner self-figurations from the speaking self of the present is marked, treasured, and in fact eroticized. Their distance (temporal, figured as intersubjective, figured in turn as spacial) seems, if anything, to constitute the relished internal space of James's absorbed subjectivity. Yet for all that the distance itself is prized, James's speculation as to what different outcomes might be evoked by different kinds of overture across the distance – by different forms of solicitation, different forms of touch, interest, and love between the less and the more initiated figures – provides a great deal of the impetus to his theoretical project in these essays. The speaking self of the prefaces does not attempt to merge with the ... younger self, younger fictions, younger heroes; its attempt is to love them.[9]

James remained the type of homosexual Freud characterised as introspective, focused on adolescent boys and young men, and on his own adolescence and early manhood, in an attempt to recapture the lost sense of a real, defining self first encountered during sexual awakening.[10] As Sedgwick says, it is the 'distance of these inner self-figurations from the speaking self of the present' that is 'marked, treasured, and in fact eroticized'. Novick has charted the physical solitariness and emotional detachment James experienced in his youth, remarks that 'almost from the moment he began to construct his secure, private little self, he felt the pain of loneliness', and shows that even at the age of 24 James's 'intimate life was locked in solitude and secrecy'.[11] In his biography, he links a series of remembrances, mostly contained in James's late memoirs, that have to do with James's early attachments before the moment when it appears he may have abandoned the idea of forming openly sexual relationships. An adolescent friendship with Gus Barker anticipated the nature of the cautiously intimate friendships James would continue to experience with younger men and boys and with a similar competing sense of denial and acceptance. By James's own account, when he first saw Gus in his military cadet uniform the latter was an exceptionally beautiful 12–year-old – red-headed, athletic and mature for his years. In 1864, when James was 19 years old, he called on his older brother William and John La Farge in the studio they were sharing, and found that they had placed Gus naked on a pedestal. James could have stayed, since he was prac-tising painting at the time; but in his confusion he walked out. He later saw Gus at Harvard, and again was struck by his elegance. This time, however, he did not greet him. A few months later he learned that Gus had been killed in the American Civil War. James had earlier asked William for the portrait of naked Gus, which he kept for the rest of his life.[12]

John Carlos Rowe has warned of the dangers of 'equating homo-erotic, adolescent, and gay sexualities', states that 'gay sexuality is not ... a "reversion" to adolescent homoerosis', and argues that moreover 'homo-erotic desires' are not 'exclusively expressions of gay sexuality'.[13] Freud of course believed homosexuality to be a symptom of arrested development, an opinion few would now endorse;[14] but there is an equal danger, when dealing with this subject, posed by political correctness. This could result in avoiding what Jonathan Freedman has established, by explaining, in his book on James's responses to aestheticism, how James's 'idealised, if not necessarily chaste, eroticising of the adolescent male is precisely the form taken by upper and upper-middle-class British homosexual discourse of the late 19th century'.[15] Richard Dellamora has similarly emphasised that a focus 'on boys by men who are attracted emotionally, and sometimes sexually, to other males is a leading figure of homo-erotic writing in the final third of the [19th] century'.[16] Throughout western literature, men are shown simultaneously to long for youths and their own youth, and to seek an ideal fusion of the resulting sexual longing and emotional nostalgia. In this sense, Freud was labelling what had been apparent to educated people for centuries.[17] But while he was right to establish such a pattern of behaviour as important for many homosexuals – Forrest Reid too has written of how material (in writing as in life) may be cyclically deployed, in his case specifically the material of homosexuality and adolescence, as when the onset of adulthood leaves the eponymous gay hero of his novel *Peter Waring* 'hopelessly shut into the little circle of my own desires and feelings'[18] – Freud was of course mistaken in believing that he was dealing only with universal human traits when he was dealing as well with socially constructed and defined behaviour. From a post-gay liberation perspective it seems hardly surprising – given what were then profoundly inhibiting external pressures of law and society – that homosexuals such as James slipped into a voluntary kind of self-suppression, and that there was a shared feeling amongst homosexuals of his generation that it was perhaps inevitable that opportunities for sexual and emotional fulfilment might not be granted. In such circumstances, glimpses of happiness could easily necessitate a return, psychologically, to a period of adolescent homosexuality and male camaraderie, before a differentiation brought about by the realisation of sexual individuation was complicated by an unsuccessful initiation into adult heterosexuality. On the other hand, there is also the universal fact that, for many homosexuals, boys and youths are considered more beautiful than older men, and that moreover an admiration of youth is a way of capturing a sense of lost youth in a narcissistic process which, for obvious reasons, would be more common to those who are attracted to members of the same sex. As Peter Swaab succinctly says in a similar context, in an essay about Gerard Manley Hopkins's admiration of boys, the 'problem for boy-enthusiasts is of course that boys won't always be boys'[19] – and, one might add, that they themselves are no longer boys. Whatever the social circumstances, whatever the psychological interpretation, the biological ageing process will always be an important and probably depressing factor for homosexual men absorbed by the beauty of increasingly indifferent – or at least in every way more distant – male youths. As I show in subsequent chapters, it is in just such a context of narcissism and retrospectiveness that James most frequently explores homosexuality in his fiction.[20]

In *Enemies of Promise* (1938), Cyril Connolly offers a theory of narcissistic homosexuality that is useful as a starting point in an attempt to define further James's own retrospective homoeroticism. 'Were I to deduce my feelings on leaving Eton,' Connolly wrote, 'it might be called *The Theory of Permanent Adolescence*.' He elaborated that 'the experience undergone by boys at the great public schools, their glories and disappointments, are so intense as to dominate their lives and to arrest their development. From these it results that the greater part of the ruling class remains ... homosexual.' Early laurels, he claimed, 'weigh like lead and of many of the boys whom I knew at Eton, I can say that their lives are over'.[21] The specific subject matter is not directly related to anything James experienced, but there is a faint echo of his recollection to Gosse and Walpole about the youthful incident marking the emergence of his 'sexual frustration', and both writers are equally aware that momentous youthful events can be defining. There is the disappointment at lost opportunities, at the passing of youth. In *The Middle Years*, James himself noted how some men remain, like himself, forever young:

> We are never old, that is we never cease easily to be young, for *all* life at the same time: youth is an army, the whole battalion of our faculties and our freshness, our passions and our illusions, on a considerably reluctant march into the enemy's country, the country of the general lost freshness; and I think it throws at least as many stragglers behind as skirmishers ahead – stragglers who often catch up but belatedly with the main body, and even in many a case never catch up at all. (AUT, 547)

The recollection Novick took to signify James's loss of virginity with Holmes, and thus to mark his sexual *'initiation première'*, is interesting in this context because of the way James again recalled the early, defining experience so many years after the event with a retrospective obsessiveness. There is the peculiar suggestion in this phrase that the experience recalled was repeatedly returned to and relived, as if always for the first time. For what initiation does *not* represent a *first* experience?

At the turn of the century James fell in love with a series of young men and achieved with them a certain level of homosexual contentment. He also, in the narcissistic pattern, used their company to compensate for his lost youth. Leon Edel wrote of James's love for Jocelyn Persse that it was 'of an ageing man for his own lost youth, and the evocation of it in a figure of masculine beauty',[22] and if Edel's reticence about James's homosexuality is remembered and James's attraction is consequently seen in a homo-erotic context, this observation becomes a valuable characterisation of late James as the kind of retrospective homosexual given defini-tion by Freud. Edel offers a similarly cautious, but nevertheless intriguing summary of the way in which James's meeting with Hendrik Anderson in 1899 in many respects corresponded to a broader pattern of nostalgia and narcissism, and was intimately related to his creative self:

> It was in Italy, where James went in 1899 after finishing *The Awkward Age*, that his vulnerable self finally experienced the sensations of love, the body's insistence on active tenderness ... Italy had always been a land of sensual delight: in his youth he had characterized it as 'a dishevelled nymph'. In Rome, in the Spring of 1899, the nymph materialized as a young American sculptor, of Norwegian descent, blond, strong, with vigorous hands that modelled clay and carved statues – not very good statues, but that mattered little to Henry James. Hendrik Anderson reminded James of the time when he himself was young and had created a fictional sculptor in this very city whom he named Roderick Hudson; he had endowed Roderick with so many tantrums of passion that he destroyed himself after falling in love. James saw in Anderson a reflection of his own early inventions – a reflection of himself as creator in his own youth.
>
> (HJL: 4, xvi)

The letters James sent to such men are love letters, overflowing with sensual and emotional yearning. They reinforce the impression given by Edel that while falling in love with others, James was falling in love with his younger self. None of the letters is sexually explicit in a crude sense; and none so far published refers to an event that could easily be interpreted as a sexual union.[23] Two extracts from those James sent to Anderson, in 1902 and 1906 respectively, are representative:

> *In* my deep hole, how I thought yearningly, helplessly, dearest Boy, of *you* as your last letter gives you to *me* and as I take you to my heart ... Now, at least, my weak arms still can feel you close. Infinitely, deeply, as deeply as you will have felt, for yourself, was I touched by your second letter ... Let yourself go and *live*, even as a lacerated, mutilated lover, with your grief, your loss, your sore, unforgettable consciousness. *Possess* them and let them possess you, and life, so will still hold you in her arms ... I respond to every throb of it, I participate in every pang ... I only, for goodnight, for five minutes, take you to my heart ... think only of my love and that I am yours always and ever.
>
> (HJL: 4, 227–8)

> In spite of the paralyzing chill of age & infirmity I am very sorry indeed to miss the chance of you that I had so hoped for ... To console me for your failure to materialize I hang up *here*, in my room, that admirable sidelong photograph of you that I have had at Lamb House these several years & place under it the Jacob wrestling with the Angel – so I feebly have you about.[24]

In the first letter the *representation* of Anderson is the object of James's affection. '[H]ow I thought yearningly, helplessly, dearest Boy, of *you* as your last letter gives you to *me*.' The italicised '*you*' and '*me*' are syntactically separated by the contents of the letter, which provide the emotional link. Only after establishing this does James say he takes Anderson 'to' his 'heart', and it is the photograph of Anderson, in the second extract, that acts as a similar emotional go-between. The reference to the sculpture of Jacob wrestling with the Angel is partly ironic – surely even James's trial of strength after his disappointment is not properly to be so compared – but it also creates an objective correlative for James's expression of his need for physical intimacy. The contrast between James's (in the first extract) 'weak arms' and (in the second) 'age & infirmity' on the one hand, and the youthful vibrancy of Anderson – whom he thinks of as a 'Boy', the standard Victorian gay euphemism for a young beloved[25] – on the other, is obvious. It lends a poignancy to the yearning in both, and reinforces the relevance of the idea of him being defined by his 'permanent adolescence'. James's advice – to 'Let yourself go and *live*, even as a lacerated, mutilated lover, with your grief, your loss, your sore, unforgettable consciousness. *Possess* them and let them possess you, and life, so will still hold you in her arms' – is paralleled by his own wish to live through that youthful energy and enthusiasm. 'I respond to every throb of it,' James confesses. 'I participate in every pang.'

How did James come to terms with his homosexuality? The evidence indicates that the self-knowledge he acquired in America did not have an association with scandal or overt disapproval. Steven Seidman writes that in Victorian America '[r]omantic friendship or love between women and, to a lesser extent, love between men, was [*sic*] fairly typical and carried no trace of wrongdoing or shame'.[26] In his youth James read the whole of Balzac, and Novick notes that he could hardly not have been struck by that most 'fascinating' of the men and women of Balzac's Paris, the 'squat, powerful, perversely attractive Vautrin', a 'lover of boys'.[27] Again, the impression must have been that writing about such things did not compromise one's literary or social standing, even in Europe: Balzac was France's most popular literary novelist. It is also worth recalling how in itself it had not been noteworthy that John La Farge and William James had placed 12–year-old Gus Barker naked on a pedestal in their studio. Later in Victorian England, as 'decadent' writers and artists became notorious for their pederasty while the new mass media reported homosexual scandals, the idea of naked young boys being admired in however artistic a context would increasingly lose its veneer of respectability. But in America, in the 1860s, it appears to have been the male physique, the classical context, that would have been the justifying context for La Farge and William's admiration of the young boy, and a private homosexual motivation in James's wish to keep the drawing evidently went either unrecognised or was accepted without negative comment.

The principal literary source of James's knowledge of homosexuality in America was Walt Whitman, and his espousal of male camaraderie. The manliness of *Leaves of Grass* had proved so valuable a shield for its homo-eroticism that Whitman could deny the existence of the latter sentiment years later,[28] and when James negatively reviewed the 1865 edition it was bad poetry he had objected to; the 'camaraderie' he accepted.[29] So it appears that James learned the rule that if there was no perceived threat to established notions of masculinity, there was unlikely to be any focus on the potentially subversive homosexual feelings. Edel explains that James was teased by William from an early age about being a 'sissy boy', meaning that he was unable to join in normal 'boyish pursuits', and that this resulted in James being acutely self-conscious about his masculinity, even to the extent that he was troubled by the 'loss of masculinity' implied in homo-eroticism.[30] Novick has shown that James remained hostile to effeminate men, whether homosexual or not, for the rest of his life,[31] and this dislike of effeminacy in men would be as important an influence on him as his admiration of masculine homosexuality would be.

James's literary knowledge of homosexuality was extended in Europe by his discovery of Walter Pater and John Addington Symonds, who saw in the rise of the study of the classics at Oxford from the 1840s an opportunity surreptitiously to explore the emerging modern concept of homosexuality.[32] James discovered Pater's *Studies in the History of the Renaissance* (1873) in a bookshop in Paris in 1873.[33] He may have met Pater as early as 1877, through a mutual acquaintance, and in the 1880s they were frequently introduced at literary parties.[34] His interest in Pater's life and letters remained sufficiently deep for him to be able to write a critical summary of his achievements when Pater died in 1894.[35] Pater's 'Winckelmann' chapter set a gay standard which others imitated. He argued that, as one of the first serious students of classical and Renaissance art, Winckelmann established an 'affinity' with eighteenth-century Hellenism in a way that was not merely intellectual:

> that the subtler threads of temperament were interwoven in it ... is proved by [his] romantic, fervent friendships with young men. He has known, he says, many young men more beautiful than Guido's archangel. These friendships, bringing him into contact with the pride of human form, and staining the thoughts with its bloom, perfected his reconciliation to the spirit of Greek sculpture.[36]

James also met, and read books authored by, Symonds (HJL: 3, 31). As England's first homosexual apologist to publish a defence of same-sex attraction, he outlined the Greek pederastic model to promote the virtues of what he saw as the natural manliness and intrinsic democratic qualities of homosexuality. Symonds also translated Michaelangelo's sonnets (restoring the male pronouns deleted from earlier editions) and wrote a life of the painter in which he also discussed homosexuality;[37] and his multi-volume *The Renaissance in Italy* (1875–86) – for which he was best known during his lifetime – similarly provided him a context in which he could explore homosexual themes, to the extent that he was criticised for making the project shape to 'his own desires and frustrations'.[38] As, most notoriously at the time, did *Studies of the Greek Poets* (1873; 1876), a passage in which Symonds believed cost him the position of Professor of Poetry at Oxford.[39] 'Greek mythology and history,' he had written, 'are full of tales of friendship, which can only be paralleled by the story of David and Jonathan in the Bible ... Among the noblest patriots, tyrannicides, lawgivers, and self-devoted heroes in the early time of Greece, we always find the names of friends and comrades received with peculiar honour.'[40]

Because in the 1860s and 1870s James lacked a contextualising vocabulary for homosexuality it now seems almost inevitable that he would have viewed adolescent male friendship as a special period allowing for innocent and undefined male bonding, and that the classical world written about by Pater and Symonds, coupled with the idea of homo-erotic 'manliness' in Whitman's poetry, would be for him important signifiers for same-sex attraction.[41] James related to his own private passions at this time in such terms, as is evident from an 1876 letter he wrote to his sister, Alice, about the Russian dilettante Paul Jukowsky, where he relates his affection to the classical and Whitmanesque ideal of an 'eternal friendship':

> The person I have seen altogether most of, of late, is my dear young friend Jukowsky, for whom I entertain a most tender affection. He is one of the pure flowers of civilization and Ivan Sergéitch says of him – 'C'est l'epicurien le plus naif que j'ai recontré' (I.S. likes him extremely). A sense of 'human fellowship' is not his forte; but he is the most – or one of the most –

refined specimens of human nature that I have ever known, a
very delicate and interesting mind ... [having] a great deal of
amiability and elevation of disposition – a considerable déver-
gontage of imagination and an extreme purity of life ... as a
figure, taken together, he is much to my taste, and we have
sworn an eternal friendship.

(HJL: 2, 49–50)

In 1898 James couched a discussion of Whitman's letters to a young
man in terms learned by Symonds and with the same use of the idea
of an 'eternal' friendship:

The person to whom, from 1868 to 1880, they were addressed
was a young labouring man, employed in rough railway work,
whom Whitman met by accident – the account of the meeting,
in his correspondent's own words, is the most charming passage
in the volume – and constituted for the rest of life a subject of
friendship of the regular 'eternal' – the legendary sort ...
Whitman wrote to his friend of what they both saw and touched,
enormities of the common ... and the record remains, by a
mysterious marvel, a thing positively delightful. If we ever find
out why, it must be another time. The riddle meanwhile is a neat
one for the sphinx of democracy to offer.[42]

In the penultimate sentence, James acknowledges that only in
'another time' will the nature of such 'positively delightful' male
friendships be able to be discussed openly, and the final sentence
admits that for the time being these friendships will have to remain
a 'riddle'. This is contextualised by an allusion to Whitman's
'sphinx of democracy', a concept based on a homo-erotic ideal of
male camaraderie outlined in *Democratic Vistas* (1877). In writing
that 'If we ever find out why, it must be another time', James was
acknowledging that, for him during his own lifetime, such open-
ness would remain for him impossible. But by 1898 he was aware
of other options, having read Symonds's second *apologia* for
pederasty, *A Problem of Modern Ethics* (1891),[43] which included a
long quotation from Whitman's *Democratic Vistas* explicitly
evoking those 'threads of manly friendship' and the related
concept of democracy to which James had alluded. Whitman had

concluded: 'I say democracy infers such loving comradeship, as its most inevitable twin or counterpart, without which it will be incomplete, in vain ...'[44]

James never raised the issue of homosexuality explicitly in the public domain; the closest he got to direct reference was in his classical allusions. As late as 1905 there was a related and revealing incident with the Irish novelist Forrest Reid, who had dedicated his novel of that year, *The Garden God*, to James as a 'slight token of my affection and admiration'. The story is concerned with memories of an English boarding school education which had been centred on the study of the Greek and Latin classics. The narrator remains attached to his adolescent schooling and the historical Greece he was then introduced to, largely because of a doomed, defining love affair at the time with another pupil. He fits the pattern of 'permanent adolescence' in the way that many other of Reid's protagonists do. Immediately James learned about this dedication, he broke off his correspondence with Reid. He also insisted that the dedication be removed.[45] In his autobiographical volume *Private Road* (1940), Reid complained that there was an injustice in James's response to his novel, since he did not object to being associated with Howard Sturgis after the latter published a novel, *Tim* (1891), which was similarly concerned with the love of two Eton boys.[46] Reid failed to understand that for James, as far as pederasty was concerned, a personal acceptance of a literary, trusted friend did not lead to his willingness publicly to be associated with his socially stigmatised type.

Many of James's contemporaries dutifully related to him in precisely the classical terms he used as a public cover. Urbian Menguin, a late friend of James, also distinguished between James's acquaintance with classical representations of homosexuality and his fervent need for the company of younger men. While he admits that James 'was never shocked to read about the customs of the Greek and Latin poets', he cannot imagine

> HJ submitting himself – yes, we must use the word submit – to such customs ... HJ would have a horror of the physical act ... Certain of his friendships, leanings, gestures, could, I know, make one think he was submitting himself ... but those gestures were in themselves a signal, and I'd say a proof, that he wasn't

capable of this kind of surrender. His affectionate manner of groping your arm, or of patting you on the shoulder, or giving you a hug – he would never have done this if his gestures had, for him, the slightest suggestion of a pursuit of physical love.[47]

It is extraordinary that the contrast between James's refined, classically educated tolerance of homosexuality and his presumed asexual actual existence has remained the obfuscating perspective adopted by those of James's critics eager to distance him from any kind of suggestion that he was meaningfully homosexual.[48] The opposite is true. In 1889, for example, James purchased in Rome a bust of a beautiful young boy, Count Alberto Bevilacqua. The sculptor was Hendrik Anderson; the creation apparently resembled him. Two weeks after James arrived back in Rye, the bust was delivered, and he wrote to Anderson:

> I shall have him constantly before me, as a loved companion and friend. He is so living, so human so sympathetic and sociable and curious, that I see it will be a lifelong attachment . . . I have struck up a tremendous intimacy with dear little Count Alberto, and we literally can't live without each other. He is the first object that greets my eyes in the morning, and the last at night.
>
> (HJL: 4, 108–9, 113)

The 'tremendous intimacy' James seeks is expressed through a reference to a classical work of art, which acts, in its presence during defining moments of James's daily routine, as a kind of surrogate lover. The classical statuette is invested with emotional qualities, 'human' and 'sympathetic' and 'social' and 'curious', which are the sort of attributes James wished to find in Anderson; and Anderson was presumably supposed to recognise himself as the longed-for 'loved companion' and 'friend', as well as that the statuette's presence was paralleled by James's desire to be alone with him at Rye.

By the Victorian period the countries of southern Europe – particularly James's beloved Italy – had acquired, along with the Orient, a reputation amongst northern European homosexuals as safe havens where an outlet could be found for potentially scandalous urges. The most famous literary example is Lord Byron, for

James the supreme authority of the Romantic Movement.[49] Later nineteenth-century writers of independent means, such as Oscar Wilde and André Gide, similarly took to travelling to classical or Oriental locations while keeping a cautious eye on Northern European customs and laws.[50] Wilfred Thesiger's *Arabian Sands* (1959), written in the tradition of nineteenth-century Oriental travel literature, contains an archetypal encounter with a boy:

> [He] was dressed only in a length of blue cloth, which he wore wrapped around his waist with one tasselled end thrown over his right shoulder, and his dark hair fell like a main about his dark shoulders. He had a face of classic beauty, pensive and rather sad in response, but which lit up when he smiled, like a pool touched by the sun. Antinous must have looked like this, I thought, when Hadrian first saw him in the Phrygian woods. The boy moved with effortless grace, walking as women walk who have carried vessels on their heads since childhood. A stranger might have thought that his smooth pliant body would never bear the rigours of desert life, but I knew how deceptively enduring were these Bedu boys who looked like girls.[51]

Rana Kabbani has argued that this passage 'contains a great many 19th-century themes', and that 'the concentration on the boy's beauty would have appealed to a Victorian reader'.[52] One can imagine it appealing to James. We know of two of his encounters with Italian boys discussed in similar classical contexts – the first was relayed by James himself in a travel essay of 1873 on Venice, the other by Mrs Humphry Ward concerning a visit in 1899 James made with her in the same country. The incidents are chronologically distant but close in tone and content, and so reveal a fundamental aspect of James's personality. Writing about a group of boys he had come across while walking in Venice, James remarked that one of the lads 'was the most expressively beautiful creature I had ever looked upon'. He continued: 'He had a smile to make Correggio sigh in his grave ... Verily nature is still at odds with propriety ... I think I shall always remember, with infinite conjecture, as the years roll by, this little unlettered Eros of the Adriatic strand.'[53] Mrs Ward recalled a visit with James to Lake Nemi, more than a quarter of a century later:

On descending from Genzano to the strawberry farm that now holds the site of the famous temple of Diana Memorensis, we found a beautiful youth at the *fattoria*, who for a few pence undertook to show us the fragments that remain. Mr. James asked his name. 'Aristodemo,' said the boy, looking as he spoke the Greek name, 'like to a God in form and stature.' Mr. James's face lit up; and he walked over the historic ground beside the lad, Aristodemo picking up for him fragments of terracotta from the furrows through which the plough had just passed, bits of the innumerable small *figurines* that used to crowd the temple walls as ex-votos ... I presently came up with Mr. James and Aristodemo, who led us on serenely, a young Hermes in the transfiguring light. One almost looked for the winged feet and helmet of the messenger God! Mr. James paused – his eyes first on the boy, then on the surrounding scene. 'Aristodemo!', he murmured smiling, more to himself than me, his voice caressing the word.[54]

In the first extract, James's casually referred to but intense involvement is qualified by a universalising reference to art, and the boy undergoes an apotheosis into Eros. Aristodemo is said by Mrs Ward to be 'like to a God in form and stature', and her reference to him as a young Hermes similarly creates a refined, classical context. She and James were, after all, strolling among Roman ruins, and the fact that they 'found' the boy further makes it seem as if he were presented as a relic from another age. Mrs Ward's context may be either playfully or innocently homo-erotic. Either way, her paragraph demonstrably traces a movement away from the sensory and towards the imaginative: from the boy to his name and finally to James's verbal manifestation of his enchantment. It is significant that Mrs Ward, a notoriously moral individual, was not scandalised by anything she witnessed: the ease with which she could relate James's admiration of Aristodemo to her classical knowledge seems to have excused both James's indulgence and her own complicity in it. In a letter to Mrs Ward, James later referred to his fond memories of 'the Nemi Lake, and the walk down and up (the latter perhaps most)', and he added that 'the strawberries and Aristodemo were the cream ... I am clear about that'.[55]

The Thesiger passage contains a specific reference to the Roman Emperor Hadrian's love for his Greek page Antinous, a love transformed to nostalgia and grief after the boy's death by drowning in the Nile.[56] In a review of 1877 of the (anonymously authored) novel *Kismet*, James also wrote about that affair:

> The tale is altogether feminine … We say this in spite of the pretty passage near the close about the Emperor Hadrian and the suicide of the beautiful Antinous, which appears to have been written by a young lady who had not a definite idea what she was saying rather than by a young man who had such an idea, and who was still determined to say it.[57]

James reveals his familiarity with classical homosexuality, and his awareness of its literary possibilities, though the explicitness is ambiguously framed by the mild rebuke. Only an ignorant woman, he would appear to be saying, would be foolish enough to be so indiscreet; and only such a woman could be forgiven for such indiscretion. To readers of early James it is his own apparent puzzlement that is puzzling. He was aware that the historical point of reference for almost all writers who discussed overtly or covertly homosexuality in the early part of the nineteenth-century was the classical world, and his own frequent recourse to such classical allusion, especially in the early fiction, was as conventional as his appreciation of Italian boys. His homosexual propensity was sublimated into his fiction, much as his contemplation of beautiful Italian boys and his love for Anderson were transfigured into contemplations of classical myths and art.

3
Whitman, Pater and the Importance of Being Manly in James's Early Fiction

Homosexuality in James's early fiction is typically related to a contrast between reason, manliness and a sensitivity to social order and convention on the one hand, and, on the other, to passionate femininity and the threat to social coherence if adolescent homo-eroticism is not grown out of in early adulthood. This is a contrast Pater himself established, when he wrote:

> Manliness in art, what can it be, as distinct from that which in opposition to it must be called feminine quality there, – what but a full consciousness of what one does, of art itself in the work of art, tenacity of intuition and of consequent purpose, the spirit of construction as opposed to what is literally incoherent or ready to fall to pieces, and, in opposition to what is hysteric or works at random, the maintenance of a standard.[1]

Gregory Woods has interpreted this passage to mean that, for Pater, 'to lack manliness is to be, or to be at risk of becoming, unconscious, artless, obtuse, purposeless, incoherent, fragmented, hysterical, random, and lacking in worthwhile standards'; but by 'thus associating artistic and intellectual control with "manliness", and thereby with male physicality, Pater proposes an aesthetic which is as much for homo-eroticism's sake as for art's alone'.[2] Richard Ellmann has pointed out that there is a recurring preoccupation in James's art criticism with the idea of 'manliness'.[3] What has hitherto remained largely unexplored is the greater extent to which this is also a concern in the early fiction, particularly 'A Light Man' (1869), *Roderick Hudson* (1875) and *Confidence* (1878), and how it relates to this Paterian equation of 'artistic and intellectual control' with 'manliness', and thereby 'with male physicality'. As Pater used the 'manliness' of pederastic relations in ancient Greece to define the essential masculinity of homosexuality, and as Symonds would draw on what Whitman in *Democratic Vistas* had called the 'threads of manly friendship … unprecedentedly emotional, muscular, heroic, and refined', so in his early fiction James alludes to classical examples of homosexuality and explicitly castigates his homosexual (or passive heterosexual) male characters for their lack of 'manliness' – characters who more complicatingly attempt to distance themselves socially from their implied homosexuality by making their behaviour in times of masculine crisis appear 'heroic', 'refined' and 'manly' to an extreme.[4]

Hugh Stevens has noted that there was a precedent for James's treatment of homosexuality in his early fiction, in the form of *Joseph and His Friends: A Study of Pennsylvania* (1870), a novel by Bayard Taylor (an author James had reviewed five years previously). In the earlier novel, the friendship of the two men is – in Stevens' phrase – 'assertively masculine'; and it articulates the difference between 'a woman's love' and a 'man's perfect friendship'. It also displays an awareness of the socially constructed reality the two men have to define their intimacy within, and anticipates later discussion of homophobia in adopting a language that would challenge such rigid definitions of gender and sexuality. It is hostile to the marriage plot; the two male protagonists are repeatedly propelled together in moments of crisis; and there is an appeal throughout to the value of 'nature' and 'instinct', rather than social norms.[5] It parallels not only the treatment of similar concerns in *Roderick Hudson* (as Stevens argues it), but more strikingly James's treatment of homosexuality and troubled male heterosexuality in 'A Light Man', a short story that actually predates *Joseph and His Friends*.

Edel wrote that James 'expressed particular fondness in later years' for his short story 'A Light Man', and almost four decades after its initial publication James revised it for inclusion in the New York Edition – an honour he bestowed upon few early stories.[6] It is concerned with the contrast between a masculine definition of 'healthy' male friendship and the feminised threat of 'unhealthy' male intimacy. There is a corresponding preoccupation with 'reason' and 'passion'.

Three men compete for one another's affection in a remote New England mansion. Rivalry develops between Max, whose journal entries form the text, and Theo, his long-standing friend. In their attempt to win over the exclusive patronage of the wealthy, infirm elderly widower, Frederick Sloane – worth about a million and in search of an heir – a question arises about what kind of masculine love it is that defines male friendship. Max is looking to make his fortune. More mysteriously, he is seeking the expression of what he terms his 'simple, natural emotion' (LM, 367). This, it becomes clear, encompasses both his hatred of male femininity and his need to express his homosexuality.

The friendship between Max and Theo derives from their school-days in Italy, which ended five years before the story begins, and the two are about to meet up again at the beginning of the story. Theo's nostalgic motivation for rejuvenating the friendship is, he tells Max, to awaken 'the touch of your old pledges of affection' (LM, 371). After reading about Max's arrival in New York from Europe, Theo invites him to visit the mansion of a Mr Sloane, who turns out to be the least disguised homosexual character in all James's fiction. Like Theo, he is fixated on his youth, and Max immediately recognises that 'He likes anything that will tickle his fancy, impart a flavour to our relations, remind him of his old odds and ends of novels and memoirs' (LM, 363). The 'friendship' Sloane forms with the young men is similarly presented in strict narcis-sistic terms: 'He understands favour and friendship only as a selfish rapture,' Max explains, 'a reaction, an infatuation, an act of aggres-sive, exclusive patronage. It's not a bestowal with him, but a transfer ...' (LM, 363). 'He has never loved anyone but himself,' (LM, 359) Max believes.

In his letter of invitation, Theo, after apologising for not having met Max off the boat in New York, writes: 'To think of your perhaps having missed the welcome you had a right to expect of me' (LM, 371). 'Perhaps' gives the sentence an uneasy, inquisitive tone, and 'you had a right' locates the uncertainty in Theo's reassurance that his simple adolescent fondness of his friend has remained, despite their long separation. This is the tension that will subsequently define the nature of their relations: Theo is unsure whether he should make explicit his fondness of Max, which has remained as a kind of innocent adolescent love – he blushes and swoons when they do meet up again (LM, 348) – while Max, aware of that innocence, exploits it for perverse sexual and financial ends. 'I shall never again care for certain things – or indeed for certain persons' (LM, 346–7) he writes, in the first of the journal entries the form of the story takes, with reference it later appears to the time he spent with Theo shortly after they finished school. Sloane's vulnerability is also noted by Max, and the question at the end of the story is whether Theo, whose vulnerability resulting from his attachment to his adolescent bond with Max leads to his being similarly exploited by the latter, has sufficiently matured to avoid falling into what had proved to be Sloane's life-long sentimental need for the company of younger men.

The story has as its epitaph a quotation from Browning's 'A Light Woman':

> And I – what I seem to my friend, you see –
> What I soon shall seem to his love, you guess.
> What I seem to myself, do you ask of me?
> No hero, I confess.

In Browning's poem, an Italian count had, like an eagle, snatched up the light woman who had been seduced by his friend. By doing this, the aristocrat had revealed the light woman's falsity, but at the same time he had exploited her and destroyed his own friendship with her intended victim. In James's reworking, the light woman, of course, is Sloane, who is seducing Theo. Max is the count, out to reveal Sloane for what he is really up to, and in the course of doing so he loses his friendship with Theo. The technical exercise of reworking Browning's poem is of interest mainly because of the homo-erotic possibilities and complications that result, a situation directly anticipated by the epitaph. What kind of love is it that needs to be uncovered? How does this relate to Max's sense of his own sexual self? And how can male friendships that have only a heterosexual counterpart for definition, and no independent linguistic existence, be defined?

The heterosexual context gave the friendship between the two men in Browning's poem a point of reference, as well as a sexual contrast to, the male–male rivalry. In James's all-male reworking, an older man seduces a younger man and a third younger man, in seeking to reveal this, becomes another seducer. Max's self-questioning – 'What am I? What do I wish? Whither do I tend? What do I believe?' (LM, 346) – quickly becomes focused on the mansion and the relationships that have been formed in it: 'Who is [Sloane], what is he, and what is the nature of his relations with Theodore? I shall learn betimes' (LM, 348). The external events of 'A Light Man' reflect the movement of Max's consciousness, and it is the accumulation of evidence proving the existent of homo-erotic seductions that is the motivation for his further investigations.

In inviting the two young men to his house, Sloane is repeating a pattern of behaviour that has resulted in his having adopted, and then with equal suddenness dropped, a series of younger '*protégés*':

> Doctor Jones, his physician, tells me that in point of fact [Sloane] has had for the past ten years an unbroken series of favourites, *protégés*, and heirs presumptive; but that each, in turn, by some fatally false movement, has fairly unjointed his nose. The doctor declares, moreover, that they were, at best, a woefully common set of people. Gradually the old man seems to have developed a preference for two or three strictly exquisite intimates, over a throng of young vulgar charmers.
>
> (LM, 358–9)

Sloane's wish to be acquainted with young men is superficially outlined in altruistic terms: he knew their parents, and therefore likes to help them in periods of financial difficulties. Having heard that impoverished Theo is responsible for taking care of his sisters, for example, Sloane offers him an independent source of income by employing him as a secretary. He claims to have known Theo's father in the past; and he suggests that he was also acquainted with Max's parents. At their first meeting, Sloane tells Max: 'how much you look like your father' (LM, 350). At its end, he appears to have forgotten which parent he had initially referred to, and he declares: 'how much you look like your mother!' (LM, 352). Alleged earlier friendships with the mother and father of both Max and Theo allowed Edel to explain away Sloane's 'femininity' by suggesting that Sloane 'acts as a kind of father-mother to both young men;

indeed he has known in the past the father of one and the mother of the other and in this way another chain of invisible brotherhood is established between [Theo and Max]'.[7] It is not clear why Edel writes 'another', because neither he nor James explicitly refers to any other such 'chain of brotherhood'. In the story, it is apparent, in any case, that Sloane is using the mother-father angle as a smoke-screen. He has been shown to be confused as to whether it was Max's mother or father that he had once known, and when he further claims that, even ten years previously, he 'knew' Max 'in knowing' his mother, Max finally retorts: 'Ah! my mother again. When the old man begins that chapter I feel like telling him to blow out his candle and go to bed' (LM, 362). It is a bit of fiction, part of Sloane's general dishonesty about himself and his motivations, and Max eventually uncovers all of this. That Sloane is acting on chari-table impulses is further undermined by Max's private impression 'that [Sloane's] cramped old bosom contains unsuspected treasures of cunning impertinence' (LM, 359), and that he 'has shown a great delicacy of tact in keeping himself free of parasites' (LM, 358). The old man is vulnerable to youthful male beauty and charm; but not to the extent that he has lost his fortune to one of the previous hangers-on. Max's challenge is to clear this final barrier. 'Apparently,' he acknowledges, 'they've been a sad lot of bunglers. I maintain that he is – how shall I say it – to be possessed' (LM, 358).

That 'how shall I say it', and the idea of possession that follows, is symptomatic of the vaguely charged language Max adopts when referring to male desire and intimacy, unless he uses the context of Sloane's femininity or draws a direct heterosexual parallel. In writing that 'The house is pervaded by an indefinable, irresistible air of luxury and privacy. Mr Sloane must be a horribly corrupt old mortal' (LM, 352), he links privacy, decadence and indefinability with a sense of irresistibility; and after declaring 'I have deliberately conceived the idea of marrying money' (LM, 355), he even draws an analogy between his own sexually charged encounters with Sloane and other young men he imagines to be in similar relationships but with women. '[M]y only complaint,' he says, 'is that, instead of an old widower, he's not an old widow (or a young maid), so that I might marry him, and dwell forever in his rich and mellow home' (LM, 356). He is able culturally to place the heterosexual alternative with reference to Hogarth, but he refers to Theo's 'immensity of dumbness' and 'affectation of mystery' when articulating his own eagerness to exploit Theo's 'indefinable' role in the love triangle:

> I firmly believe that a large portion of his happiness rests upon his devout conviction that I really care for him. He believes in that, as he believes in all the rest of it – in my culture, my latent talents, my underlying 'earnestness', my sense of beauty and love of truth. Oh, for a *man* amongst them all – a fellow with eyes in his head – eyes that would know me for what I am and let me see that they had guessed it. Possibly such a fellow as might get a 'rise' out of me.   (LM, 355)

'Theodore's a *man*,' Max later repeats. 'Well, that's what I want. He wants a fight – he shall have it. Have I got, at last, my simple, natural emotion?' (LM, 367). The italics particularise a type, because Max wants to fight not with any man but specifically with Theo. By rejecting Theo and the adolescent, homo-erotic bond between them, he will also distance himself sexually from feminine men as a group. Associating his 'natural emotion' with a forbearance of anything weak-headed or sentimental while remaining aware of his own homosexual propensity, Max sublimates his homo-erotic desires through a scheme of hateful, 'manly' exploitation. In eventually usurping his friend's position as Sloane's favourite, he moves one step further towards his fortune, which simultaneously brings him one step closer to a final showdown and therefore to the probability of that sexually charged 'rise'.

There is a great deal of reference to 'reason' and 'passion' in this story, and in the Paterian way Max equates 'reason' with control, security and homosexual repression, and 'passion' with vulnerability, femininity and homosexual indulgence. He is presented as being enviably full of 'reason' and as logical, for example when he reports that he 'came within an ace of obeying my foremost impulse' of casting Sloane's will into the fire. 'Fortunately,' he says, 'my reason overtook my passion, though for a moment 'twas an even race' (LM, 368). Of Sloane, however, it is said that, upon recovering his fortune after briefly losing it years before, 'The control and discipline exercised during these years upon his desires and his natural love of luxury, must have been the sole act of real resolution in the history of [his] life' (LM, 358). Sloane's lurking passion, in the form of a susceptivity to male charm and beauty, and therefore a potential lack of control, is what Max is hoping to exploit. Sloane had once before lost all his money by squandering it (LM, 357), and Max's hope is that he can make Sloane lose his money once again – this time by making him homosexually passionate and therefore to lose his 'control and discipline', rather than as before because of simple economic recklessness. Conversely, Max proves that he is able to control and manipulate his own homosexual drive – that he is defined by his masculine 'reason' rather than a feminine 'passion' – for objective ends, and even declares that he has 'a passion for nothing – not even for life' (LM, 355).

Sloane's study is described as 'sort of female', and Max comments, 'You perceive the place to be the home, not of a man of learning, but a man of fancy' (LM, 350). Sloane is also said, on two occasions in the only such repetition in the story, to be 'of the real feminine turn' (LM, 357; 363). He is the source of considerable humour for his role as the aesthete, and anticipates James's description of Ned Rosier in *The Portrait of a Lady* (1881), which is similarly camp: 'He had some charming rooms in Paris, decorated with old Spanish altar-lace, the envy of his female friends, who declared that his chimney-piece was better draped than the high shoulders of many a duchess' (PL, 186). Madame Merle's taunting comments, later in the novel, suggest a link between Rosier's dubious sexuality and his surroundings by pushing the terms of the narrator's earlier comment, in the same way that Theo is categorising Sloane according to his physical surroundings:

> When Madame Merle came in she found him standing before the fireplace with his nose very close to the great lace flounce attached to the damask cover of the mantel. He had lifted it delicately as if he were smelling it.
>
> 'It's old Venetian,' she said; 'it's rather good.'
>
> 'It's too good for this; you ought to wear it.'
>
> 'They tell me you have some better in Paris, in the same situation.'
>
> 'Ah, but I can't wear mine,' smiled the visitor.
>
> 'I don't see why you shouldn't! I've better lace than that to wear.'
>
> (PL, 302)[8]

'I honestly believe,' Max says of Sloane, 'that I might come into his study in my night-shirt and he would smile upon it as a picturesque *désebillé* {sic}' (LM, 363). Nowhere else in James's *oeuvre* is the suggestion of homosexual seduction so unambiguously stated. Given that Sloane's only encounter with heterosexuality was with a woman he married for her money when he was young, who 'considerately' (LM, 357) died three years afterwards and left him her fortune, it might be assumed that the memoir Sloane is writing in some way documents an 'alternative' lifestyle. It is said that he 'likes to sit in his chair, and read scandal, talk scandal, make scandal' (LM, 357). Theo's primary function as 'guide' and 'philosopher', as well as note-taker for Sloane's memoirs, is to get Sloane to 'leave things out' (LM, 349). 'His patron's lubrications have taken the turn of all memoirs,' Max reports, 'and have become *tout bonnement* immoral' (LM, 349). Elsewhere it is casually reported, in the context of a discussion of his writings, that he has had 'intimate friends of both sexes' (LM, 358), and the fact that the younger men he has previously known are referred to as 'strictly exquisite intimates' and 'young vulgar charmers' is certainly homosexually suggestive, as, correspondingly, is Max's allusion to his travels in southern Europe and the Orient – travelling to such places was, as we have seen, the option open to those of independent means to find a safe outlet for pederastic impulses:

'Excuse me, my dear fellow,' I said, 'you know, for the last ten years I have lived in Catholic countries.'

'Good, good, good!' cried Mr Sloane, rubbing his hands and clapping them together, and laughing with high relish.

'Dear me,' said Theodore, smiling, but vaguely apprehensive, too – and a little touched, perhaps by my involuntary reflection on the quality of his faith, 'I hope you're not a Roman Catholic.'

I saw the old man, with his hands locked, eyeing me shrewdly, and waiting for my answer. I pondered a moment in mock gravity. 'I shall make my confession,' I said. 'I have been in the East, you know. I'm a Mohammedan!'

Hereupon Mr Sloane broke out into a wheezy ecstasy of glee.
(LM, 351)[9]

Friendships between males is the subject of an extraordinarily revealing exchange between Max and Sloane at the first moment the love triangle of Sloane, Max and Theo is brought fully into play:

> The *bonhomme* still kept my hands. 'I wish very much,' he said, 'that I could get you to love me as well as you do poor Theodore.'
> 'Ah, don't talk to me about love, Mr. Sloane. I'm no lover.'
> 'Don't you love your friend?'
> 'Not as he deserves.'
> 'Nor as he loves you perhaps?'
> 'He loves me, I'm afraid, far more than he deserves.'
> 'Well, Max,' my host pursued, 'we can be good friends, all the same. We don't need a hocus-pocus of false sentiment. We are *men*, aren't we – men of sublime good sense.' And just here, as the old man looked at me the pressure of his hands deepened to a convulsive grasp, and the bloodless mask of his countenance was suddenly distorted with a nameless fear. 'Ah my dear young man!' he cried, 'come and be a son to me – the son of my age and desolation! For God's sake don't leave me to pine and die alone!'
> I was amazed – and I may say I was moved. It is true, then, that this poor old heart contains such measureless depths of horror and longing?

> (LM, 362)

The physical contact between the two men lasts throughout the conversation, and the suggestion is that Max gains evidence to support his theory that it is a physical kind of relationship that Sloane seeks. The move in Max's mind from the idea of loving Theo to being or not being 'a lover' is playful and flirtatious, and not in keeping with the strict notions of 'brotherhood' Edel considered as the only explanation for intimacy between the younger men (which could anyway be a Whitmanesque signifier for something deeper). When Sloane returns to the subject of friendship, his 'mask' becomes 'distorted with a nameless fear': again it is the sense of the nameless and the unspoken that takes emotional precedence once a certain level of honesty and explicitness is neared. Sloane recovers his sense of self-protectiveness with his comment, 'We're *men*, aren't we?', which refers them back safely to the acceptable, definable masculine discourse they had momentarily strayed away from. The idea of 'brotherhood' is not sufficient to explain why each of the young men is said to be or not to be the other's 'lover'. Sloane's final outburst, when he calls for Max to be a 'son of his age and desolation', also makes 'son' sound like a substitute for something far more intense and physical that would justify 'pine' – the traditional state of yearning by a lover in the absence of a beloved. In making clear that he 'pines' for Max, Sloane subtly shifts the definition from being a father-figure to a son to being 'a lover' or 'piner', just as Max had earlier shifted from the idea of 'friendship' to that of being 'a lover'.

Having gained the knowledge that Sloane is to be 'had', Max turns his attention to Theo. He has decided to stay on at the mansion to complete his work as secretary to Sloane, despite the fact that it has become obvious to him that Max has usurped his position as Sloane's favourite and that Sloane consequently will take little interest in him. After hearing of Theo's intention nevertheless to stay, Max says that he has 'ceased to be puzzled' by Theo's conduct, which

> is suddenly illuminated with a backward, lurid ray. Here are a few plain truths, which it behooves me to take to heart – commit to memory. Theodore is jealous of me. Theodore hates me. Theodore has been seeking for the past three months to see his name written, last but not least, in a testamentary document ... For this he sets his teeth and tightens his grasp; for this he'll fight. Merciful powers! it's an immense weight off one's mind. There are nothing, then, but vulgar, common laws; no sublime exceptions, no transcendent anomalies. Theodore's a knave, a hypo – nay, nay; stay, irreverent hand! – Theodore's a *man*! Well, that's what I want. He wants a fight – he shall have it. Have I got, at last, my simple, natural emotion?'
>
> (LM, 363)

Max's elation at discovering that Theo is – as far as Max understands it – as scheming and insincere as himself is associated with his self-justification that if sentimentality, honesty and selflessness are absent even from individuals such as Theo – who was earlier said to have 'angelic charity' (LM, 352) – then he himself need not have constraints on his behaviour or feel guilty about its negative consequences. It is from this position of scepticism and solipsism that

Max is shaken at the end of the story, when he learns that Theo had acted out of pure love rather than rivalry. At this point, however, Theo's supposed jealousy and hatred of Max arises, as far as Max understands it, from the probability that Max will now inherit Sloane's fortune; but in responding to this imagined cause Max envisages a confrontation which has more to do with a need to confront Theo physically, in the form of a fight, than with money. He is brought back to his overriding need to experience his 'natural, simple emotion'.

The parallels – between his superficial scheme to make money and his more profound but much less-well defined homo-erotic yearning for a masculine confrontation; between materialistic self-advancement and emotional and sexual intercourse – are made explicit in a later scene involving Max and Sloane, when Max pretends he is to depart:

> I repaired to Mr. Sloane, who had not yet gone to bed, and informed him that it is necessary I shall at once leave him, and seek some occupation in New York. He felt the blow; it brought him straight down on his marrow-bones. He went through the whole gamut of his arts and graces; he blustered, whimpered, entreated, flattered. He tried to drag in Theodore's name; but this I, of course, prevented. But finally, why, *why*, WHY, after all my promises of fidelity, must I thus cruelly desert him? Then came my supreme avowal: I have spent my last penny; while I stay, I'm a beggar. The remainder of this extraordinary scene I have no power to describe: how the *bonhomme*, touched, inflamed, inspired, by the thought of my destitution, and at the same time annoyed, perplexed, bewildered at having to commit himself to any practical alleviation of it, worked himself into a nervous frenzy which deprived him of a clear sense of the value of his words and actions; how I, prompted by the irresistible desire to leap astride of his weakness, and ride it hard into the goal of my dreams, cunningly contrived to keep his spirit at the fever point, so that strength, and reason, and resistance should burn themselves out. I shall probably never again have such a sensation as I had to-night – actually feel a heated human heart throbbing, and turning, and struggling in my grasp; know its spasms, its convulsions, and its final senseless quiescence.

> (LM, 367–8)

Sloane's 'strength, and reason, and resistance' 'burn themselves out' and Max is 'prompted by the irresistible desire to leap astride of his weakness' to continue the pressure, until Sloane finally breaks down. Since the contrast is between reason and control, between weakness and manliness, the broader point is not only that this is a literary metaphor for actual sexual intercourse between Max and Sloane, but that the images and passions associated with the build-up to sexual climax exist only in Max's mind. Even in this highly sexualised assault he is in full control of his 'reason', and what excites Max is Sloane's very loss of reason – clearly meaning here his lack of self-control and his sudden homosexual vulnerability. As in earlier instances when a movement towards homosexual explicitness resulted in 'nameless fears' and a confusion about terms and vocabulary, so in this most explicitly homosexual scene Sloane is 'bewildered at having to commit himself to any practical alleviation' of his being 'touched, inflamed, inspired, by the thought' of Max's destitution, and he 'worked himself into a nervous frenzy which deprived him of a clear sense of the value of his words and actions'. Words become meaningless, because the actions incorporate homosexual 'acquiescence'. Max triumphs because he has managed to distance himself from an effeminate homosexual while simultaneously indulging in what is (at the very least) an erotically charged confrontation. Sloane afterwards dies, and having triumphed in one area Max turns his attention to Theo, who opens his heart to his old friend:

> For whom but you would I have gone as far as I did? For what other purpose than that of keeping our friendship whole would I have borne you company into this narrow pass? A man whom I loved less I would long since have parted company with. You were indeed – you and your incomparable gifts – to bring me to this. You ennobled, exhalted, enchanted the struggle ... With another man that you I never would have contested such a prize. But I loved you, even as my rival. You played with me, deceived me, betrayed me. I held my ground, hoping and longing to purge you of your error by the touch of your old pledges of affection. I carried them in my heart.
>
> (LM, 371)

This parallels Sloane's physical acquiescence. Theo is finally made to state his love for Max in explicit terms, sounding off the words of resentment in a traditional lover's spat: 'I loved you, even as my rival.' Old pledges of affection have finally been manipulated to their most extreme emotional end: Theo has been used as much as anybody could have been by a friend, but insists on stating that it was only his love for Max, dating from their schooldays together, that made him hold out a hope of discovering Max's goodness. Max's 'reason' once again takes over:

> I never pretended to love you. I don't understand the word, in the sense you attach to it. I don't understand the feeling, between men. To me, love means quite another thing. You give it a meaning of your own; you enjoy the profit of your invention; it's no more than just that you should pay the penalty.
>
> (LM, 372)

'A Light Man' revolves around Max's manipulation of his knowledge that Theo loved him and that Sloane could be made to love him. He was able to play off one against the other because of an awareness that a lack of vocabulary about male desire, and the necessity of remaining silent about a subject which beyond the secluded mansion would be scandalous, meant his own motivations would not be too closely examined. Max finally betrays Theo in the cruellest imaginable way: when the homo-eroticism he has been manipulating is made even more explicit by Theo than even Max had managed to make it, it is immediately rejected in Max's false claim that he has no 'knowledge' of the kind of 'love' he knew Theo had been obsessed with from the beginning.

In the penultimate chapter of *Roderick Hudson* Roderick's rejection of Rowland is almost identical to that of Theo by Max at the end of 'A Light Man'. Roderick, too, questions the emotional claims of male intimacy that have been made on him throughout the novel by his older patron, Rowland Mallet, and – again like Max – Roderick has exploited the intense but ultimately unnameable and inexpressible affection bestowed upon him by another man. 'Your love – your suffering – your silence – your friendship,' he shouts at Rowland. 'I declare I don't understand!' (RH, 375). 'They were the sacrifices of friendship and they were easily made,' Rowland retorts, 'only I don't enjoy having them thrown back in my teeth' (RH, 375). 'Come, be more definite,' (RH, 375) Roderick insists, and Rowland replies that it has been 'a perpetual sacrifice to live with a transcendental egotist!' (RH, 376). There follows, as in 'A Light Man', a traditional lover's spat – traditional, that is, if between a man and woman. *Roderick Hudson* is principally concerned with why the friendship between the two men has been brought to this low point – a friendship which, again as in 'A Light Man', is explored in terms of a Whitmanesque signifier of broadly defined 'camaraderie', though one which is related specifically in *Roderick Hudson* to Rowland's famous 'moral passion':

> Rowland had found himself wondering ... whether possibly his brilliant young friend were without a conscience; now it dimly occurred to him that he was without a heart. Rowland as we have already intimated was a man with a moral passion, and no small part of it had gone into this adventure. There had been from the first no protestations of friendship on either side, but Rowland had implicitly offered everything that belongs to friendship, and Roderick had apparently as deliberately accepted it. Rowland indeed had taken an exquisite satisfaction in his companion's easy inexpressive assent to his interest in him. 'Here is an uncommonly fine thing,' he said to himself; 'a nature unconsciously grateful, a man in whom friendship does the things that love alone generally has the credit of ...'
>
> (RH, 189–90)

It is this position of undefined intimacy and camaraderie – where there is 'easy inexpressive assent' and an 'unconscious' gratitude of a friendship that can do the thing 'love alone generally has the credit of' – that is made explicit at the end of the novel, when Roderick directly calls into question Rowland's motivations in having befriended him so impulsively and emotionally. Shortly afterwards, Roderick is killed, signifying that as soon as the nature of Rowland's affection is made a specific issue the friendship between the two men ends. As homosexuality had always become a linguistically insurmountable problem in 'A Light Man' whenever it was expressed with particular intensity or explicitness, there remains no way of giving it definition, in either positive social or self-explanatory personal terms, in *Roderick Hudson* – at least outside the Whitmanesque 'manly friendship' and 'camaraderie' that by the end of the novel have become redundant. The tragic ending can be compared to the positive ending of *Watch and Ward* (1873), James's first novel, in which the protagonist adopts not a boy but a young girl, whom eventually he will marry; a happy ending significant moreover because it allows for the reconciliation of the idea of 'permanent adolescence' (as central to *Watch and Ward* as it is to *Roderick Hudson*) through a heterosexual scenario. In the earlier novel, the central relationship between two cousins, Hubert and Roger, is defined as follows: 'He and Roger had been much together in early life and had formed an intimacy strangely compounded of harmony and discord ... Roger was constantly differing, mutely and profoundly, and Hubert frankly and sarcastically; but each, nevertheless, seemed to find in the other a welcome counterpart and complement to his own personality.'[10]

When Rowland hears from Roderick that he is engaged to be married to Mary Garland, the woman for whom Rowland himself is supposed to harbour a romantic attachment, he listens 'with a feeling that fortune had played him an elaborately-devised trick. It had lured him out to mid-ocean and smoothed the sea and stilled the winds and given him a singularly sympathetic comrade, and then it had turned and delivered him a thumping blow in mid-chest' (RH, 102). The emphasis in this passage, as elsewhere in the novel, is on Rowland's loss of his 'singularly sympathetic comrade', rather than on the effects any love he may hold for Mary, which nowhere is articulated or expressed. Later, when thinking of Roderick, Rowland feels a 'flood of comradeship rise in his heart' (RH, 109), and this is occasionally reciprocated, as when Roderick acts 'as if there had never been a difference of opinion between them; as if each had been for both, unalterably, and both for each' (RH, 333). However, after Rowland has as good as given up on Roderick, it is said that he 'began to feel that it was perfectly idle to appeal to his comrade's will; there was no will left; its place was a mocking vacancy' (RH, 351–2). It is this movement, away from Rowland seeing Roderick as a 'singularly sympathetic comrade' towards his realisation that such sympathy, if it ever existed, has been replaced by a 'mocking vacancy', which culminates with the altercation already quoted, that defines the thematic progression in *Roderick Hudson*.

The treatment of the theme of masculine, homo-erotic desire in *Roderick Hudson*, when compared to 'A Light Man', is complicated by the Paterian Italian setting and the consequent classical points of reference. Ellmann has written of how James discovered Pater's *The Renaissance* in a bookshop in Paris in 1873, while in the middle of writing *Roderick Hudson*. He argues that, given James's homosexual propensity, he 'could not fail to observe how Pater's book covertly celebrated such a propensity by dwelling on Leonardo, Michelangelo and Winkelmann'. While James took alarm and wished to inscribe himself as 'neither aesthetic nor homosexual', he also 'knew and wanted to portray homosexuals', conflicting reactions reconciled by his representing homosexuals 'negatively as aesthetes'. In *Roderick Hudson*, it is therefore Roderick, the 'aesthete *gloriosis*', Ellmann concludes, who is the Paterian victim. He dutifully burns himself out and dies, punished for his aesthetic excesses.[11] Roderick is certainly Paterian, and there are clear echoes in Roderick's speech of Pater's infamous call on the young to 'burn with a hard, gem-like flame': 'What becomes of all our emotions, our impressions ... all the material of thought that life pours into us at such a rate during such a memorable three months as these? There are twenty moments a week – a day, for that matter, some days – that seem supreme, twenty impressions that seem ultimate, that seem to form an intellectual era' (RH, 105). However, Pater's influence on the novel is less negative than Ellmann recognised, and is mostly evident in Rowland's difficulty in trying to live through Roderick while Roderick himself, with increasing recklessness, lives first for the Paterian moment and then for Christina Light. The most useful summary of Rowland's motivations in befriending Roderick is in Pater's essay on Winckelmann, which has been quoted above but which is worth quoting in full again: 'the subtler threads of temperament were interwoven into [his interest in Hellenism] ... is proved by [his] romantic, fervent friendships with young men. He has known, he says, many young men more beautiful than Guido's archangel. These friendships, bringing him into contact with the pride of human form, and staining the thoughts with its bloom, perfected his reconciliation to the spirit of Greek sculpture.'[12] In *Roderick Hudson* there is a passage that could be derivative of the Winckelmann essay. It defines Rowland's sense of benevolent camaraderie when in the company of Roderick.

While revealing Rowland to be another of James's 'permanent adolescents', who like Sloane in 'A Light Man' is reliving his own lost youth in the company of younger men, the passage also reads as if it were a celebration of the boyish charm of certain expressive and gifted young men, and is evocative of Pater's Winckelmann in the added sense that the context is a 'pilgrimage to Rome' by an older man with his younger artistic *protégé*:

> Roderick was so much younger than he himself had ever been! Surely youth and genius hand in hand were the most beautiful sight in the world. Roderick added to this the charm of his more immediately personal qualities. The vivacity of his perceptions, the audacity of his imagination, the picturesqueness of his phrase when he was pleased – and even more when he was displeased – his abounding good-humour, his candour, his unclouded frankness, his unfailing impulse to share every emotion and impression with his friend; all this made comradeship a high felicity, and interfused with a deeper amenity the wanderings and contemplations that beguiled their pilgrimage to Rome.
>
> (RH, 107)

In the novel, this 'comradeship' is given an explicitly homo-erotic classical subtext, revealing a combined influence of Whitman and Pater. In New England Rowland's cousin Cecilia first introduces his future charge by presenting a statue created by Roderick, with the comment: 'If I refused last night to show you a pretty girl, I can at least show you a pretty boy' (RH, 59). The statue is of a 'naked youth drinking from a gourd', and the narrator elaborates that 'The figure might have been some beautiful youth of ancient fable – Hylas or Narcissus, Paris or Endymion' (RH, 59). Robert K. Martin has written that

> Endymion evokes Keats's poem, of course, and its story of the quest for ideal beauty; it foreshadows Roderick's infatuation with Christina Light, who plays Moon-goddess to Roderick's shepherd. Paris evokes fatal love and beauty, since Paris abandons his first lover, the nymph Oenone, elopes with Helen, and is killed in the Trojan war; it foreshadows Roderick's abandonment of

Mary, his love for Christina, and his death. Narcissus evokes the fatal love of the self, with which Roderick is certainly imbued, and suggests the metaphor of drowning which runs throughout the novel. Hylas is the least obvious and most significant of these allusions. Hylas was the beloved of Hercules and his companion on the 'Argo'; it is Hylas's death by drowning which causes Hercules to abandon the expedition. His mention here has no other function than to make the reader aware of a homosexual (or homo-erotic) relationship between the two men.[13]

Critics have traditionally couched their discussion of the relationship between Rowland and Roderick strictly in artist–patron terms, even emphasising the *lack* of homo-eroticism.[14] But that Rowland falls in love with Roderick's person, as well as his genius, is actually very clearly spelled out: 'Roderick was acutely sensitive, and Rowland's intelligent praise had absorbed him; he was ruminating the full-flavoured verdict of culture. Rowland took a great fancy to him, *to his personal charm and his probable genius*. He had an indefinable attraction – the something tender and divine of unspotted, exuberant, confident youth' (RH, 68; emphasis added). So Rowland, connoisseur of the arts, lives through the young artist Roderick's youth and beauty, as Winckelmann the scholar had found a real-life parallel for his appreciation of Greek art in the 'romantic, fervent friendships with young men' Pater refers to. The irony in *Roderick Hudson* is that, though Roderick conveniently declares that 'The Greeks never made anything ugly, and I'm a Hellenist' (RH, 123), and though Rowland appreciably finds him to be 'a tall slender young fellow', is struck by his 'remarkably handsome' face, swoons at the 'extraordinary beauty' of the 'fair slim youth', and observes how he displays a charming combination of 'boyish unconsciousness and manly shrewdness' (RH, 64–5), Roderick when in Italy refuses to confine himself, like a good Greek boy should, to his indulgent patron, and instead falls in love with Christina Light, whom Rowland consequently grows to despise. The added irony is that Rowland remains in any case too much of a prudish New Englander to be able to act on his Hellenistic impulses, even if, one imagines, Roderick were to offer himself.

As Max in 'A Light Man' had transferred his homosexual seduction of Sloane onto the idea of a Hogarthian 'mercenary marriage', so in *Roderick Hudson* there is a direct transferral, this time of

Rowland's wish for an ideal kind of camaraderie or fellowship onto Christina, who states that

> 'One doesn't want a lover one pities, and one doesn't want – of all things in the world – a picturesque husband! I should like Mr. Hudson as something else. I wish he were my brother, so that he could never talk to me of marriage. Then I could adore him. I would nurse him, I would wait on him and save him all disagreeable rubs and shocks. I am much stronger than he, and I would stand between him and the world. Indeed with Mr. Hudson for my brother I should be willing to live and die as an old maid!'
>
> (RH, 311)

This is precisely what Rowland had wished for, but has since been denied partly because of the arrival of Christina, and when Rowland hears what Christina says he unsurprisingly weighs 'his sympathy against his irritation' and feels it 'sink in the scale' (RH, 311). Priscilla L. Walton has usefully remarked of *Roderick Hudson*: 'Homosexuality is implicit in the text, but cannot be made explicit, for its explication would be more ideally devastating even than the explication of feminine sexuality. To elide this new problem, the text avoids further detailed description of Rowland and Roderick's relationship and introduces new women who can, presumably, deflect attention away from its homosexual implication.'[15] This is precisely Christina Light's role.

In the first paragraph of the novel, we are told that Rowland has 'accepted the prospect of bachelorhood' and that he has 'a lively suspicion of his uselessness' (RH, 49–50). Shortly afterwards, he tells Cecilia:

> I am tired of myself, my own thoughts, my own affairs, my own eternal company. True happiness, we are told, consists in getting out of one's self; but the point is not only to get out – you must stay out; and to stay out you must have some absorbing errand. Unfortunately I have no errand, and nobody will trust me with one. I want to care for something or for somebody. And I want to care with a certain ardour; even, if you can believe it, with a certain passion.
>
> (RH, 53)

'What an immense number of words,' Cecilia says, 'to say you want to fall in love!' (RH, 53). Then Rowland asks about the availability of local 'excellent' and 'pretty girls' (RH, 53), and it is in this context that Cecilia afterwards introduces Rowland to a 'pretty boy'. At the end of the novel, after Roderick has died, the narrator says: 'Now it was all over Rowland understood how exclusively, for two years, Roderick had filled his life. His occupation was gone' (RH, 387). It is clear that it is Roderick, and not Mary Garland, with whom Rowland falls in love: the emphasis on 'exclusivity' is otherwise too strong a sentiment for a character who is supposed to have been in love with somebody else during those previous two years, and it is understandable that, in his biography, Novick condemned the Mary–Rowland love angle to a footnote, where he proceeded to dismiss it is an unconvincing plot device.[16] However, Mary is of significance in the novel, not as the beloved of Rowland but – like Christina Light – as a third party used by Roderick and Rowland to distance themselves from the emotional complications of their male intimacy, which neither of them is able to confront until Roderick explicitly raises the motivations behind Rowland's friendship at the end.

There is a great deal of discussion of the idea of 'manliness' in *Roderick Hudson* – not only of what it is right and wrong for men to feel for one another, but the extent to which, in Rowland, there exists any passion for women at all. Rowland is described as being 'unlike other men' (RH, 98), and is said to know 'little ... about women' (RH, 182). He admits that 'some men perhaps would even say' that he is 'making a mighty ado about nothing' over Roderick, but that he is 'fond of the poor devil' and so despite everything he 'can't give him up' (RH, 228). At one point, Rowland, a 'trifle annoyed', is on the brink of saying to Roderick 'Be a man ... and don't, for heaven's sake, talk in that confoundedly querulous voice!' (RH, 144), but he manages to stop. He berates himself in similar terms for his own lack of manliness:

He often felt heavy-hearted; he was sombre without knowing why; there were no visible clouds in his heaven, but there were cloud shadows in his mood. Shadows projected they often were, without his knowing it, by an undue apprehension that things after all might not go so ideally well with Roderick. When he caught himself fidgeting it vexed him, and he rebuked himself for taking things unmanfully hard.

(RH, 160)

Two incidents involving a daring escapade to pluck a flower reveal both their vulnerability about their masculinity and the absurdly adolescent and clichéd response they both have to women. On the first occasion, Rowland overhears a conversation between Christina and Roderick, during which the former accuses the latter of being 'weak'. 'No, I am not weak,' Roderick retorts. 'I maintain that I am not weak! I am incomplete perhaps; but I can't help that. Weakness is a man's own fault!' (RH, 214). 'Ah the man who is strong with what I call strength,' Christina replies, 'would neither rise nor fall by anything I could say! I am a poor weak woman; I have no strength myself, and I can give no strength' (RH, 215). 'Give me something to conquer,' implores Roderick, and he soon notices that Christina is looking at a flower that has 'sprouted from the top of an immense fragment of wall some twenty feet from Christina's place' (RH, 207):

'I will bring it to you,' he said.
    She seized his arm. 'Are you crazy? Do you mean to kill your-self?'
    I shall not kill myself. Sit down!'
    'Excuse me. Not till you do!' and she grasped his arm with both hands.
    Roderick shook her off and pointed with a violent gesture to her former place. 'Go there!' he cried fiercely.
    'You can never, never!' she murmured beseechingly, clasping her hands. 'I implore you!'
    Roderick turned and looked at her, and then in a voice which Rowland had never heard him use, a voice almost thunderous, a voice which awakened the echoes of the mighty ruin, he repeated, 'Sit down!' She hesitated a moment, and then she dropped on the ground and buried her face in her hands.
    Rowland had seen all this, and he saw what followed . . . If the thing were possible, he felt a sudden admiring glee at the thought of Roderick doing it. It would be finely done, it would be gallant, it would have a sort of masculine eloquence as an

answer to Christina's sinister persiflage. But it was not possible! Rowland left his place with a bound and scrambled down some neighbouring steps, and the next moment a stronger pair of hands than Christina's were laid upon Roderick's shoulders ...

Roderick wiped his forehead, looked back at the wall, and then closed his eyes, as if with a spasm of retarded dizziness. 'I won't resist you,' he said. 'But I have made you obey,' he added, turning to Christina. 'Am I weak now?'

(RH, 217–19)

The paradox is that Rowland admires the 'masculine eloquence' of Roderick – here being used to impress Christina and therefore assert Roderick's heterosexual and masculine credentials – precisely because this is how Rowland relates to his own homo-erotic attraction to Roderick. The display may be with the intention of impressing Christina, but Rowland nevertheless feels an 'admiring glee' at the thought of Roderick getting the flower, because it would be 'gallant'. Then his own hands, 'stronger ... than Christina's', are placed on Roderick's shoulders. Gregory Woods's earlier quoted remark – that by associating artistic and intellectual control with 'manliness', and with male physicality, 'Pater proposes an aesthetic which is ... for homo-eroticism's sake' – is particularly relevant here. Rowland has taken control of the situation and replaced Christina as Roderick's manly intimate. Distancing himself from the 'weakness' he has been accused of has led Roderick into the arms of Rowland, and Christina remains, to both of these reunited manly comrades, the provocatively 'weak' female outsider, who perpetually threatens – like Mary – to reveal to the men their heterosexual hesitations and 'weakness' for one another.

The second flower scene, in which Rowland attempts to impress Mary with his masculinity in the way Roderick had wanted to impress Christina, and for the same reason in that he fears the consequences of being viewed as weak and unassertive, sadly but amusingly parodies the earlier one:

Suddenly as he stood there he remembered Roderick's defiance of danger and of Christina Light, at the Coliseum, and he was seized with a strong desire to test the courage of his own companion. She had just scrambled up the grassy slope near him, and had seen that the flower was out of reach. As he prepared to approach it she called to him eagerly to stop; the thing was impossible! Poor Rowland, whose passion had been terribly underfed, enjoyed immensely the thought of having her care for three minutes of what would become of him. He was the least brutal of men, but for a moment he was perfectly indifferent to her suffering.

'I can get the flower,' he called to her. 'Will you trust me?'

She looked at him and then the flower; he wondered whether she would shriek and swoon as Christina had done. 'I wish it were something better!' she said simply; and then stood watching him while he began to clamber. Rowland was not a trained acrobat and his enterprise was difficult; but he kept his wits about him, made the most of narrow footholds and coigns of vantage, and at last secured his prize. He managed to stick it into his button-hole and then he contrived to descend ... Mary's eyes perhaps did not display perhaps the ardent admiration which was formerly conferred by the queen of beauty at a tournament; but they expressed something in which Rowland found his reward. 'Why did you do that?' she asked gravely.

He hesitated. He felt it was physically possible to say, 'Because I love you!' but it was not morally possible. He lowered his pitch and answered simply, 'Because I wanted to do something for you.'

'Suppose you had fallen?'

'I believed I should not fall. And you believed it I think.'

'I believed nothing. I simply trusted you, as you asked me.'

'*Quod erat demonstrandum*!' cried Rowland. 'I think you know Latin.'

(RH, 350–1)

The remembrance of Roderick's 'defiance of danger' is the source of Rowland's recollection of the previous flower scene, and he merely wants Mary to think of what will become of him for 'three minutes'. Whereas Christina had been made to accept that Roderick was not 'weak', Mary – apparently quite baffled – states that she wishes Rowland was doing 'something better!' Again, it is not how Mary reacts, but what would be represented by how she ought to react – particularly in relation to Rowland's memory of Roderick – that is important to Rowland: 'She looked at him and then the flower; he wondered whether she would shriek and swoon as Christina had done.' He is unable to move beyond such clichés, but even on that level he is to be disappointed: 'Mary's eyes did not display perhaps the ardent admiration which was formerly conferred by the queen of beauty at a tournament.' All that is left for him is the final defeatist absurdity of a Latin exclamation.

The most revealing exchange about 'manliness' occurs between Rowland and Roderick after the latter has finally become exasperated by the former's constant justification for his every motivation by alluding to his 'moral passion' and responsibilities as patron. The accusation is that things, if looked at strictly in those heterosexual and 'moral' terms, just do not add up. The subject is both Rowland's apparent lack of passion for women, and the possible deeper motivation for his obsessive reaction to Roderick's love for Christina:

'... You ask too much, for a man who himself has no occasion to play the hero. I don't say that invidiously; it's your disposition and you can't help it. But decidedly there are certain things you know nothing about.'

Rowland listened to this outbreak with open eyes, and Roderick, if he had been less intent upon his own eloquence, would probably have perceived that he turned pale. 'These things – what are they?' Rowland asked.

'They are women, principally, and what relates to women. Women for you, from what I can make out, mean nothing. You have no imagination, no sensibility – nothing to be touched!'

'That's a serious charge,' Rowland said gravely.

'I don't make it without proof!'

'And what is your proof?'

Roderick hesitated a moment. 'The way you treated Christina Light. I call that grossly obtuse.'

'Obtuse?' Rowland repeated frowning.

'Thick-skinned, beneath your good fortune.'

'My good fortune?'

'There it is – it's all news to you! You had pleased her. I don't say she was dying of love for you, but she took a fancy to you.'

'We will let this pass!' Rowland said, after a silence.

'Oh, I don't insist. I only have her own world for it.'

'Her own word?'

'You noticed, at least, I suppose, that she was not afraid to speak! I never repeated it, not because I was jealous, but because I was curious to see how long your ignorance would last if it were left to itself.'

'I frankly confess it would have lasted for ever. And yet I don't consider that my insensitivity is proved.'

'Oh don't say that,' cried Roderick, 'or I shall begin to suspect – what I must do you the justice to say that I never suspected – that you too have a grain of conceit! Upon my word when I think of all this, your protest, as you call it, against my following Christina Light seems to me thoroughly offensive. There is something monstrous in a man's pretending to lay down the law to a sort of emotion with which he is quite unacquainted – in his asking a fellow to give up a lovely woman for conscience's sake when *he* has never had the impulse to strike a blow for one for passion's!'

'Oh, oh!' cried Rowland.

'It's very easy to exclaim,' Roderick went on; 'but you must remember there are such things as nerves and senses and imagination and a restless demon within that may sleep sometimes for a day, or for six months, but sooner or later wakes up and thumps at your ribs till you listen to him! If you can't understand it, take it on trust and let a poor visionary devil live a life as he can!'

Roderick's words seemed at first to Rowland like something heard in a dream; it was impossible they had been actually spoken – so supreme an expression were they of the insolence of egotism. Reality was never as consistent as that! But Roderick sat there balancing his beautiful head, and the echoes of his strident accents still lingered along the half-muffled mountain-side. Rowland suddenly felt that the cup of his chagrin was full to overflowing, and his long-gathered bitterness surged into the simple wholesome passion of anger for wasted kindness ...

(RH, 373–5)

'Reality was never as consistent as that!' Rowland exclaims, and the inconsistency is found in the fact that the kind of 'simple wholesome passion' which here is expressed in 'anger for wasted kindness' has until this point been sublimated by Rowland into his friendship with Roderick. As Novick writes: 'The scene would have been a great deal stronger, and Roderick's dismayed reaction more probable, if Rowland had been able to say: "I have loved you from the beginning, you ass!"'[17] The point remains, though, that this is precisely what Rowland was unable to say, and it is this fact that has resulted in Roderick being able to milk Rowland dry, both financially and emotionally: he would never have to deal with the resulting strains on their friendship because their 'manly' bond, as with that between Max and Theo in 'A Light Man', would always remain conceptually indefinable and verbally inexpressible, or if it were to be made explicit it would make Rowland, rather than Roderick, vulnerable.

When Rowland does afterwards attempt to contextualise his behaviour, by referring to his supposed love for Mary, it is primarily 'to rebut' Roderick's charge that he is 'an abnormal being' (RH, 378). The fact of his actual love for Mary, if indeed there be any, is secondary. Roderick accepts the explanation, but appends a revealing disclaimer: 'though you have suffered, in a degree,' he tells Rowland, 'I don't believe you have suffered as some other men would have done' (RH, 378). While Rowland needed to prove that he is not 'abnormal', he also felt 'an immense desire to give [Roderick] a palpable pang' – as when in 'A Light Man' Theo had wished to provoke Max into a manly fight so that he could give expression to his homo-erotic 'simple, natural emotion' in a way that would superficially leave him appearing even more masculine and heroic than before. Like Max, Rowland rejoices 'keenly, it must be confessed, in his companion's confusion' (RH, 377), and Mary herself, along with any feelings Rowland may hold for her, are again defined by their absence.

Rowland's motivation for confessing his muted love for Mary goes deeper still. Much earlier in the novel, on the first occasion that Rowland had felt a sense of 'wasted hope and faith' in Roderick (who is showing too much interest in Christina), the narrator explains that Rowland

> felt, in a word, like a man who has been cruelly defrauded and who wishes to have his revenge. Life owed him, he thought, a compensation, and he should be restless and resentful until he

found it . . . In his melancholy meditations the idea of something better than all this, something that might soften, richly inter-pose, something that might reconcile him to the future, something that might make one's tenure of life string and zealous instead of mechanical and uncertain – the idea of concrete compensation in a word – shaped itself sooner or later in the image of Mary Garland.

Very odd, you may say, that at this time of day Rowland should still be brooding over a girl with no brilliancy, of whom he had but the lightest of glimpses two years before; very odd that so deep an impression should have been made by so lightly pressed an instrument. We must admit the oddity, and remark simply in explanation that his sentiment apparently belonged to that species of emotion of which by the testimony of the poets the very name and essence are oddity.

(RH, 250)

Very odd, we may indeed say. Mary is viewed as a compensation once the eternal friendship with Roderick begins to seem transitory. Rowland has his 'revenge' at the end of the novel by stating that he is in love with Mary, and his chief motivation is to get that 'palpable pang' from Roderick. This inexpressible, in explicit terms, oddity is nevertheless structurally crucial to the novel, and it results in an imbalance: Rowland is presented as being in love with Mary but we simply do not believe it, while he is presented as being objective in his patronage of Roderick in a way that is equally unconvincing. In this particular passage, James is attempting, rather unsuccessfully, to find a way of justifying in conventional terms what would remain an 'oddly' inexpressible truth.

James returns to the scenario of a male friendship strained by the presence of a woman in his little-read short novel *Confidence*, but unlike in *Roderick Hudson* he reconciles the homo-erotic bond of masculine affection rooted in adolescence with the necessity of being free from the emotional and psychological limitations of such male adolescent bonding once adulthood arrives and marriage is therefore expected. The novel is concerned with how to gain the necessary experience, and thereby acquire the 'confidence', to face an adult world in which an adolescent kind of homo-erotic mascu-line bonding is no longer socially acceptable. The two principal characters, Bernard Longueville (an artist) and Gordon Wright (a scientist), 'had formed an alliance of old, in college days, and the bond between them had been strengthened by the simple fact of its having survived the sentimental revolutions of early life ... [I]t had never been very definitely been proposed to these young gentlemen to distinguish themselves. On reaching manhood, they had each come into property sufficient to make violent exertion superfluous' (C, 1053). They are experiencing the 'precious remnant of their youth' (C, 1157), a male adolescent companionship which, for James, always had a precious homo-erotic sentiment. Although there is no evidence that James had the play in mind when writing the novel,[18] a useful starting point when thinking about *Confidence* is Shakespeare's *The Winter's Tale*, in which Leontes and Polixenes are said, by the latter, to have been like

> ...Two lads, that thought there was no more behind
> But such a day tomorrow as today
> And to be boy eternal ...
> We were as twinn'd lambs that did frisk i' th' sun,
> And bleat the one at th' other: what we chang'd
> Was innocence for innocence: we knew not
> The doctrine of ill-doing, nor dream'd
> That any did.
>
> (I.ii. 64–70)

In the play, it is Leontes' inability to accept that his friendship with Polixenes has been superseded by higher concerns, and that it has therefore become dependent on a greater degree of complexity and trust than the previous simple pledges of boyish camaraderie had allowed for, which is at the root of his jealousy and their subsequent falling out. The play is partly about how these two characters are wrenched apart, to be reconciled again in a way that makes them recognise the responsibilities and duties of an adult heterosexual environment.

In *Confidence*, Gordon is the Leontes figure. He provokes a falling-out between himself and Bernard by (absurdly, if the novel is mistakenly viewed in terms of realism rather than as a fable) insisting that Bernard become intimately involved with his wish to choose a bride, Angela – just as Leontes had insisted on an easy intimacy between his wife and Polixenes only to suspect them of infidelity immediately afterwards. Women are referred to in the novel as 'necessities' (C, 1078), but Bernard admits that he is 'as ignorant of women as a monk in a cloister' (C, 1085). Conversely, he is said to have 'a great affection for his friend – an affection to which it would perhaps be difficult to assign a definite cause' (C, 1054). The narrator states: 'The reasons for [Gordon] appreciating Bernard Longueville were much more manifest ... He was very good-looking – tall, dark, agile, perfectly finished, so good looking that he might have been a fool and yet forgiven' (C, 1054). What follows, when Bernard instead of Gordon falls in love with Angela and subsequently marries her, is the 'violent exertion' which is hitherto said to have been 'superfluous' to their friendship, and the homo-erotic undertones of that friendship are paradoxically brought to the fore, because, by marrying, Gordon is hoping to test the adolescent loyalty established between himself and Bernard. 'I want to see how she will affect you,' (C, 1052) he says, and the narrator soon afterwards talks of the 'candid, manly, affectionate nature of his comrade' (C, 1054).

Manliness, camaraderie and loyalty become, as previously in 'A Light Man' and *Roderick Hudson*, increasingly prominent preoccupations. Initially, Bernard is conscious of 'the duty and loyalty to his friend' when he meets Angela, and dutifully tells Gordon that he thinks Angela will marry him. 'I am much obliged to you,' Gordon says. 'That's my idea of friendship. You have spoken out like a man' (C, 1125). Shortly afterwards, Gordon leaves Baden-Baden for no apparent reason, but presumably to give Bernard and Vivian the opportunity to enjoy one another's company, during which time Bernard will be obliged further to test his own sense of loyalty. However, now that Gordon has gone, '[Bernard] felt a sudden and singular sense of freedom. It was a feeling of unbounded expansion, quite out of proportion, as he said to himself, to any assignable cause. Everything suddenly appeared to have become very optional; but he was quite at a loss as to what to do with his liberty' (C, 1130). This 'freedom' eventually leads to Bernard becoming engaged to Angela, when he decides after three years that he is in love with her and that such a love should supersede his responsibilities to an adolescent male friendship. Gordon learns the news and exclaims:

It's horrible, most horrible, that such a difference as this should come between two men who believed themselves – for whom I believed, at least – the best friends in the world. For it is a difference – it's a great gulf, and nothing will ever fill it up. I must say so; I can't help it. You know I don't express myself easily; so, if I break out this way, you may know what I feel. I must say to her that you have no right to marry her; and beg of her to listen to me and let you go.

(C, 1231)

Referring to the news of the engagement, Gordon had earlier told Bernard that 'This thing is between ourselves' (C, 1230), thus relegating Angela – as Rowland had always relegated Mary – to a convenient cause for an argument between manly friends. In the longer passage, Gordon is talking to Bernard as though he ought, if this were a conventional heterosexual novel, to be talking to Angela: he proposes to ask *her* to give *him* up. It is the friendship he wishes to save, rather than his marriage. The novel afterwards descends into farce, as Angela seeks out Gordon in Paris to convince him that he is in fact in love with another woman, brainless Blanch. Angela succeeds, and Gordon makes it up with Bernard:

'That's over now,' said Gordon. 'I came to welcome you back. It seemed to me I couldn't lay my head on my pillow without speaking to you.'

'I'm glad to get back,' Bernard admitting, smiling still. 'I can't deny that. And I find you as I believed I should.' 'Then he added, seriously – 'I knew Angela would keep us good friends.'

'Yes, for that purpose it didn't matter which of us should marry her. If it had been I,' he added, 'she would have made you accept it.'

'Ah, I don't know!' Bernard exclaimed.

'I am sure of it,' Gordon said earnestly – almost argumentatively. 'She's an extraordinary woman.'

'Keeping you good friends with me – that's a great thing. But it's nothing to her keeping you good friends to your wife.'

Gordon looked at Bernard for an instant; then he fixed his eyes for some time on the fire.

'Yes, that's the greatest of all things. A man should value his wife. He should believe in her. He has taken her, and he should keep her – especially when there's a great deal of good in her. I was a great fool the other said,' he went on. 'I don't remember what I said. I was weak.'

'It seemed to me feeble,' said Bernard. 'But it's quite within a man's rights to be a fool once in a while, and you had never abused of the license.'

'Well, I have done it for a lifetime – for a lifetime.'

(C, 1249–50)

The implication is that the chief purpose of marriage is to strengthen masculine bonds of friendship, and 'for that purpose it didn't matter' whether Gordon or Bernard had married Angela (in the same way that, if this had been an ending for *Roderick Hudson*, it would not have mattered whether Rowland or Roderick had married Mary so long as they were allowed to continue their own intimacy with a sense of being given their own space). In *Confidence*, unmanly 'weakness' and 'feebleness' are no longer issues at the end of the novel, as they were in *Roderick Hudson*: they are laughed at rather than avoided or covered up, then discarded. The final lines of *Confidence* reveal that 'on his arrival in Cairo, while [Gordon] waited for his dragoman to give the signal for starting, he found time, in spite of the exactions of that large correspondence which has been more than once mentioned in the course of our narrative, to write Bernard the longest letter he had ever addressed to him. The letter reached Bernard in the middle of his honeymoon' (C, 1252). In this way James finds a way of permanently extending the sense of an adolescent, homo-erotic bonding between Gordon and Bernard in a way that he had found it impossible to do with Rowland and Roderick.

In 'Daisy Miller', the heterosexual hesitations that define Rowland in *Roderick Hudson* and Gordon in *Confidence* are directly confronted by the protagonist Winterbourne, who at the end of the tale steps out of his enforced role of a dutiful chaser of the flirtatious eponymous girl. Like both Gordon and Rowland, Winterbourne fits with surprising exactitude the pattern of 'permanent adolescence'. The first thing we learn about him is that 'he had an odd attachment for the little metropolis of Calvinism; he had been put to school there as a boy, and he had afterwards gone to college there – circumstances which had led to his forming a great many youthful friendships. Many of these he had kept, and they were a source of great satisfaction to him' (DM, 4–5). This is the only unambiguous 'satisfaction' Winterbourne is granted by James, and the story is framed by the retrospectiveness to the extent that, at its end, Winterbourne symbolically complains that he has 'lived too long in foreign parts' (DM, 202) to be able to understand American women and he returns to Geneva. Geneva therefore serves two purposes. Geographically real and culturally specific, its connection with Calvinistic dryness and repression also allows it to be used as an objective correlative for (the symbolically named) Winterbourne's psychology – in the same way that he asks himself whether Daisy's 'extravagance' was 'generic, national' or 'personal' (DM, 195), and that America is obviously the defining environment out of which Daisy's subjective temperament has emerged. On this symbolic level, Geneva should be equated with Winterbourne's adolescence, and Rome (where he deepens his 'observation' of Daisy) with the initiating social and sexual world of adulthood. The drama of the story centres on Winterbourne's failure to experience a socially defined heterosexual maturation, which is paralleled by his geographical movement from Geneva to Rome and back again, at the end of the story, to his unthreatening adolescent haven Geneva.[19]

Winterbourne's interest in Daisy's little brother, Randolph, reinforces the impression of his narcissism and retrospectiveness: 'Winterbourne wondered if he himself had been like this in his infancy, for he had been brought to Europe at about this age' (DM, 156). He sees the boy before he sees Daisy (DM, 155), the boy introduces him to her (DM, 157), and Winterbourne sees the boy again after Daisy dies (DM, 200). The story is framed by Winterbourne's encounters with the child, encounters which anticipate, because of an added emphasis by James on the potential of a teacher–pupil intimacy between them, the pederastic couplings of Pemberton and Morgan in 'The Pupil' (1891) and Quint and Miles in *The Turn of the Screw* (1898). 'Don't you want to come and teach Randolph?' (DM, 175) Daisy asks Winterbourne. Randolph is also the same type of boy as Morgan and Miles: he, too, wears knickerbockers and stockings (DM, 156); he is isolated and extremely mature (DM, 160); he has an 'aged expression of countenance' (DM, 155); he is said by his mother never to have been 'much like an infant' (DM, 179); and he tells adults truths about themselves which they are unable to deal with – for example, when he clarifies for Winterbourne that Daisy has dyspepsia (DM, 178).

Winterbourne famously analyses, categorises and objectifies his relationship – or more precisely, his potential relationship – with the eponymous hero of the story, but never acts. He is essentially innocent, and 'Daisy Miller' is concerned with whether he will mature into a 'gallant' heterosexual: 'he wondered what were the regular conditions and limitations of one's intercourse with a pretty American flirt. It presently became apparent that he was on his way to learn' (DM, 162). He is even said to be 'afraid – literally afraid' of certain ladies – a trait he shares with Clifford in *The Europeans* (1878),[20] written at the same time as 'Daisy Miller' – but conversely has 'a pleasant sense that he should never be afraid of Daisy Miller' (DM, 192). One reason that he might never be afraid of her is that she does not exist, physically speaking: with irritating repetition we learn only that she is 'strikingly, admirably pretty'; that her eyes are 'wonderfully pretty'; that she has 'extremely pretty hands'; a 'pretty figure'; and even 'pretty teeth' (DM, 157; 158; 160; 173; 180).

Jean Goodner has written: 'Winterbourne's appraisal of Daisy is, of course, the dramatic centre of the story. From the start it is ambivalent. . . . For a man of urbanity and wit he seems remarkably afraid of being compromised.'[21] Since everything is presented from Winterbourne's point of view, it is indeed his sense of self, and how his self-perception changes, that gives the story its narrative momentum. The 'compromise' he is most afraid of is being made to confront the fact that he has no 'instinctive' romantic feelings for Daisy. He displays instead only an eccentric and objective 'interest': 'He had a great relish for feminine beauty; he was addicted to observing and analysing it' (DM, 158). Elsewhere, his reactions to Daisy are sometimes couched entirely in the negative: 'That she should seem to wish to get rid of him would have helped him to think more lightly of her, and to be able to think more lightly of her would make her less perplexing' (DM, 184). Moreover, whenever his wish to be thought about by her is expressed, it is in the context of how she might boost his self-esteem: 'The news that Daisy Miller was surrounded by half a dozen wonderful moustaches checked Winterbourne's impulse to go straightway to see her. He had perhaps not definitely flattered himself that he had made an inef-faceable impression upon her heart, but he was annoyed at hearing of a state of affairs so little in harmony with an image of a very pretty girl looking out of an old Roman window and asking herself urgently when Mr Winterbourne would arrive' (DM, 177). Like Roderick and Rowland in *Roderick Hudson*, Winterbourne is concerned about living up to what he believes to be appropriate manly behaviour in the company of a woman whose actions he is also needing to interpret and categorise. Despite the fact that he has 'lost his instinct in this matter, and his reason could not help him' (DM, 161), he becomes obsessed with the idea of what it means to be 'gallant'. The central contrast in the story is between Giovanelli – Daisy's assumed, low-class, handsome, moustachioed and 'instinctive' lover – and 'stiff' (DM, 189) Winterbourne, a contrast brought out by the repeated use of the word 'gallant'.

The importance of this word is highlighted by the fact that James introduced it to a number of sentences when he revised the tale for its inclusion in the New York Edition. When Winterbourne first approaches Daisy, he (in the New York Edition) 'wondered whether he had gone too far, but decided that he must gallantly advance rather than retreat',[22] and the first time he challenges social convention – by going against his aunt's disparaging opinion of Daisy – it is said to reveal a 'questionable mixture of gallantry and impiety' (DM, 168). Daisy challenges Winterbourne about what she suspects is his attempt to save her 'reputation' by discouraging her from getting into a carriage with Giovanelli, but Winterbourne 'himself had in fact to speak in accordance with gallantry' (DM, 186). Shortly afterwards, in an addition to the New York Edition, Winterbourne observes 'the gallant Giovanelli' take out Daisy's parasol and open it.[23] A few pages on, the narrator confirms that Giovanelli bears himself 'gallantly' when he performs 'all the proper functions of a handsome Italian at an evening party' (DM, 189), and Winterbourne finally admits that 'holding oneself to a belief in Daisy's "innocence" came to seem ... more and more a matter of fine-spun gallantry' (DM, 195). When the fact that Giovanelli is his 'rival' is spelled out, Winterbourne admits to Daisy in an addition to the New York Edition: 'I'm not as fortunate ... as your gallant companion.'[24] Gallantry for Winterbourne is behaving like a 'gentleman' (DM, 183), but is also something deeper to do with passion and an instinctive way with women, which he knows he does not have but Giovanelli does, to the extent that it allows the latter to be an apparently successful suitor at Winterbourne's expense and humiliation. Winterbourne makes explicit his jealousy when he says of Giovanelli: 'damn his good looks!' (DM, 182). He wants what Giovanelli has, despite his protestation that Giovanelli is a 'spurious gentleman' (DM, 183). Finally, in the New York Edition, James has Winterbourne admit to Daisy that he feels that he is not 'as fortunate' as her 'gallant companion'.

The relationship, as much as it can be called one, that Winterbourne does establish with Daisy is best compared to that of Rowland and Mary in *Roderick Hudson*, as much as that too could be called a relationship. What Winterbourne is most concerned about is what is also Rowland's chief preoccupation: socially behaving in a way that would seem 'gallant' to Christina and 'have a sort of masculine eloquence' (RH, 218), in order for him publicly to distance himself from his inner turmoil. And again like Rowland wanting Mary to 'swoon' at his masculine daring, Winterbourne can only relate to Daisy in terms of romantic clichés: 'he had never yet enjoyed the sensation of guiding through the summer starlight a skiff freighted with a fresh and beautiful young girl' (DM, 171); or when, 'as he looked at her dress and, on the great staircase, her little rapid, confiding step, he felt as if there were something romantic going forward. He could have believed he was going to elope with her. He passed out with her among all the idle people that were assembled there; they were all looking at her very hard ...' (DM, 173). Winterbourne ends up begging Daisy: 'flirt with me, and me only'. She pointedly replies: 'you're the last man I should think of flirting with' (DM, 190). In a repeat of both Roderick and Rowland's attempts in *Roderick Hudson* to dominate 'weak' Christina and Mary respectively in the two flower scenes, Winterbourne attempts to assert his masculinity and dominance by ordering Daisy: 'You won't leave me!' But on this occasion, as when in Rowland attempted to dominate Mary, Waterborne fails. He merely provokes a 'little laugh' and the amusing retort: 'Are you afraid you'll get lost – or run over?' (DM, 182).

Winterbourne's casting away of his psychological mask provides the climactic moment to the story. He is relieved at no longer having to face the confusion of dissembling romantic interest.

James made substantial and important changes to this paragraph for the New York Edition, and it is therefore useful to quote both and then to explore the difference in emphasis:

> Winterbourne stopped, with a sort of horror; and, it must be added, with a sort of relief. It was as if a sudden illumination had been flashed upon the ambiguity of Daisy's behaviour and the riddle had become easy to read. She was a young lady whom a gentleman need no longer be at pains to respect. He stood there looking at her – looking at her companion, and not reflecting that though he saw them vaguely, he himself must have been more brightly visible. He felt angry with himself that he had bothered so much about the right way of regarding Miss Daisy Miller. Then, as he was going to advance, he checked himself; not from the fear that he was doing her injustice, but from a sense of the danger offering unbecomingly exhilarated by this sudden revulsion from cautious criticism. He turned away towards the entrance of the place; but as he did so he heard Daisy speak again.
>
> 'Why, it was Mr. Winterbourne! He saw me – and he cuts me!'
>
> (DM, 198)

Winterbourne felt himself pulled up with final horror now – and, it must be added, with final relief. It was as if a sudden clearance had taken place in the ambiguity of the poor girl's appearances and the whole riddle of her contradictions had grown easy to read. She was a young person about the shades of whose perversity a foolish puzzled gentleman need no longer trouble his head or his heart. That once questionable quantity had no shades – it was a mere black little blot. He stood there looking at her, looking at her companion too, and not reflecting that though he saw them vaguely he himself must have been more brightly presented. He felt angry at all his shiftings of view – he felt ashamed of all his tender little scruples and all his witless little mercies. He was about to advance again, and then again checked himself; not from the fear of doing her injustice, but from a sense of the danger of showing undue exhilaration for his disburdenment of cautious criticism. He turned away toward the entrance of the place; but as he did so he heard Daisy speak again.

'Why it was Mr Winterbourne! He saw me and he cuts me
dead!' (New York Edition)[25]

That this is a thematic, as well as a structural, climax is emphasised
by the repeated 'final' in the opening sentence of the revised
version. The new observation that though Winterbourne 'saw them
vaguely he himself must have been more brightly presented', rather
than (in the original) 'more brightly visible', reflects the fact that,
for the reader, Winterbourne's reactions and observations are being
'presented' as the main subject. The 'sudden clearance' in Daisy's
'appearance' does not arise as a result of the erasure of some
intrinsic complexity or ambiguity in Daisy's behaviour – she has
always been a daringly innocent flirt and is now being daringly and
innocently flirtatious – but because this is the first occasion when
Winterbourne views her with (albeit negative and dismissive)
sincerity. In the New York Edition, Daisy's final words are changed
from 'he cuts me' to 'he cuts me dead', and Bell has written of how
Daisy's 'individuality, such as it is, is doomed by Winterbourne's
decision to "cut her dead" and the stiff box into which his categor-
ical mind has thrust her is, in effect, her coffin'.[26] The juxtaposition
of 'horror' with 'relief' in the first sentence of both versions locates
the following 'disburdenment' in the dual consciousness of
Winterbourne, and the addition of the word 'dead' in 'cuts me
dead' indicates that James wanted to associate, in a more obvious
way than was the case when he first published the story, that
Daisy's metaphorical and then literal death results in an awakening
in Winterbourne associated with his rejection not of Daisy but
his own insincerity. It is Winterbourne's internal contradictions
that disappear.

A phrase included in both versions, 'not from fear of doing her
injustice', reverses an earlier self-deprecation by Winterbourne that
he 'by instinct' should not 'appreciate [Daisy] justly'. This previous
'vexation' was linked to his being 'impatient to see her again' (DM,
166), and his inner conflict was the result of his attempt to express
responses that contradicted his 'instinctive' feelings. In the
climactic scene, Winterbourne ceases to consider what would be
just for Daisy and acts instead on what he thinks is 'just' to himself.
This newly discovered assertiveness leads to feelings of 'exhilaration' and a later paragraph opens: 'Winterbourne – to do him

justice, as it were ...' (DM, 200). Finally, the sentence 'She was a young lady whom a gentleman need no longer be at pains to respect' in the original version is replaced by 'She was a young person about the shades of whose perversity a foolish puzzled gentleman need no longer trouble his head or his heart' in the revised one. The idea of Winterbourne's 'puzzlement' is introduced, and instead of his simple lack of a need to be at 'pains to respect' Daisy it is said that he no longer needs to 'trouble his head or his heart'. Again, this emphasises his elation at no longer having to dissemble romantic feelings.

The general effect of the revisions is to increase Winterbourne's puzzlement while emphasising the role his romantic attachment to Daisy has had in creating that now-resolved perplexity. While it would indeed be an 'abuse of speculation' to label Winterbourne homosexual, he does – unlike Clifford in *The Europeans*, who is conventionally married off (E, 191), and Rowland in *Roderick Hudson*, who retreats behind the protective shield of his phoney interest in Mary – unambiguously reject the conventions of compulsory heterosexuality. In this rejection, and especially considering his interest in Daisy's little brother Randolph, Winterbourne points the way to James's later treatment of exclusively homosexual characters, who start from the position of rejecting compulsory heterosexuality that 'Daisy Miller' shows Winterbourne moving towards.

The single defining characteristic of the unnamed protagonist of 'The Diary of a Man of Fifty', published one year after 'Daisy Miller', is his melancholy retrospective narcissism, which is associated with his sense of personal and social failure as a heterosexual. While Winterbourne rejects compulsory heterosexuality and admits his lack of 'instinctive certitude' about women, the protagonist of this later story contemplates the kind of life Winterbourne could perhaps be contemplating 27 years hence:

They told me I should find Italy greatly changed; and in seven and twenty years there is room for changes. But to me everything is so perfectly the same that I seem to be living my youth over again; all the forgotten impressions of that time come back to me. At that moment they were powerful enough; but they afterwards faded away ... I have not been miserable; I won't go as far as to say that – or at least to write it. But happiness – positive happiness – would have been something different ... I should have had a wife and children, and I should not be in the way of making, as the French say it, infidelities to the present. Of course it's a great gain to have had an escape, not to have committed an act of thumping folly; and I suppose that, whatever serious steps one might have taken at twenty five, after a struggle, and with a violent effort, and however one's conduct might appear to be justified by events, there would always remain a certain element of regret; a certain sense of loss lurking in the sense of gain; a tendency to wonder, rather wishfully, what *might* have been. What might have been, in this case, would, no doubt, have been very sad, and what has been has been very cheerful and comfortable; but there are nevertheless two or three questions I might ask myself. Why, for instance, have I never married ...?

(DMF, 334–5)

The overwhelming sense is that true happiness – 'positive happiness' – can only be found by gaining 'a wife and children', and that, however great the risk of committing 'a great act of thumping folly' in getting married, the result of not doing so is an inevitable constant wish that somehow things could have been different. Like Rowland in *Roderick Hudson* and Winterbourne in 'Daisy Miller', this man has rejected the compulsory world of heterosexual relations; but he has not found a credible alternative lifestyle and so is crippled by the consequences. Like Winterbourne, he was 'too cautious – too suspicious – too logical' (DMF, 360) and 'afraid' (DMF, 348) of the woman in question, who – as with Daisy Miller – only liked men 'who are afraid of nothing' (DMF, 343). James left Rowland and Winterbourne at the moment their lack of passion for women and 'gallantry' could be seen to have social and personal consequences. In 'The Diary of a Man of Fifty', he explores what those consequences might have been, and in so doing anticipates the stories of the middle period, which present the consciousness of men who have rejected a compulsory heterosexual world and are having to deal with the consequences.

In 'The Diary of a Man of Fifty' the protagonist befriends Stanmer, a handsome younger man, and the superficial justification for his developing interest in this younger man is that he is in love with the daughter of the woman the protagonist himself was in love with at the age of 25. When the protagonist discovers by chance this 'analogy', it is so 'complete' (DMF, 340) that he feels compelled to save the young man from the same unhappy fate as himself – of being bewitched by a 'consummate coquette' (DMF, 345) – though he evidently feels that his failure to marry has resulted in an even greater unhappiness and emptiness than might perhaps otherwise have been the case. And as the details emerge of why he did not marry, it becomes increasingly apparent that he is eager to thwart Stanmer's marriage to the daughter because of his jealousy, and a kind of homo-erotic yearning for Stanmer himself, as much as through a concern about the unhappiness that threatens to engulf the younger man if he does indeed decide on matrimony.

The circumstances surrounding the protagonist's fear of what the mother represented, and what she expected him to represent, is a macho duel her husband had fought with a man with whom she was having an affair, who killed her husband and then continued the affair (DMF, 355). Later the protagonist discovered that they were to be married: 'I had been ready to marry the woman who was capable of that!' (DMF, 356) he exclaims. This is a credible retrospective justification for his inability to marry, but since he did not gain the knowledge of the scandalous marriage at the time it is not a sufficient reason for his *initial* inability to marry. The result of that inability, however, is clear enough: he has remained fixated on his youth. 'I live in the past,' (DMF 348) he admits unambiguously. He is another of James's 'permanent adolescents' and his keen but deflected interest in Stanmer, who resembles his own younger self, strikingly relates to the narcissistic psychological definition of homosexuality Freud would encapsulate as a focus on young men and early manhood by men who are attempting to recapture the lost sense of a defining self first encountering in sexual maturation. 'You remind me of my younger self,' (DMF, 338) the protagonist says to Stanmer, and goes on to explain that in meeting him he is encountering 'not only myself' by 'my whole situation over again' (DMF, 339). In this sense, the story anticipates James's more homo-erotically charged, and all-male 'The Great Good Place' (1990), in which an older man is similarly metamorphosed into the younger man he once was through a meeting with a mysterious Brother figure, who again very much resembles that own younger self.

However, the homo-erotic themes in 'The Diary of a Man of Fifty', in keeping with their treatment elsewhere in James's earlier fiction, are obliquely presented in a superficially heterosexual scenario.

There is something clearly sinister in the way the protagonist uses the analogy of his own past situation and what Stanmer is presently experiencing in order at once to create a homo-erotic bond between himself and the young man and then to attempt to deny the latter the opportunity of heterosexual happiness. His admiration of Stanmer is expressed in the language of Rowland's admiration of Roderick: 'Whether it was that I had seen him before, or simply that I was struck with his agreeable young face – at any rate, I felt myself, as they say here, in sympathy with him' (DMF, 337). And they enjoy the same kind of instantaneous and physical friendship. Stanmer initially hesitates 'very properly' to 'talk with a perfect stranger' (DMF, 337), but after the protagonist has declared him to be a 'handsome young Englishman' and asserted his own heterosexual credentials, 'Instantly, instinctively, [Stanmer] raised his hand to my arm' (DMF, 338). Shortly afterwards, the protagonist passes his 'hand into [Stanmer's] arm' (DMF, 339), and off they stroll. This now reads like homosexual cruising.

The focus of the story quickly shifts from the 'analogy' towards the protagonist's annoyance at not being able to keep Stanmer away from the daughter, just as Rowland had become increasingly exasperated at Roderick's infatuation with Christina. There is an exchange which echoes that between Rowland and Roderick at the end of *Roderick Hudson*, when Roderick complains that Rowland has been interfering in his personal love affairs more than the context of a simple male friendship justifies. Here, it is Stanmer who is doing the complaining:

'What you mean, then, is that the daughter is a finished coquette?'
'I rather think so.'
Stanmer walked along some moments in silence.
'Seeing that you suppose me to be a – a great admirer of the Countess,' he said at last, 'I am rather surprised at the freedom with which you speak of her.'
I confessed that I was surprised at it myself. 'But it's on account of the interest I take in you.'

'I am immensely obliged to you,' said the poor boy.

Ah, of course you don't like it. That is, you like my interest – I don't see how you could help liking that; but you don't like my freedom. That's natural enough; but, my dear young friend, I want only to help you. If a man had said to me – so many years ago – what I am saying to you, I should certainly also, at first, have thought him a great brute. But, after a little, I should have been grateful – I should have felt that he was helping me.'

'You seem to have been very well able to help yourself,' said Stanmer. 'I think this, at any rate – that you take an extraordinary responsibility in trying to put a man out of conceit of a woman who, as he believes, may make him very happy.'

I grasped his arm, and we stopped, going on with our talk with a couple of Florentines.

'Do you wish to marry her?'

He looked away, without meeting my eyes. 'It's a great responsibility,' he repeated.

'Before Heaven!' I said, 'I would have married the mother! You are exactly in my situation.'

'Don't you think you rather overdo the analogy?' asked poor Stanmer.

(DMF, 347)

As with Rowland, the protagonist carefully couches his argument in a strictly heterosexual context; but just as Roderick had asserted that even if Rowland had indeed loved Mary, he had not suffered 'as other men would have', so Stanmer later directly confronts the protagonist of 'The Diary of a Man of Fifty' with the assertion that he 'couldn't have been much in love' (DMF, 356). Exasperated at his inability to persuade Stanmer not to marry, the protagonist finally compensates for his peculiar sense of defeat by consoling himself that their marriage will be nightmarish: 'It would really be very interesting to see Stanmer swallowed up. I should like to see how he would agree with her after she had devoured him – (to what vulgar imagery, by the way, does curiosity reduce a man!)' (DMF, 353). This is perhaps in part a transferral of his own wish to 'swallow' Stanmer, and in his jealousy he can only see negative consequences if the daughter does so instead. He is moreover governed by 'curiosity', rather than his sense of the 'analogy', and is jealous of the increasingly intimate (and therefore excluding) behaviour of Stanmer and the daughter, which eventually leads to the protagonist confessing that 'it *does* irritate me – the way he sticks!' (DMF, 358). Finally, he declares: 'His happiness makes him clever. I hope it will last! – I mean his cleverness, not his happiness' (DMF, 359). In the closing paragraph, the protagonist admits to himself what Stanmer had known all along: that the analogy was not as exact as he had at first led Stanmer to believe, and that his drawing it had more to do with his own insecurity and self-denial than his wish to help the younger man:

> ... the boy's words have been thrumming in my ears – 'Depend upon it you were wrong. Wasn't it rather a mistake?' *Was* I wrong – *was* it a mistake? Was I too cautious – too suspicious – too logical? Was it really a protector she needed – a man who might have helped her? Was the poor woman very unhappy? God forgive me, how the questions come crowding in! If I married her happiness, I certainly didn't make my own. And I might have made it – eh? That's a charming discovery for a man of my age!
>
> (DMF, 360)

4
John Addington Symonds and 'The Author of *Beltraffio*'

The only surviving letter from James to Symonds was written in 1884 and concerns the 'unspeakably tender passion' they shared for Italy. 'I sent you the *Century* more than a year ago with my paper on Venice,' James wrote, meaning the year he had lunched with Symonds and during which Symonds had published the first defence of homosexuality to appear in England, *A Problem in Greek Ethics*. James explains that he sent the paper

> because it was a constructive way of expressing the good will I felt towards you in consequence of what you had written about the land of Italy – and of intimating to you, somewhat dumbly, that I am an attentive and sympathetic reader. I nourish for the said Italy an unspeakably tender passion, and your pages always seemed to say to me that you were one of a small number of people who love it as much as I do – in addition to your knowing it immeasurably better. I wanted to recognize this (to your knowledge); for it seemed to me the victims of a common passion should exchange a look ... I spent last winter in the United States and while I was there another old and excellent friend of mine, Sergeant Perry ... read me a portion of a note he had had from you, in which you were so good as to speak (in a friendly – a very friendly way) of the little paper in the *Century* ...
>
> I imagine that it is scarcely ever in your power to come to England, but do take note of my whereabouts, for this happy (and possibly, to you, ideal) contingency. I should like very much to see you... and (I will say it) I think of you with

exceeding sympathy. As a sign of that I shall send you everything I publish.

(HJL: 3, 29–30)

Although the travel article published in the *Century* sent to Symonds contained the reference to the group of nearly naked boys James encountered, one of whom underwent in James's vision an apotheosis into Eros, it could be argued that this letter had nothing to do with homosexuality. Then a number of questions would be raised, particularly since James wrote it more than a decade before stylistic obscurity and indulgence became the trademark of his writing – questions such as why James wrote in such a coded way, why the information he is offering is for Symonds's 'knowledge' only, why the 'passion' for Italy should be described as 'unspeakably tender', why this utterance of it is made 'somewhat dumbly', and why that same 'passion' should later be referred to in the context of a reference to a small number of 'victims' looking out for, or 'glancing', at one another. Then there is the '(friendly – a very friendly way)' to be accounted for, as well as the frank admission, at the end of the letter, of what James had for no obvious reason being circuitously approaching. After the obscure parenthetical peculiarity of '(I will say it)' there is the statement: 'I think of you with exceeding sympathy.' Why the theatrical build-up? And why 'sympathy'? Why the sense of danger from exposure when all James was writing was doing was writing a personal letter?

It is not known whether James read *Greek Ethics* immediately, but it is more likely that he heard about it rather than was sent a copy because the polemic appeared in a privately printed edition of just ten copies.[1] Symonds, however, had confided his homosexuality to Gosse, and the homosexual Gosse had already been in correspondence with James about Symonds and had made specific reference to the latter's homosexuality (HJL: 3, 72). We know from James's letter and from other sources that he took a deep interest in Symonds's work and that he wanted Symonds to reciprocate that interest, and while we do not know whether James kept his word and did indeed forward Symonds all his subsequent books, Edel notes that eventually James did have almost all of Symonds's books in his own private library (HJL: 3, 31). Writing to Symonds at this time, James was eager to deepen his intimacy with a man he knew to be openly homosexual, interested in homosexual legal reform, and in promoting the more general belief that there could be an intellectual understanding about and tolerance of homosexuality in England.

Symonds was the bridge in Victorian England between the sublimated and coded Hellenistic approach to homosexuality in Whitman and early Pater (and James's early fiction) and the more open movement promoting homosexual legitimacy associated with the aesthetes that would gather pace after Symonds published his *Modern Ethics* in 1891 but then meet with a powerful and ultimately successful homophobic counter-reaction which culminated in the Wilde trial of 1895. This situation coincided with the emergence of sensational reports of homosexuality in the new mass-circulation newspapers and magazines. Weeks says that a series of scandals in the early 1880s served to link 'homosexuality and prostitution with sexual decadence, and in 1884 there was a full-scale homosexual scandal involving high officials in Dublin Castle'. Particularly important when thinking about the shift in James's subsequently fiction is the way that, according to Weeks, 'homosexuality became an explicit subject in its own right' and 'the labelling process threatened to undermine traditional male camaraderie'.[2]

The Criminal Law Amendment Act was placed on the statute book the year after the Dublin Castle scandal, extending the legal prohibition of the act of sodomy to virtually all male homosexual activity or speech in public or private; and the concept associated with it – of a definable, identifiable male exclusively judged and criminalised by his sexual attraction to other males – began to take hold. The medical profession 'began to break down the formerly universal execrated forms of non-procreative sex into a number of "perversions and deviations", so that, for the succeeding generations, the prime task of theory seemed to be the classification of new forms, the listing of their manifestations, the discussion of their causes'. Weeks concludes that it is in this process that 'homosexuality gradually emerges as a specific category'.[3] Eric Haralson writes that, as the letter James sent to Symonds in 1884 was written more than ten years before the Wilde trials, it is not clear why it should be read 'as if it were informed by an emotional state and a political climate that would not fully obtain until ... a decade later'.[4] Weeks does indeed make it clear that by 1884 the process of the emergence of homosexuality by way of social scandal was well under way, and it should be remembered that Wilde's trial was as much a culmination of what went on before it as it would prove to be a marker for those who had to live in its wake. Indeed, a recently published letter, sent to Theodore Child on 19 November 1884, confirms James's awareness and curiosity. 'The demoralization of your country seems to me complete,' he writes ironically. 'Escape before the doom of Gomorrah descends on it – escape to this virtuous clime [England] where I see that the Very Rev. the Dean of Hereford was yesterday arrested for indecent behaviour – with a young man! – in Hyde Park' (HJLL, 165–6).

In extending the hand of friendship to Symonds in 1884, James placed himself at the very centre of this new (and usually negative) discussion of homosexuality. Haralson has succinctly documented what became James's intimate involvement with leading associated figures with the debate about homosexuality, beginning in 1885 with Labouchère, whose parliamentary amendment of that year had criminalised homosexuality, and

> whose aggressive politics James discussed with his sister Alice and whose journalistic exposés struck him as rudely 'staring one in the face'; Lord Rosebury, one of the 'Snob Queers' reviled by the Marquess of Queensbury en route to his confrontation with Wilde; George Curzon, who would humiliate Wilde for publishing *The Picture of Dorian Gray*; W.E. Henley, whose review deemed Dorian Gray fit for only 'outlawed noblemen and perverted telegraph boys'; Frank Lockwood, the Solicitor-General whose zealous prosecution turned the tide against Wilde and who inspired one of James's late stories; 'the atrocious Alfred D[ouglas]', as James came to regard Wilde's companion; and finally Robbie Ross, another of Wilde's intimates, who remained a special friend of the American author. Not least, of course, there was Oscar Wilde himself, familiar to James as society phenomenon, potential rival, and antipodal creature since 1882.[5]

When Gosse later sent to him a copy of Symonds's second *apologia*, *A Problem in Modern Ethics*, in 1893, James thanked him for having forwarded the 'marvellous outpourings', and added:

J.A.S. is truly, I gather, a candid and consistent creature, & the exhibition is infinitely remarkable. It's, on the whole, I think, a queer place to plant the standard of duty, but he does it with extraordinary gallantry. If he has, or gathers, a band of the emulous, we may look for some capital sport. But I don't wonder that some of his friends are haunted with a vague malaise ...

(HJL: 3, 398)

After calling Symonds a 'great reformer', James says that, for him, it seems 'a queer place to plant the standard of duty'. But Symonds does it with 'extraordinary gallantry'; his writings are 'infinitely remarkable'. James admits to Gosse that if Symonds 'has, or gathers, a band of the emulous, we may look for some capital sport'. In making a reference to a 'band of the emulous', James was reflecting the new idea that there could be a definable group of people for whom homosexuality, or at least an interest in homosexuality, would be seen as a 'representative characteristic'. This was an idea, as we have seen, that he was always personally resistant to, and is possibly the reason he considered Symonds's 'band of the emulous' to be 'haunted by a vague malaise'.

This shift towards a legal and psychological categorisation that accompanied the negative public perception of homosexuals, and consequently away from the previous casual acceptance of male 'camaraderie' exploited by writers such as Whitman and Pater as a way of discussing homosexuality, is reflected for the first time in James's fiction in 'The Author of *Beltraffio*' (1884), based on the knowledge James had acquired about Symonds's homosexuality (HJL: 3, 72). The Whitmanesque signifier 'camaraderie' so evident in the early fiction is replaced in this story by an awareness of homosexual scandal, and what would come to be called a 'homosexual consciousness' is also reflected, all of which parallels social changes outlined by Weeks. Though obviously having still to live in a defining heterosexual social environment, homosexuals in James's fiction begin, as with homosexuals in Victorian society more generally, to define themselves independently of the simple and limiting contrast between same-sex attraction and heterosexual norms and expectations.

James's new understanding of the potentially scandalous consequences of a lack of caution, and that an individual's 'innermost cause' of his psychological state could be viewed in terms of his deviant sexual inclination, is apparent in 'The Author of *Beltraffio*', the only of James's tales or novels – apart from 'The Turn of the Screw' (1898) – that deals significantly with homosexuality but not in the context of a 'permanent adolescence', which suggests that he was shaken from his usual way of contextualising the subject by his encounter with Symonds and other related events of the early 1880s, and then later by the Wilde trial, during which James conceived the original idea of 'The Turn of the Screw'.[6]

In having the protagonist, Mark Ambient, write a scandalous text entitled *Beltraffio*, James was drawing a subtle parallel between Symonds's adaptation of his role as art historian for subversive sexual-theoretical ends (in *Studies of the Greek Poets* and elsewhere) and the protagonist Ambient's evocation of the historical Beltraffio (or 'Boltraffio', as he was better known) in the fictionally infamous text. Boltraffio idealised his male subjects to the point of causing minor scandals, as in the famous *Portrait of a Young Man*, where the 'ambiguous beauty that Boltraffio gave to the sitter ... led to the suggestion that the portrait is that of a woman'.[7] There is also a biographical parallel between James's expressed wish to see Symonds in his letter about Italy and the way that the narrator in 'The Author of *Beltraffio*' expresses his wish to meet Ambient:

> I went to the Continent, spent the following winter in Italy and returned to London in May. My visit to Italy had opened my eyes to a good many things, but to nothing more than the beauty of certain pages in the works of Mark Ambient ...
>
> [I] sent with my friend's letter a note of my own, in which I asked his leave to come down and see him for an hour or two some day to be named by himself. My proposal was accompanied by a very frank expression of my sentiments, and the effect of the entire appeal was to elicit from the great man the kindest possible invitation.
>
> (AB, 58–9)

The narrator's position corresponds in other ways to James's reaction to Symonds. Like James, he initiated the contact between himself and Ambient. He immerses himself in the subject matter of Ambient's books in the way James had with books by Symonds and would continue to over the next decade. He goes on to tease information from Gwendolen Ambient about her brother in the way that James would tease from Gosse news about his intimate friend Symonds. But ultimately, again like James, he refuses to align himself to the cause. Given these parallels, it is unsurprising that James wanted (falsely) to insist to his brother William that he should not be thought of as being too closely associated with the narrator. He even lied about the fact that he had lunched with Symonds. 'I am told on all sides, here,' he wrote in 1885, 'that my *Author of Beltraffio* is a living and scandalous portrait of J.A. Symonds and his wife, whom I have never met' (HJL: 3, 71). Despite this caution, James was resolutely determined to explore his earlier-admitted 'curiosity'.

Ambient is presented as a bridge between a subversive (even if by then familiar) classical way of relating contemporary homosexuality to Greek pederasty and the new association of it with 'aestheticism', in the way that Symonds in real life proved to be. Even his ostracism is said to result from a conflict between Christian and Pagan cultures, 'which have never succeeded in getting on with one another' (AB, 90). Here James is reflecting – either intuitively or because he did indeed read it when it appeared in 1883 – a contrast Symonds himself had explicitly explored, in the final short chapter of *Greek Ethics*,[8] and which he would make the principal subject of the first chapter of *Modern Ethics*.[9] Ambient meanwhile remarks that his wife thinks him 'no better than an ancient Greek' (AB, 90). His book, however, is seen in more contemporary terms, as an 'aesthetic war cry' (AB, 57). It has caused one of those 'scandals' (AB, 57) so prevalent in the early 1880s, and Dolcino, his son, is also 'stamped with some social stigma' (AB, 64). There is, moreover, specific mention of the new mass-circulation 'newspapers', which were 'always abnormally vulgar about' Ambient (AB, 87). And in a comment that anticipates James's own later distinction between the 'mass' and the 'élite' on the unsuccessful first night of his play *Guy Domville* (1895), Ambient announces: 'There's a hatred of art; there's a hatred of literature – I mean of the genuine kind. Oh the shams – *those* they'll swallow by the bucket!' (AB, 92).

The social and domestic worlds represented in the story extend the debate about aestheticism through the hostilities of Ambient's wife, a Christian and family-centred woman about whom it is said that she wants above all else to protect Dolcino from his father's influence. Weeks, writing of how other changes in the late nineteenth-century both encouraged and paralleled changes in attitudes towards homosexuality, explains that childhood lengthened and there was an increasing emphasis on the need to protect the innocence of children. 'Childhood sexuality became an important political issue,' he writes. 'The 1885 Act had succeeded in raising the age of consent for girls to 16, and Labouchère at least claimed that his most famous Amendment [extending legal restrictions for homosexual behaviour] was directed at preventing the corruption of youth.'[10] In *Modern Ethics*, which Symonds explained was 'limited to the actual conditions of contemporary life',[11] there is the acknowledgement that it is 'the common belief that boys under age are specially liable to corruption'.[12] Symonds refuted this claim, but since he was discussing Greek *paederastia* in *Greek Ethics* he himself inevitably limited the discussion, somewhat paradoxically, to sexual relationships formed between, as he put it, 'a man and a boy'.[13]

The general emphasis on childhood innocence, on the need to protect boys in particular from predatory pederasts, is not specific to the 1880s and 1990s. But as far as Symonds's discussion of pederasty is concerned, it is the case that he wrote about how male homosexuals do indeed have a sexual preference for younger boys. In this sense, the Christian, middle-class wife's fear of predatory pederasts was justified (though whether sex between men and boys is, in a wider sense, always 'corrupting' is of course debatable). She specifically will not let her husband see Dolcino at bed time (AB, 79), locks the door when he tries to enter the bedroom (AB, 81) and believes 'she can't begin to guard him too early' (AB, 80). Ambient's undesirable influence is related in terms of it being 'a subtle poison or contagion – something that would rub off on his tender sensibility when his father kisses him or holds him on his knee' (AB, 84). Again, it is the threat of his physical expressiveness, this time in the form of his 'kisses', that is emphasised, and in the end his wife lets the boy die, 'to prevent him from ever being touched' (AB, 110). Earlier, in a wonderfully playful moment, Mrs Ambient said that it might be 'very awkward' for Dolcino if he read his father's books 'when he was about fifteen, say' (AB, 89). Despite, or perhaps because of, that 'say', this amusingly reflects the fact that, in the

Greek ideal of *paederastia* Symonds had written so extensively
about, it was very much the case that 15–year-old boys (say) would
be sought as lovers by older men. Haralson makes a broader point
by observing that, as Symonds had only daughters, 'the fact that his
fictional counterpart has only a son reveals James's dramatic intuition at work: patriarchal culture has more at stake, in the proper
molding of Dolcino'.[14]

Novick claims that the way James portrayed Symonds in 'The
Author of *Beltraffio*' shows that he 'had an almost physical repul-
sion from the immorality that Symonds's marriage represented to
him. The man's selfishness was expressed in his perverse appearance and manner'.[15] There is no biographical evidence that James
said Symonds or his marriage was 'immoral', and Ambient's dress
sense strikes one as more in keeping with what effeminate Sloane
wore in 'A Light Man' of 1869 than that of the 'perverse appearance
and manner' of a raving decadent of the 1880s. Novick and others
critics have also failed to point out that in the story the narrator is
on Ambient's 'side':

> My ingenious sympathy received at any rate a shock from three
> or four of his professions – he made me occasionally gasp and
> stare. He couldn't help forgetting, or rather couldn't know, how
> little, in another and dryer clime, I had ever sat in the school in
> which he was master; and he promoted me as to a jump to a
> sense of its penetralia. My trepidations ... were delightful; they
> were just what I had hoped for, and their only fault was that they
> passed away too quickly; since I found that for the main points I
> was essentially, I was quite constitutionally, on Mark Ambient's
> 'side' ... It was his fate to make a great many still more 'prepared'
> than me not to inconsiderably wince; but there was no grain of
> bravado in his ripest things (I've always maintained it, though
> often contradicted), and at bottom the poor fellow, disinterested
> to his finger tips and regarding imperfection not only as an
> aesthetic but quite also as a social crime, had an extreme dread
> of scandal.
>
> (AB, 77–8)

Conversely, Mrs Ambient is said to be 'a true eccentric' (AB, 103)
and she lets Dolcino die rather than risk him being influenced by

his father (AB, 109), which in no way is represented as morally justifiable. In this sense she is clearly the villain with the 'perverted' and destructive views, and at the end of the story, after Dolcino has died, she 'converts' to her husband's beliefs by accepting the need to read and understand his books (AB, 112). Ambient, on the other hand, is consistently determined to see that 'nothing shall ever hurt' (AB, 91) Dolcino. He even had to slip past Mrs Ambient to bound 'upstairs to judge for himself of his child's condition' (AB, 82).

What makes 'The Author of *Beltraffio*' still seem troublingly relevant is James's ambiguous and complicated treatment of the theme of pederasty as presented though the behaviour of the narrator. The 'extraordinary beautiful' (AB, 64) Dolcino is a little boy who may indeed be provoking sexual desire in the way feared by his mother, and perhaps not even anticipated by his father. Since Dolcino is 'not more than seven years old' (AB, 64) – a fact that Leland S. Person, in a discussion of the story which locates a pederastic motivation behind the narrator's interest in Dolcino, does not consider worthy of commentary[16] – this subversive subtext is as disturbing now as it was (to judge from James's letter to William in 1885 about the 'scandal' the story had caused) when it first appeared.

As well as specifically drawing on new social ways of relating to homosexuality, James was bringing into play in 'The Author of *Beltraffio*' those anxieties about the 'corruption' of children that were intimately related to the debate around that emerging concept of the homosexual. 'She thought me,' the narrator says of Ambient's sister Gwendolen, 'an obtrusive and designing, even perhaps a depraved, young man whom a perverse providence had dropped upon their quiet lawn to flatter his worst tendencies' (AB, 87). The 'depraved' and 'perverse', when taken with the idea of 'flattering' another man's 'worst tendencies', is homosexually suggestive, considering the assertion by Weeks that by the early 1880s such categorisations – he specifically refers to 'perversions and deviations' – were an increasingly common way of referring to subversive sexuality generally, and sometimes homosexuality in particular. The general fear of two like-minded individuals meeting to further, or 'design', their subversive aesthetic goals anticipates James's comment to Gosse concerning Symonds's *Modern Ethics* that he may gather around him a 'band of the emulous', while these references to the narrator's 'perversity' and 'depravation' prepare for his intimate exchange of looks with the child. Since that visual exchange takes place in the same paragraph as these labels appear, they should obviously be thought directly relevant to an understanding of what follows:

I found myself looking perpetually at the latter small mortal, who looked constantly back at me, and that was enough to detain me. With these vaguely-amused eyes he smiled, and I felt it an absolute impossibility to abandon a child with such an expression. His attention never strayed; it attached itself to my face as if among the small incipient things of his nature throbbed a desire to say something to me. If I could have taken him on my own knee he perhaps would have managed to say it; but it would have been a critical matter to ask his mother to give him up, and it has remained a constant regret for me that on that strange Sunday afternoon I didn't for a moment hold Dolcino in my arms ...

I remained there with Mrs. Ambient, though even our exchange of twaddle had run very thin. The boy's little fixed white face seemed, as before, to plead with me to stay, and after a while it produced still another effect, a very curious one, which I shall find it difficult to express. Of course I expose myself to the charge of an attempt to justify by a strained logic after the fact a step which may have been on my part but the fruit of a native want of discretion; and indeed the traceable consequences of that perversity were too lamentable to leave me any desire to trifle with the question. All that I can say is that I acted in perfect good faith and that Dolcino's friendly little gaze gradually kindled the spark of my inspiration ... the plea ... issued from the child's eyes and seemed to say: 'The mother who bore me and who presses me here to her bosom – sympathetic little organism that I am – has really the kind of sensibility she has been represented to you as lacking, if you only look for it patiently and respectfully. How is it conceivable she shouldn't have one? How is it possible that I should have so much of it – for I'm quite full of it, dear strange gentleman – if it weren't also in some degree in her? I'm my great father's child, but I'm also my beautiful mother's, and I'm sorry for the difference between them!' So it had shaped itself before me, the vision of reconciling Mrs. Ambient with her husband, of putting an end to their ugly difference. The project was absurd of course ... I went on to remark that it seemed an immense pity so much that was interesting [in Ambient's books] should be lost on [Mrs. Ambient].

'Nothing's lost upon me,' she said in a tone that didn't make the contradiction less. 'I know they're very interesting.'

'Don't you like papa's books?' Dolcino asked, addressing his mother but still looking at me. Then he added to me: 'Won't you read them to me, American gentleman?'

(AB, 99–100)

On one level, this is consistent with James's earlier fiction. When the issue of male intimacy and desire becomes explicit, 'the traceable consequences of that perversity' appear 'too lamentable to leave me any desire to trifle with the question'. The narrator will 'find it difficult to express' what he felt when he responds to the 'boy's little fixed white face', which 'seemed, as before, to plead with me to stay'. However, there is an important difference between this moment of narrative and stylistic denial and those in the earlier fictions in that it is explicitly referred to as a 'perversion', rather than, as before, immediately sublimated into a heterosexual context or a discussion about 'masculinity' or 'camaraderie'. The question of the narrator's motivations and feelings becomes a matter for the reader to explore and make judgements about, and the narrator's denial of anything sinister is made solely for the benefit of the reader. The superficial reason for this retrospective focus on these moments of intimacy is that, later on, the narrator was aware that Dolcino is going to die, and that this was perhaps the one chance he had to save the child from his 'lamentable' fate; and he especially feels compelled to profess that 'all that I can say is that I acted in perfect good faith'. But why would there be any need for such self-conscious denial if there were no implication of guilt? And what kind of guilt is it that he is implying there is a necessity for? After all, he was merely visiting an admired author.

The main reason why the issue of his 'good faith' seems important is that he himself feels compelled to raise it, which suggests that there is more to the depiction of the child's sensuality than merely a use of it to reflect the wife's goodness in order in turn to create an obligation in the narrator to deal fairly – not just to use them solely for his own gratification but to free them to live fulfilled lives. That point could not be made, narratively speaking, directly; and so James has the child transmit it through the child's improbably sensitive intuition (a common enough Jamesian device).

The passage still seems otherwise troubling, however, and this uneasiness stems from the narrator's need to deny whatever it is that results from his initial response to the longing in the beautiful little boy's fixed gaze, which the boy's imaginary pleading then obfuscates. The boy's pleading, that is to say, is a smoke screen, as well as a sort of magical transferral of his mother's emotion. This is further emphasised by the fact that the narrator then dismisses the 'project' of reconciling the mother and father as 'absurd' much more quickly than would have been the case if he had sensed in the boy what he later claims he did. The whole idea of reconciliation is too suddenly dropped, only to make way for a re-establishment of the relationship linking the narrator, the boy and the scandalous text.

Even if it were convincing, the idea of saving the boy does not sufficiently explain the sensuousness underlying the narrator's experience of dealing with the child. 'If I could have taken him on my own knee, he perhaps would have managed to say it; but it would have been a critical matter to ask his mother to give him up, and it has remained a constant regret for me that on that strange Sunday afternoon I didn't for a moment hold Dolcino in my arms . . .' Though this is a long way away from a desire for sexual congress, a fear of the desire such men as Ambient and his friends might hold for physical intimacy with her child is the defining characteristic of Mrs Ambient, and since the narrator has already been labelled 'an obtrusive and designing, even perhaps a depraved, young man whom a perverse providence had dropped upon their quiet lawn to flatter [Ambient's] worst tendencies', his own desire to hold the child in his arms and to have him on his knee would surely have been regarded as intriguingly sinister by most middle-class readers when the story first appeared, and it is admitted by the narrator that Mrs Ambient herself would regard it in such a way. The idea that the boy is being corrupted by a pederast in the way feared by the mother (and that society generally was becoming increasingly hysterical about) is finally underlined when Dolcino himself asks, at the end of the exchange, whether the narrator will read him his father's decadent books. The impression supports the mother's assertion that she cannot begin to protect the boy 'too early'.

After receiving a note from Edmund Gosse about the influence of Symonds on 'The Author of *Beltraffio*', James teasingly replied:

> Perhaps I have divined the innermost cause of J.A.S.'s discomfort
> – but I don't think I seize, on P. 571, exactly the allusion you
> refer to. I am therefore devoured with curiosity as to the further
> revelation. Even a postcard (in covert words) would relieve the
> suspense of the perhaps already-too-indiscreet.
>
> (HJG, 32)

This response characterises what would come to be James's increasingly dualistic personal response to the emerging category of the homosexual, particularly in the 1890s. He would remain 'devoured with curiosity' about homosexuality, but, with equal measure, he would insist on the need for 'covert words' whenever that curiosity was given expression to. When Symonds died in 1893, James declined to write an appreciation. To do so 'either ironically or explicitly', he explained, 'would be a Problem – a problem beyond me'[17] – clearly alluding to Symonds's gay *apologias*, and making clear in the process that specific discussion of the subject of homosexual reform, outside of a covert fictional context, was not and never would be an option for him. He had, however, remained sympathetic; and he admitted that he had always been a 'curious onlooker'. Once again manifesting his two sides, he declared in another letter to Gosse that

> I had never even (clearly) seen him – but somehow I too can't
> help feeling the news as a pang – & with a personal emotion. It
> always seemed as if I might know him – & of few men whom I
> didn't know has the image so much come home to me ... He
> must have been very interesting – & you must read me some of
> his letters. We shall talk of him ... Do let me know of any
> circumstance about Symonds – or about his death – that may be
> interesting.
>
> (HJL: 3, 409–10)

James could not deny to Gosse that he had met Symonds, as he had
denied the fact to William in the letter about the scandal caused by
'The Author of *Beltraffio*'. Gosse was a long-standing friend of
Symonds (HJG, 32; n. 3) and so would have known about James's
meeting. The earlier assertion to William by James, that he had
'never seen' Symonds, is therefore broken by '(clearly)' in this later
attempt by James publicly to distance himself from his private
sympathies. The admission that 'of few men whom I didn't know
has the image so much come home to me' confirms, though, that
James's focus on Symonds's life and literary projects remained
profoundly intense; and there is perhaps also the impression given
that James was unhappy that the simple matter of Symonds's
homosexuality could have become a source of constant personal
anxiety. This defining dualism centred on a personal and literary
interest in and a general sympathy for Symonds's project on the
one hand, but a total public distancing from its social ramifications
on the other, eventually resulted in James taking the decision to
return to Gosse, at the height of the Wilde trial, his copy of
Symonds's *Modern Ethics*. He explained that

> these are days in which one's modesty is, in every direction,
> much exposed, and one should be thankful for every veil that
> one can hastily snatch up or that a friendly hand precipately
> [*sic*] muffles one withal. It is strictly congruous with these
> remarks that I should mention that there go to you tomorrow
> a.m. in 2 registered envelopes, at 1 Whitehall, the fond pourings
> of poor J.A.S.
>
> (HJG, 126)

On the back of the envelope James scribbled: 'Quel Dommage – mais
quel Bonheur – que J.A.S. ne soit plus de ce monde!' (HJG, 126).

5
Public Scandals, Private Dilemmas

The Cleveland Street Scandal of 1889–90, involving a boy-brothel, telegraph boys, their high-class gentlemen clientele and possibly Prince Albert Victor, son of the Prince of Wales, made the front pages of the new mass-circulation newspapers in England for months.[1] Throughout the 1880s the series of other trials and scandals, 'whose every twist and turn was broadcast by a developing press',[2] had already helped to establish in the public consciousness a negative concept of homosexuality as a distinct type of 'deviance' that threatened traditional family values, childhood innocence and the strict English class system. This general movement towards a focus on alternative lifestyles was subtly reflected in the shift in emphasis in Symonds's two *apologias*. The first, *Greek Ethics*, mostly written in 1876 but privately published in 1883,[3] concentrated on Greek homosexuality in an abstract, historical, classical context. The second, *Modern Ethics* of 1891, was concerned with 'contemporary life' and the 'inverted sexual instincts' or 'sexual inversion' of a particular group of individuals oppressed by social norms and unjustly prohibitive legislation. This change in perspective in Symonds's work, from Greek to Modern, represented 'a shift from a *form of behaviour*, love between males, to a *condition*, "inverted sexuality"'.[4]

An important, if unforeseen, consequence of the pursuit of a specific policy of condemnation of homosexuality was that it heightened the awareness of that marginalised group or under-world amongst those men who defined themselves as such. The boundaries created by the stigma that separated this underworld from mainstream society could, that is to say, paradoxically act as

protection against a hostile 'mass' which, in the din of its condem-
natory jeering, could relate to homosexuality only in terms of social
scandal and effeminate or 'aesthetic' stereotypes. In the developing
homosexual underground of late Victorian society, men began 'to
learn the rules for picking up and watching for the law as well as
places to go. They could imbibe the rituals of social contact and
behaviour, the codes for communicating, and the modes of living a
double life'.[5] Of James's stories and novels of this period, *The Tragic
Muse* (1890) and 'The Great Good Place' (1890), 'The Pupil' (1891)
in particular explore this new 'double life' – initially more
cautiously reflected in 'The Author of *Beltraffio*' – centred on a sensitivity to public hostility towards homosexuality and aestheticism
on the one hand, and, on the other, an intensely private homosexual existence. They do so in more socially realistic ways than do
the tales of 'writers and artists' James also wrote during these years
that feature an obscure male author and his young male disciple,
which occasionally appeared in *The Yellow Book*, and which have
recently received attention from critics charting James's responses
to the emergence of the modern concept of homosexuality as a
cause of social and literary anxiety at the Victorian *fin de siècle*.[6] The
other, less discussed tales and novels do not deal with scandal as
such, or with the particular problem of literary representations of
homosexuality; nor are they greatly preoccupied with the notion of
notorious authorship. Instead, their chief preoccupation, when
they deal with homosexual themes, is the *threat* of scandal, and
conversely the potential for happiness in adopting the alternative
lifestyle those scandals helped, in however negative a context, to
highlight. In these fictions James subtly but subversively insisted on
the legitimacy of male–male attraction. What makes them seem still
remarkable – quite aside from the question of their literary value –
is both the depth of that implicit insistence and the corresponding
degree to which James emphasised positive social and personal
consequences that can result from a refusal to define behaviour
according to strict heterosexual norms and expectations. James may
have viewed Symonds with a sympathetic but always slightly
mocking detachment, but in his fiction he began to deal with
homosexuality in precisely the terms it has been said he dealt with
the women's liberation movement as well, believing that in the end
'repression is finally worse than rebellion' (AC, 254).

The lead characters of *The Tragic Muse*, 'The Great Good Place' and 'The Pupil' distinguish themselves from the earlier characters in James's fiction who were similarly aware of their homo-eroticism or questionable manliness, such as Rowland Mallet in *Roderick Hudson* and Gordon Wright in *Confidence*, in that they have inter-nalised the psychological and emotional conflicts arising from their decisions to abandon mainstream society and its conven-tional demands on manhood to contemplate instead the possibility of achieving a privately cultivated moral (as opposed to merely conventional) outlook. This new emphasis in James's fiction paral-lels that shift in Symonds's two polemical works, away from a *form of behaviour* (attraction of males to males) to a *condition* ('inverted sexuality'), and of course reflects as well the broader movement towards Modernist subjectivity. It parallels in a related way a similar change in emphasis during these years in the works of Pater and Wilde. After the scandal caused by his Conclusion to *The Renaissance*, and in a climate of growing intolerance, Pater continued to affirm male–male desire, but with increasing atten-tion to the social functions of homophobia.[7] While Wilde's early poetry had drawn, like James's early fiction, on classical examples of homosexuality,[8] with *The Picture of Dorian Gray* and *The Importance of Being Earnest* (1894) he began to produce more of a 'transgressive literature that thrived on the conditions of oppres-sion and yet courted the approval of the oppressor'.[9]

Pater and Wilde were sources for the high-aesthete Gabriel Nash in *The Tragic Muse*, as would have been apparent to contemporary readers who had witnessed throughout the 1880s the satirical press directing its scathing humour at Wilde and the more decadent version of Pater's aestheticism, for which Wilde's name had become a trademark.[10] As with Ambient in 'The Author of *Beltraffio*', Nash has until recently been too easily summed up by those who have written about this novel – particularly Ellmann – as an essentially negative portrait of the kind of formless, amoral Oxford aestheti-cism James did, personally, always seek to distance himself from.[11] The narrator of 'The Author of *Beltraffio*' was clearly on Ambient's 'side', and in *The Tragic Muse* the subversive ideals of Nash are like-wise viewed positively by his friend and disciple, Nick Dormer. In part, Nick relates to Nash through a novel the latter has written (TM, 35), and a literary link between Nick and his 'Mentor or oracle'

(TM, 83) is one of a number of loose but revealing similarities between their relationship and that formed between the narrator and Ambient in 'The Author of *Beltraffio*'. Ambient's influence was related in terms of it being 'a subtle poison or contagion', and Nick says to Nash: 'At Oxford you were very bad company for me, my evil genius; you opened my eyes, you communicated the poison. Since then, little by little, it has been working within me; vaguely, covertly, insensibly at first, but during the last year or so with violence, pertinacity, cruelty. I have taken every antidote in life; but it's no use – I'm stricken' (TM, 143). The narrator of 'The Author of *Beltraffio*' does not relate to Ambient in such negative terms. Nor, on the whole, does Nick relate to Nash in this way. His self-consciously negative reactions at such moments could be viewed in light of the fact that Nash's aestheticism has more potential for scandal than did Ambient's, expressed as it is not only outside a literary and domestic context (always Ambient's defining context) but with blatant disregard for any social or personal consequences. Ambient, moreover, was married, which at least helped give to the outside world an impression of respectable heterosexuality. Nash however explains, when Nick asks him about the possibility of his being in love with the 'tragic muse' of the title, Miriam Rooth, that he is 'never another man' to a woman (TM, 407).

The newspapers had always been 'abnormally vulgar about' Ambient. In the later 'age of publicity' reflected in *The Tragic Muse*, which 'never distinguished as to the quality of events' (TM, 403) – when 'deafening newspaperism' is the age's 'most distinctive sign' (TM, 410–11) – newspapers are so much reporting 'abnormally vulgar' *behaviour* that those writing on Nash's aesthetic circle are 'restrained by decorum from touching upon the worst of their aberrations' (TM, 549). By 1890 aestheticism had come to be identified with more than a fancy way with clothes and literary style. It also signified sexual and moral decadence, and when thinking about Nash and contemporary reactions to him as a character it should of course also be remembered that *The Tragic Muse* was published at the height of the Cleveland Street Scandal. What probably saved James from the kind of condemnation *The Picture of Dorian Gray* met with one year later was his guarded private life and his resulting public image as a typical Victorian bachelor, as well as the lack of a beautiful boy in the novel itself as an object of Nash's (always sexually vaguely defined) affections and deviations – a scenario which was central to Wilde's novel in the form of Basil Hallward's infatuation with Dorian. In *The Tragic Muse*, Nash is presented as narratively important, but he is always a socially marginalised – even stigmatised – influence on the mainstream upper-middle-class social and political world with which James's readers could have easily identified. In Wilde's novel, Hallward is of course very much the defining consciousness.[12]

The various introductions made by Nash in the opening chapters of *The Tragic Muse* allow for all the subsequent action of significance, meaning that James afforded him a crucial role inconsistent with Ellmann's suggestion that he is a narratively and thematically marginalised character. Nick, who is hovering between his desire to be married and a successful Member of Parliament and his stronger (and in the end overriding) wish to remain single and pursue his passion for portrait painting, welcomes (albeit with certain important qualifications) Nash's influence; and that Nash is not also welcomed by those around Nick gives deeper significance and meaning to the latter's rebellious acceptance of him. Nick's younger sister Bridget's initial bewilderment at encountering Nash, for example, is given a focus by her cautiously bold question 'Are you an aesthete?' (DM, 39). Nick nevertheless remains stubborn in his belief, expressed both to Bridget and to his hostile mother, that Nash 'won't hurt us. On the contrary, he'll do us good' (DM, 36). At the end of the novel Nash fades, both as a character and an image from the canvas on which Nick had begun to paint his portrait; but that should not be interpreted in the way Ellmann interpreted it – as an indication that Nash should be viewed as a wholly rejected influence.[13] Rather, it suggests that Nash has done his job: he has 'rescued' (TM, 550) Nick, not to lead him towards the 'aesthetic' lifestyle – that is never Nash's objective, and Nick never wavers in his rejection of the excesses of Nash's aesthetic circle – but away from conformist social mores weak Nick, on his own, had the moral strength to confront but not reject. Nash in the end is unambiguously said to have 'converted' Nick 'from a representative into an example' (TM, 550) – and it is this conversion that defines the thematic progression of, and then the conclusion to, *The Tragic Muse*. To put it in the loosest terms: the novel evidences a social movement away from traditional class and social boundaries in favour of Modernist diversity and subjectivity and subversiveness.

The pattern of permanent adolescence is more intricately woven into *The Tragic Muse* than in any other of James's novels or tales. All of Nick's important personal relationships date from his childhood or late adolescence: with his diplomat cousin Peter Sherringham, with Julia Dormer (whom Nick is expected to marry), with his late father's closest friend Mr Carteret, as well as with Nash. The different way in which the substance of each relationship is presented with reference to its roots reinforces the impression that James was particularly sensitive to the way male friendship cultivated in late adolescence and early manhood can have homo-erotic undertones that in later adult life remain as sources of emotional and psychological security. Nick first met Nash at Oxford. Though they have since 'diverged' (in the sense that they do not often see one another), Nick explains that he has 'not so much' lost touch with his friend as Nash perhaps believes, on account of his having read Nash's 'very clever book' (TM, 35). He is moreover aware that there are risks involved in being so intimate with Nash, but demands – almost with an embarrassing insistence – that he 'must keep' Nash by his side, that they 'must stick together – forever and ever' (TM, 35; 322).

This dependence on and sympathy with Nash is sharply contrasted with his attitude both to Julia and Peter, which is in both instances profoundly cold. The specific contrast between Nash and Peter, in light of their relations with Nick, is that while Nash and Nick cultivated their friendship at Oxford Peter and Nick separated at a much earlier age – crucially before they had reached adolescence. 'One of our young men had gone to Eton and the other to Harrow (the scattered school on the hill was the tradition of the Dormers), and the divergence had taken its course later, in university years' (DM, 73). The key phrase, when thinking about the difference in the relationships Nick forms with Peter and Nash, is 'the divergence had taken its cause later, in university years', since Nick had earlier insisted that his 'divergence' from Nash since Oxford had not in any way lessened their emotional and intellectual bond. The opening chapters of *The Tragic Muse*, which show Nick clinging to Nash, reveal him refusing even to make the effort to arrange to see Peter. He says to his mother: 'Oh hang Peter ...

Leave him out of account ...' To this, Bridget replies: 'I must say –
about [Peter] – you're not nice ...' (TM, 21).

A similar, but more complex, sense of an irreparable divergence
defines Nick's relationship with his childhood friend Julia:

> If it be thought odd that [Nick] had not been able to read the
> character of a woman he had known since childhood, the answer
> is that that character had grown faster than Nick Dormer's obser-
> vations. The growth was constant, whereas the observation was
> but occasional, though it had begun early. If he had attempted
> to phrase the matter to himself, as he probably had not, he might
> have said that the effect that she produced upon him was too
> much a compulsion; not the coercion of design, of importunity,
> nor the vulgar pressure of family expectation, a suspected desire
> that he should like her enough to marry her, but something that
> was a mixture of diverse things, of the sense that she was impe-
> rious and generous – but probably more the former than the
> latter – and of a certain prevision of doom, the influence of the
> idea that he should come to it, that he was predestined.
>
> (TM, 79)

The opening, 'If it be thought odd ...', echoes the passage in
Roderick Hudson that revealed the difficulty James had in explaining
Rowland's essentially emotionless attraction to Mary, a woman
with whom he too was supposed to be in love – and who, like Julia,
had no difficulty in recognising her suitor's insincerity. In *Roderick
Hudson*, it was admitted by the narrator: 'Very odd, you may say,
that at this time of day Rowland should still be brooding over a girl
with no brilliancy, of whom he had but the lightest of glimpses two
years before; very odd that so deeply impression should have been
made by so lightly pressed an instrument. We must admit the
oddity ...' In *The Tragic Muse*, James is again awkwardly avoiding
explicitly stating what elsewhere in the novel is made clear by
implication and inference: that Nick is not in love with Julia,
despite having experienced that long period of intimacy with her
which Rowland is said not to have experienced with Mary, and that
Nick does not want to get married or to cohabit with a female any
more than Rowland did. What the narrator lists as the possible
reasons that should be discounted when thinking about Nick's

hovering – 'the coercion of design, of importunity ... the vulgar
pressure of family expectation, a suspected desire that he should
like her enough to marry her' – are, furthermore, precisely what the
broader narrative points to as the cause of his wavering, and in this
important sense Nick's rebelliousness parallels that of Miriam
Rooth, who Rowe persuasively argues is a 'magnificent example of
what the New Woman can do once she has freed herself from the
delusions of romantic love, 19th-century femininity, national character, and family heritage'.[14] Nick moreover tells Nash quite frankly
that he is not 'in the least' (TM, 142) in love with Julia, and later
when he makes the 'discovery' that he is indeed suddenly in love
with this woman he has known since childhood (TM, 209) it is no
more convincing than had been either Rowland's love for Mary in
Roderick Hudson or Bernard's discovery in *Confidence* that, after three
years of knowing her, he is in love with Angela. James cannot *do*
men falling in love with women. Such male–female relationships
are unconvincing because they are obviously plot contrivances,
which James makes only the faintest effort to disguise.

There is nothing in *The Tragic Muse* to suggest that Nick has a
clearly defined homosexual sensibility – apart, that is, from his
peculiar attraction to ostracised Nash, who obviously has. Nick's
sexuality is so consistently unapparent, indeed, that it is best
described as intriguingly ambiguous, and he resembles those other
of James's male protagonists – such as Winterbourne in 'Daisy
Miller' (1878), Newman in *The American* (1877) and Strether in *The
Ambassadors* – who are similarly presented as having no apparent
sexual attraction towards women, and who are inept, crippling self-
conscious and troubled by the prospect of forming permanent
attachments to them. In *The American*, Mrs Tristram especially
wants to know if Newman 'had ever been in love – seriously,
passionately – and, failing to gather any satisfactions from his allusions, she at last directly inquired. He hesitated awhile, and at last
said: "No!" She declared that she was delighted to hear it, as it
confirmed her private conviction that he was a man of no feeling'
(AM, 66–7). At the beginning of *The Ambassadors* the daughter of
the woman with whom Strether is in some way supposed romanti-
cally to be involved is said to have (just as Mrs Tristram was said to
have of Newman) 'at best' a 'scant faith in [Strether's] ability to find
women'. 'It wasn't even,' the narrator elaborates, 'as if he had found

her mother – so much more, to her discrimination, had her mother performed the finding' (A, 117–18). In *The Tragic Muse*, Nick's sister Grace similarly laments the fact that he 'never mentions [Julia] of himself', and Nick's mother replies: '"Sometimes I think he's thinking of her; then at others I can't fancy what he's thinking of"' (TM, 43). Peter admits that Nick has 'never said a word' to him about Julia (TM, 46), and Nick's mother later wonders whether Julia herself must be 'already tired of the way this young gentleman treated her' (TM, 68). Julia confirms this fear when she complains to Nick directly that he loves her 'with so little!' (TM, 207), and that he gives the impression moreover that he 'owes' her his affection (TM, 213). She continually postpones their marriage because she does not believe in his commitment, and Nick himself reinforces Julia's impression that he sees his possible marriage to her in purely economic terms when, on one of the few occasions Nick seems to be willing to take the plunge but Julia herself then begins to waver, he unambiguously exclaims: '"You'll make me lose a fortune"' (TM, 328). *The Tragic Muse* is on one level about the way that social hypocrisy and cruel limitations on personal freedom arise when marriage is considered merely as a convenient economic arrangement. Lady Agnes, Nick's mother, could have walked out of any novel by Jane Austen, with the important ironic difference (for Lady Agnes as well as for Nick) that she is desperate to sell off her son, rather than her daughters (TM, 191).

Nick's failure to marry Julia is the cause of friction between himself and Mr Carteret, an old and wealthy friend of his father who has guaranteed Nick a considerable income if he chooses to marry and enter the House of Commons. Mr Carteret, who has 'forsworn the commerce of women', is another of James's renounced celibates, or permanent adolescents:

[Mr Carteret] rested his mild eyes on [Nick], who had a sense of seeing in them for a moment the faintest ghost of an old story, the dim revival of a sentiment that had become the memory of a memory. The glimmer of wonder and envy, the revelation of a life intensely celibate, was for an instant infinitely touching. Nick had always had a theory, suggested from a vague allusion from his father, who had been discreet, that their benevolent friend had had in his youth an unhappy love affair which had led him to forswear forever the commerce of women. What remained in him of conscious renunciation gave a throb as he looked at his bright companion, who proposed to take the matter so much the other way.

(TM, 226–7)

Nick proposes to do no such thing, and the question of why his prospective bachelorhood would prove difficult if he entered public life – in a way that it never had for Mr Carteret – points to the radical *fin de siècle* sexual dynamics brought into play in *The Tragic Muse*. Mr Carteret is the upper-class celibate of the Victorian period personified. There is no evidence for his homosexuality, but that he is repressed in a way that defines his sense of his masculinity and security is undoubtedly the case. His salon is described as 'unfeminine' (TM, 220) and Nick thinks, when visiting the old man, that it 'might as well be 1830' (TM, 219). Mr Carteret himself expresses his bafflement at the social and sexual uncertainties and anxieties of the 1880s by claiming they were not even issues half a century before:

'Everything has altered: young people in my day looked at these questions more naturally,' Mr Carteret declared. 'A woman in love has no need to be magnanimous. If she is, she isn't in love,' he added shrewdly.

'Oh Mrs Dallow's safe – she's safe,' Nick smiled.

'If it were a question between you and another gentleman one might comprehend. But what does it mean, between you and nothing?'

'I'm much obliged to you, sir,' Nick returned. 'The trouble is that she doesn't know what she has got hold of.'

'Ah, if you can't make it clear to her!'

'I'm such a humbug,' said the young man. His companion stared, and he continued: 'I deceive people without in the least intending people.'

'What on earth do you mean? Are you deceiving me?'

'I don't know – it depends on what you think.'

'I think you are flighty,' said Mr Carteret, with the nearest approach to sternness that Nick had ever observed in him. 'I never thought so before.'

'Forgive me; it's all right. I'm not frivolous; that I affirm I'm not.'

'You have deceived me if you are.'

'It's all right,' Nick stammered with a blush.

'Remember your name – carry it high.'

'I will – as high as possible.'

(TM, 231)

The seriousness of the exchange is revealed in the narrative observation that Mr Carteret speaks 'with the nearest approach to sternness that Nick had ever observed in him'. Everything for the old man has changed: the values he once took for granted have been replaced by an unfathomable moral vacuum. Nick is insulted as 'flighty' and 'undisciplined', and although he attempts to win Mr Carteret over there is in his final words about carrying his name *only* 'as high as possible' the hint that it will not be carried as high as the old man would like. Mr Carteret's inability to read anything he can understand into Nick's hesitations and procrastinations over Julia is reflective of the new sexual politics of Nick's generation his own finds itself suddenly excluded from, and which homosexual Victorian bachelors would be as fearful of as would be the mainstream society in which they had managed to find a niche.

Showalter lists the types of character that often peopled the new genre of single-volume novels of the 1880s and 1890s as 'the celibate, the bachelor, the "odd woman", the dandy, and the aesthete'.[15] In *The Tragic Muse*, Mr Carteret is, as we have seen, the quintessential celibate and bachelor. He defines Nick as a dithering dandy. If Miriam Rooth is the New Woman, then Mr Carteret reacts against Julia as an 'odd' one, inexplicably refusing to take a man's honest word as guide and truth and insisting in having her say regarding whom she will marry, and for what reason. Nash 'the aesthete' is so outrageous to Mr Carteret's generation that Nick probably would not even be able to mention the former's name in the presence of the latter. So it is clear that, rather than being a book principally concerned with the world of politics and portrait painting – as it has largely been read by James's critics[16] – *The Tragic Muse* is very much a product of the radical changes in thinking about sexuality and gender in the years surrounding its composition.

Pulled between the tradition Mr Carteret represents and the related responsibilities of carrying on the family name, and whatever it is that the high-aesthete Nash represents, Nick's dilemma of whether to be a politician or a painter (neither activity is realistically portrayed in the novel) symbolises those new and troublesome choices for artistic young men not content with convenient marriages and careers, choices they had been made aware of by the Paterian generation at their beloved Oxford and which for both Nash and Nick seem (again like those Oxford aesthetes who came before them) to have to do at least in part with homosexuality. Nick defines himself to his mother in schizophrenic terms:

> 'The difficulty is that I'm two men: it's the strangest thing that ever was,' Nick pursued, bending his bright face upon her [his mother]. 'I'm two quite distinct human beings, who have scarcely a point in common; not even the memory, on the part of one, of the achievements or the adventures of the other. One man wins the seat – but it's the other fellow who sits in it.'
> 'Oh Nick, don't spoil your victory by your perversity!' Lady Agnes cried, clasping her hands to him.
>
> (TM, 186)

Shortly afterwards, the narrator relates these two 'sides' of Nick to his friendship with Nash:

> There were two sides which told him that all this was not really action at all, but only a pusillanimous imitation of it: one of them made itself fitfully audible in the depths of his own spirit and the other spoke, in the equivocal accents of a very crabbed hand, from a letter of four pages by Gabriel Nash ...
> Sometimes ... it seemed to him that he had gone in for Harsh because he was sure he should lose; sometimes he foresaw that he should win precisely to punish him for having tried and for his want of candour; and when presently he did win he was almost frightened at his success. Then it appeared to him that he had done something even worse than not choose – he had let others choose for him. The beauty of it was that they had chosen with only their own object in their eye: for what did they know about his strange alternative?   (TM, 197–8)

When Lady Agnes talked of Nick's 'perversity', as when Nick refers to his own 'strange alternative', there is a subtle indication that James is pointing to something more than merely the act of painting – particularly as Nick is said not even to know whether he has any ability as an artist (TM, 141). Julia later tells him that it is his 'innermost preference' and his 'secret passion' (TM, 322) that disturbs her, and again this superficial reference to Nick's wish to paint conveys a deeper meaning. Nash and Nick both explain their sense of exclusion, moreover, in a way that would become common in 'coming out' novels one hundred years after *The Tragic Muse*. Nash says: '"I have feelings, I have sensations: let me tell you that's not so common. It's rare to have them; and if you chance to have them it's rare not to be ashamed of them. I go after them – when I judge they won't hurt anyone"' (TM, 140). There is nothing specifically homosexual indicated, but when read alongside the portrait of Nash as a whole this confession is suggestive of the discovery of homosexual inclinations, and just as importantly of the need to be true to that discovery. Since Nick is obsessively drawn to Nash while at the same time continually repulsed by the idea of marrying Julia, his divided self should similarly be seen as possibly having at its foundation a recognised but socially denied homosexuality. The least that can be said is that James treated the subject of Nick's sexuality with such deliberate ambiguity that it warrants – indeed, invites – this kind of speculation. The narrator echoes Nash's description of being set apart by a subjective sense of doubleness with reference to Nick, again hinting at more than a mere passion for portrait painting to the extent that it cannot easily be explained only by referencing Nick's family expectation that he should carry on their father's name in the world of politics: 'He was conscious of a double nature; there were two men in him, quite separate, whose leading features have little in common and each of whom insisted on having an independent turn at life' (TM, 197). A useful context to bear in mind when viewing both Nash and Nick's concern about their discovery of an all-encompassing 'other self' is Michel Foucault's observation that 'the 19th-century homosexual became a personage, a past, a case history, and a child-hood, in addition to being a type of life'.[17] More specifically relevant to *The Tragic Muse* is Brian Reade's comment that, during the period in which this novel was composed, the admission of homosexuality by individuals 'grew into a belief that the more acute sensibility of the "artistic temperament" was often allied to the frustrated senses of the homosexual', and to be 'homosexually inclined thus became one of the secondary qualifications for declaring oneself an "artist"'.[18] Nash admits that Nick's wish to be a painter is only the excuse he needs to draw Nick away from his family and his proposed marriage to Julia towards a vaguely defined 'independent' way of life indulged in by people on 'his side', and forces Nick to confess that he is a 'freak of nature':

> 'Do you think I can do anything?' Nick inquired.
>   'Paint good pictures? How can I tell till I've seen some of your work? Doesn't it come back to me that at Oxford you used to sketch very prettily? But that's the last thing that matters.'
>   'What does matter, then?' Nick demanded, turning his eye on his companion.
>   'To be on the right side – on the side of beauty.'
>   'There will be precious little beauty if I produce nothing but daubs.'
>   'Ah, you cling to the old false measure of success. I must cure you of that. There will be the beauty of having been disinterested and independent; of having taking the world in the free, brave, personal way.'
>   'I shall nevertheless paint decently if I can,' Nick declared.
>   'I'm almost sorry! It will make your case less clear, your example less grand.'
>   'My example will be grand enough, with the fight I shall have to make.'
>   'The fight – with whom?'
>   'With myself, first of all. I'm awfully against it.'
>   'Ah, but you'll have me on the other side,' smiled Nash ...
>   'I don't know what I am – heaven help me!' Nick broke out, tossing his hat down on his little tin table with vehemence. 'I'm a freak of nature ...'
>
> (TM, 141–2)

The question is what Nash, 'on the other side', actually represents. Ellmann was mistaken to write that the aesthetic theory he proffers 'is a Paterian one, with no sign that he caught up with Wilde's post-aestheticism'.[19] At the beginning of the novel, Nash does speak as though he has just walked out of the pages of Pater's *The Renaissance*: '"I drift, I float ... my feelings direct me – if such a life as mine may be said to have a direction. Where there's anything to feel I try to be there!"' (TM, 34). But Nash drops this Paterian gibberish later on, to the extent that it is even said of him that he talks 'like an American novel' (TM, 408). What makes Nash a particular product of the 1880s – and so personify everything Mr Carteret cannot understand about the modern world he is metaphorically living out his last days excluded from – is not so much his occasional Paterian musings as how he is compartmentalised, as Wilde was compartmentalised, as leading a secret homosexual life, which in turn *The Tragic Muse* places in a broader mainstream social context, which both Nick and the old man are very much a part of. In creating the character of Nash, then, James was at once reflecting new social attitudes towards homosexuality as a 'type' of behaviour threatening to undermine family values and social stratification, while simultaneously incorporating the new self-definition by homosexuals such as Pater, Symonds and Wilde – and thousands of anonymous others – who viewed positively the fact that homosexuality had the potential to break down class distinctions, and who believed that homophobia rather than homosexuality as the problem needing to be addressed. Haralson correctly writes that in this and other ways *The Tragic Muse* penetrates to 'the unspeakable doubt at the core of "successful" Victorian manhood' by asking what happens if 'the construct of the (re)productive gentleman is just that, a construct manufactured in performance and thereby liable to inauthenticity, to sudden rupture and self-emptying, perhaps even to inversion in parts?'[20]

The fact that Nash fades at the end of the novel can be related to James's real-life reactions to the aesthetes, and to this sense of vulnerable Victorian masculinity Haralson locates. When Nick says that he

'had forbidden himself for the present to think of absence, not only because it would be inconvenient and expensive, but because it would be a kind of retreat from the enemy, a concession to difficulty', and that 'the enemy was no particular person and no particular body of persons ... [I]t was simply the general awkwardness of his situation. This awkwardness was connected with the sense of responsibility that Gabriel Nash so greatly deprecated – ceasing to roam, of late, on purpose to miss as few scenes as possible of the drama, rapidly growing dull, alas, of his friend's destiny ...'

(TM, 524)

the phrases about not allowing for any 'concession to difficulty', and the linking of 'awkwardness' and 'responsibility' in a way that marginalises Nash, parallels James's own reaction to Wilde and the aesthetes: he learned a great deal from them; many of his novels and stories could not have been written without his various reactions to them; but ultimately he rejected them as a group because of their lack of literary and novelistic rigour and discipline. Woods astutely comments that *'The Picture of Dorian Gray* could have been a great novel – if only it had been written by Henry James. But he was too busy writing *The Tragic Muse* ...,'[21] and Nick's broader reaction against too close an intimacy with the aesthetic-homosexual circle Nash is a representative of similarly reflects James's refusal publicly to associate himself with Symonds, Wilde or any other writer whose homosexuality was so open as to make him vulnerable. When the narrator of *The Tragic Muse* explains that 'Nick had an instinct, in which there was no consciousness of detriment to Nash, that the pupils, perhaps even the imitators of such a genius would be, as he mentally phrased it, something awful. He could be sure, even Gabriel himself could be sure, of his own reservations, but how could either of them be sure of others?' (TM, 548), he could be a James biographer explaining James's own reactions to Wilde.

Nash justifies such caution on Nick's part when he neatly defines himself according to social perceptions of his type by remarking, after Nick has alluded to the names people call him, that '"The observer is nothing without his categories, his types and varieties"' (TM, 39). Bridget places him quite separately from herself and her family, explaining that to her mind he belongs to an 'under-world' (TM, 37). The narrator also explains that Nash 'had a club, the Anonymous' (TM, 549), and his exclusivity and secret subterranean existence is troubling to Nick precisely because of how it would be interpreted negatively by those closest to him: 'it would probably have been hard ... to persuade Lady Agnes, or Julia Dallow, or Peter

Sherringham, that he was not at home in some dusky, untidy, dimly-lit suburb of "culture", peopled by unpleasant phrasemongers who thought him a gentleman and who had no human use but to be held up in the comic press' (TM, 549). However, when Nick tells Nash that this striving towards complete independence is 'always provoking', Nash defiantly replies:

> 'So it would appear, to the great majority of one's fellow-mortals; and I well remember the pang with which I originally made the discovery. It darkened my spirit, at a time when I had thought no evil. What we like, when we are unregenerate, is that a new-comer should give us a password, join our little camp or religion, get into our little boat, in short, whatever it is, and help us to row it. It's natural enough; we are mostly in different tubs and cockles, paddling for life. Our opinions, our convictions and doctrines and standards, are simply the particular thing that will make the boat go – *our* boat, naturally, for they may very often be just the thing that will sink another. If you won't get in, people generally hate you.'
>
> (TM, 133)

As a novelist, James was too interested in how real-life social and psychological restrictions on freedom and personal expression related to fictional form to be taken over by polemical gay liberation ideals. But in *The Tragic Muse* he illustrates how a subversiveness associated with decadence, aestheticism and sexual 'deviance' may have a beneficial, diversifying influence on those who live their lives in the social mainstream but who are willing to listen to cries of dissent. Rowe says that 'up to the very end of the novel, James gives hints that the new social relationships he has described … have some positive effects on more conventional social relations,'[22] and in such a context Nash could be recognised as a hitherto unacknowledged subversive hero of the novel: the moral guide Nick needs to confront imaginatively stifling conventions associated with dominant mothers, worthy careers and economic marriages.

Edel's summary of James's short story 'The Great Good Place', published one year after *The Tragic Muse*, provides a useful starting point for a much fuller reading. It also illustrates how Edel and others' traditional reticence on the subject of James's homosexuality limited their ability to offer more penetrating interpretations:

> In his story the good and great place is more than a private retreat. A mixture of monastery, hotel, club, country house, it is an ideal cushioned silent refuge, accessible to the Protestant as a 'retreat', yet not of the religious sort: a place of material simplification.
>
> The interest of the story, on its biographical side, is not only in its obvious wish for respite from worldly pressure, but in James's desire for an exclusive man's world, a monastic Order, a sheltering Brotherhood. The admiring acolyte who comes to the great writer, George Dane, puts a hand on his knee, and gives him at once a 'feeling of delicious ease' ... Above all there is the blessing of anonymity.
>
> George Dane ... identifies himself with his young Acolyte: the great good place is also the place of youth. James's fantasy expresses the wish to be young again, the brother that he had once been.[23]

Peter Gay has written of how the Victorian upper-class gentleman's club provided men an exclusive male hideaway, where they would not be compelled to grow up or be forced into abandoning their persistent adolescent ties with their 'distinctly, though largely unconscious, homo-erotic pleasures'.[24] The 'great good place' in James's story is just such an all-male preserve, though the men are said to look at one another in a way 'different from the looks of friends in London clubs' (GGP, 21). The homo-eroticism is more strongly intimated in the story by the metaphorical evocation of that other Victorian bastion of same-sex indulgence, from which all those gentleman in the clubs would have originated: the English public school. In particular, there is the imagined experience of communal bathing: 'He didn't want, for the time, anything but just to *be* there, to stay in the bath,' the narrator says of Dane as he talks to the sympathetic Brother figure. 'He was in the bath yet, the broad, deep bath of stillness. They sat in it together now, with the water up to their chins' (GGP, 20). Elsewhere, Dane and the Brother talk 'as innocently as small boys confiding to each other the names of toy animals' (GGP, 23); and these boy-eternals, moreover, are said to act together as though they were a couple of 'regular boarders' (GGP, 31). Dane is enjoying the 'permanent adolescence' so many other of James's homosexual protagonists, and James himself, have been seen to have been longing to experience.

At the beginning of the story, Dane is shown to be in despair at the prospect of having to keep a number of social engagements with women later in the day (GGP, 15–16). His mood changes, however, when he is reminded by his servant that he has invited a young male Acolyte to breakfast. The latter arrives. As Dane fantasises about changing places with the young man – who, of course, in his admiration for the novelist himself finds the idea of becoming Dane equally liberating – Dane falls asleep:

> The mere sight of his face, the sense of my hand on his knee, made me, after a little, feel that he not only knew what I wanted, but was getting nearer to it than I could have got in ten years. He suddenly sprang up and went over to my study-table – sat straight down there as if to write me my passport. Then it was – at the mere sight of his back, which was turned to me – that I felt the spell work. I simply sat and watched him with the queerest, deepest, sweetest sense in the world – the sense of an ache that had stopped. All life was lifted; I myself was at least somehow off the ground. He was already where I had been.
>
> (GGP, 29)

The resulting escape, from the dread clutches of an imposing and restrictive and vulgar reality to an idyllic all-male haven, is not presented, on the surface of the text, as being exclusively homosexual. 'It's a simple story of the old, old rupture – the break that lucky Catholics have always been able to make, that they are still, with their innumerable religious houses, by going into "retreat",' the Brother explains, in an attempt to define precisely why they feel the need for their own haven. 'I don't speak of the pious exercises,' he then qualifies himself. 'I speak only of the material simplification' (GGP, 24). Elsewhere, the narrator refers to the need more simply as a desire to experience 'the uncontested possession of the long, sweet, stupid day' (GGP, 32). However, the yearning to be psychologically and literally distanced from the influence of the popular and the crass and in the process to be able to regain a sense of selfhood purely spiritual and sensuous is developed in 'The Great Good Place' in a decidedly homo-erotic atmosphere. When Dane meets in his study the young man who resembles his own younger self, the sight of this 'indescribably beautiful' (GGP, 28) youth propels him into the fantasy world of the 'retreat'. Correspondingly, the place Dane escapes to is defined as 'the scene of his new consciousness' (GGP, 19), and that 'consciousness' is related to the consciousness of the other men there – all of whom are shown to be intuitively in sympathy with other males seeking an escape from a world 'not to be trusted for tact or delicacy' (GGP, 15). In the 'general refuge' there is a 'an image of embracing arms, of liberal accommodation' (GGP, 31); 'every act of the mind was a lover's embrace' (GGP, 34). Such male sympathy and camaraderie recall Nash's theory in *The Tragic Muse* that like-minded 'unregenerates' seek out one another and then support one another, and this is rephrased by Dane as he lays a hand on his companion's arm and reflects: 'It's charming, how, when we speak for ourselves, we speak for each other' (GGP, 25). 'The conditions settle us – they determine us' (GGP, 37) Dane adds later, as Nash had argued that 'the observer is nothing without his categories, his types and varieties'.

Nash's positive self-definition in the face of social condemnation also finds its parallel in 'The Great Good Place'. Dane argues that he is not 'ill' but only, as far as others are concerned, too '"beastly well"' (GGP, 37). There is also the question of the lack of a clear linguistic definition for whatever emotion or action or feeling it is that binds Dane to the other men. The narrator admits that the 'charm' the retreat holds for the men who populate would not have been 'easily phrased' (GGP, 19); it is something they never 'named' (GGP, 30); and the 'real exquisite was to be without the complication of an identity' (GGP, 32) – which at least reminds one of how James would have preferred society to relate to sexuality (including his own sexuality) in ways that did not categorise people or falsely sum them up. There is moreover everywhere that 'blessing of anonymity' that Edel correctly pointed to as a contextualising factor (while giving no explanation for why there might be the need to experience it). And while Edel also wrote, as though such a comment was sufficient in itself, that the biographical interest of 'The Great Good Place' lies in 'James's desire for an exclusive man's world', of related interest is the way that the fantasy of this retreat anticipated James's real-life move to Rye five years later and how, shortly afterwards, James fell in love with a series of younger men who, as Edel himself acknowledges elsewhere, resembled James's younger self and thus gave him the liberating sense of once again being young. James there found his great good place, and the context was – as in the story – very much one of narcissistic homo-erotic devotion.

'The Pupil' has provided a focal point for the discussion of the theme of homo-eroticism – or the lack thereof – in James's fiction. Horne's essay attacking queer theorists focused on the story and was primarily a negative reaction to an earlier essay by Helen Hoy.[25] Horne argued against the suggestion, advanced by Hoy, that the relationship between the tutor Pemberton and his charge Morgan should be recognised as pederastic, and in this specific instance one can sympathise with Horne's criticisms. Hoy's essay best serves as an illustration of the negative, reductive consequences on James criticism when the theoretical jargon of 'queer theory' is employed at the expense of more worthy practical criticism, historical contextualising and sensible biographical speculation. As Horne points out, in her crude ambition to unearth a gay subtext to the tale Hoy makes mistakes in her citations which afterwards she crucially draws on to substantiate her thesis.[26]

As well as pointing out the limitations of queer theory, Horne also – but less self-consciously – points to a way of reading the story that can reveal the homosexual theme to be a crucial part of the narrative. 'The real test,' writes Horne, 'would be a "fuller" account of "The Pupil" in which a homo-erotic reading came into serious and interesting tension with the complex balance of other more explicit strains in the story, about duty and sacrifice, money and honour, education and experience.'[27] In fact, these other strains are not nearly as explicit as the homosexual one, which is given substantially more emphasis; and unlike with those other concerns, James uses the relationship between Pemberton and Morgan as the defining context of the story.

Morgan, who matures from an 11-year-old to a 15-year-old, is the most significant, unifying character, but everything is presented from Pemberton's point of view. His decisions and assessments, particularly when directly associated with the question of money and honour, are clearly made, without exception, in response to an action, utterance or perceived thought by, or an anxiety about the logical consequences on, his charge. His conflicted feelings for the boy, and how those feelings result in his otherwise inexplicable inability to reject the Moreen family because they repeatedly refuse to pay him, is the central dilemma of 'The Pupil'. The story, that is to say, is about money, honour *and* pederasty.

The general, abstract theme that defines the intellectual and emotional bonding of Pemberton and Morgan is childhood, and the story explores a great Jamesian question: what children can and should know about the conflicts and complications of the adult world, what a proper adult response to 'knowledges and intuitions' (TP, 411) expressed by a child like Morgan should be, and whether for a child confused ignorance can be more corrupting than the knowledge of a world he is either considered too sensitive to be incorporated into or too vulnerable not to be protected against – or, even more troublingly, is at once cruelly drawn into and yet manip-ulatively denied an opinion about or control over. Morgan retorts, when Pemberton suggests that it was his former nurse who 'made' him 'very shrewd': 'Oh, that wasn't Zénobie; that was nature. And experience!' (TP, 435), and James then makes Pemberton's general difficulty of dealing with the way Morgan challenges his under-standing of childhood and children explicit:

> When [Pemberton] tried to figure to himself the morning twilight of childhood, so as to deal with it safely, he perceived that it was never fixed, never arrested, that ignorance, at the instance one touched it, was already flushing faintly into knowl-edge, that there was nothing that at a given moment you could say a clever child didn't know. It seemed to him that *he* both knew too much to imagine Morgan's simplicity and too little to disembroil his tangle.
>
> (TP, 437)

Morgan is peculiarly mature and perceptive, but only according to the social codes and ideas about normality Pemberton's experiences have, until his meeting with Morgan, led him to understand: 'During the first weeks of their acquaintance Morgan had been as puzzling as a page in an unknown language – altogether different from the obvious little Anglo-Saxons who had misrepresented childhood to Pemberton' (TP, 414). That 'misrepresented' is profound, and, as there is no qualifier – 'appeared to have misrepresented', 'seemed to have misrepresented' – attached to it, it suggests an understanding of the state of childhood as a social construct, and a view of children as inveterately resistant to the romantic attributes of natural innocence, vulnerability and dependency common since Rousseau but which began to wane with the harsh progress of the industrial revolution.[28] The object of Pemberton's attraction is, it is worth remembering, physically little more than a child even when the story ends; but James, through the presentation of Pemberton and Morgan's knowing glances, their physical closeness and the repeated articulation of their desire to run away with one another, presents every level of their companionship as in some way reciprocated. That is not to suggest, of course, that James sees Morgan – or indeed any other child in his fiction – as simply a little adult. Rather, Morgan combines an adult sophistication, sense of humour and level of intelligence with mystical qualities particular to James's fictional children, which Pemberton refers to in the early chapters as Morgan's 'supernatural' and 'superstitious' qualities (TP, 418; 419). Pemberton also notices 'that from one moment to the other [Morgan's] small satiric face seemed to change its time of life. At this moment it was infantine; yet it appeared also to be under the influence of curious intuitions and knowledges' (TP, 411); and that the boy declares things with a 'humour that made his sensitiveness manly' (TP, 441). The narrator even goes as far as to say that in his appearance there was 'something elderly and gentlemanly in Morgan's seediness' (TP, 423), and in an early, general summing up it is said that Morgan

> was a pale, lean, acute, undeveloped little cosmopolite, who liked intellectual gymnastics and who, also, as regards the behaviour of mankind, had noticed more things than you might suppose, but who nevertheless had his proper playroom of superstitions, where he smashed a dozen toys a day.
>
> (TP, 419)

The relationship between Pemberton and Morgan is openly encouraged by the boy's mother, and the 'love' Pemberton unquestionably holds for Morgan[29] is directly paralleled by that which the mother also feels for the child. It is similarly said to derive from the same kind of impulsive, uncontrollable feelings that a female nurse, Zénobie, had formerly held for Morgan. Pemberton's love of and interest in Morgan is not, however, entirely explainable by referencing the mother's maternal, or the former nurse's devotional, love. The substance of the mother's love is itself questionable, since she uses the love the boy himself arouses in others for fraudulent ends, and even bizarrely accepts the idea of its transferral: 'you've made him so your own,' she tells Pemberton after urging him to take the boy for himself, 'that we've already been through the worst of the sacrifice' (TP, 459); while Pemberton, conversely, is sufficiently confused by his sincere love for the boy consistently to overlook or find ways of dealing with that fraudulence. But Zénobie, after staying 'ever so long – as long as she could' (TP, 434–5), as Morgan recalls it, in the end did after all realistically decide that she had suffered enough, whereas Pemberton only decides to leave so that he can earn enough money eventually to keep him and Morgan independently of the Moreens. 'I'll get some work that can keep us both afloat,' he tells the boy, later repeating: 'I'll earn a lot of money in a short time, and we'll live on it' (TP, 435; 447). In neither instance is there cause to question the seriousness of the expressed intention. Indeed, it is only when the idea becomes completely acceptable to, and even encouraged by, both Morgan and his family that 'for the first time' Pemberton begins to feel 'sore and exasperated' at the 'escape' (TP, 455).

Pemberton chooses, when he is at Oxford tutoring another boy, to send by post 60 francs to Mrs Moreen; and then he returns to the family after hearing that the boy has become ill. So while Zénobie decided to leave, and the mother in the ends begs Pemberton to take the boy away with him, Pemberton is conversely defined initially by his inability actually to let the boy go, and then afterwards by his inability finally to take the boy when he is presented with the clear opportunity to do so. Appropriately, he is said to be left in a 'queer confusion of yearning and alarm' (TP, 456) at the inexorably doomed progress of the Moreens. Like a troubled lover who has sacrificed all for his beloved, he privately exclaims at one point, 'Morgan, Morgan, to what pass have I come for you?' (TP, 447), and at another, 'Where shall I take you, and how – oh *how*, my boy?' (TP, 452).

The parallel between the boy and Zénobie and Mrs Moreen on the one hand, and the boy and Pemberton on the other, is therefore obviously more one of contrast rather than similarity. Pemberton's relationship with the 'opulent youth' at Oxford provides another contrast, which sets the Pemberton–Morgan situation against its more normal and objective and strictly financial and educational equivalent: 'When Pemberton got to work with the opulent youth, who was to be taken in hand for Balliol, he found himself unable to say whether he was really an idiot or it was only, on his own part, the long association with an intensely living little mind that made him seem so' (TP, 449). Finally, while a love interest on Pemberton's part in Morgan's two sisters, Lisa and Amy, would not be considered appropriate in the strict aristocratic conventions of the story (he has not got any money, so there is no point in his trying), there is nevertheless something eccentric about the narrator's generic description of them, which provides another contrast to Pemberton's immediate fascination with the boy: 'The girls had hair and figures and manners and small fat feet ...' (TP, 413–14).

As Maxwell Geismar succinctly put it, 'The Pupil' is 'a study of the dangers of compassion',[30] and the question is whether the nature of Pemberton's compassionate interest in Morgan, and Morgan's idealisation of Pemberton, is sufficiently developed to give rise to a worthwhile discussion of its pederastic nature – and, if so, how it in turn can lead, in Horne's terms, to a 'fuller' reading. There are a number of reflections and actions by Pemberton, and towards Pemberton by Morgan, which relate to nothing apart from the feelings they hold for one another. At their first meeting Pemberton 'caught in the boy's eyes the glimpse of a far-off appeal' (TP, 412), and it is the idea of 'loving' Morgan that provides for his imagination 'an element that would make tutorship absorbing' (TP, 413). At the end of the first meeting, Pemberton indulgently reflects, after being charmed by some of Morgan's witticisms: 'After all, he's rather nice' (TP, 413). The two are said to develop a 'democratic brotherhood' (TP, 423), in the way that Rowland Mallet is said to find in Roderick Hudson a 'singularly sympathetic comrade'; and their intimacy is made explicit when towards the end of an evening strolling in Nice, Pemberton is seen affectionately to draw Morgan 'closer' after the boy had been 'clinging to his arms', begging him to 'hang on to the last' (TP, 421). Their behaviour becomes so informal in public that Pemberton fears that they were 'looked askance at, as though it might be a case of kidnapping' (TP, 423). When it is finally decided that Pemberton will leave for Oxford, 'Pemberton held [Morgan] fast, his hands on his shoulders – he had never loved him so'. And Morgan thinks of his tutor as a 'hero' (TP, 435), giving him an 'effusive young foreign squeeze' (TP, 450) when he returns from Oxford. His idea that the two of them should 'escape' is described as a 'romantic utility' (TP, 455). Finally, there is Morgan's reflection on the treatment he received when Pemberton was away, which gives rise to moments of tenderness:

> Morgan's comments, in these days, were more and more free; they even included a large recognition of the extraordinary tenderness with which he had been treated while Pemberton was away. Oh, yes, they couldn't do enough to be nice to him, to show him they had him on their mind and make up for his loss. That was just what made the whole thing so sad, and him so glad, after all, of Pemberton's return – he had to keep thinking of their affection less, had less sense of obligation. Pemberton laughed out at this last reason, and Morgan blushed and said: 'You know what I mean.' Pemberton knew perfectly what he meant; but there were a good many things it didn't make any clearer.
>
> (TP, 454–5)

The contrast between 'obligation' and 'affection' is poignant and embarrassing; ultimately unspeakably so. The lack of general clarification, even after Pemberton accepts that he knew 'perfectly well' what the boy was referring to, suggests that the issue of their feelings is distinct from money, the other theme of the story. That is indeed explicitly referred to by the boy to the tutor; but the complication of their love is not. More striking are Pemberton's memories, which are referred to by the narrator on two separate occasions:

> If it were not for a few tangible tokens – a lock of Morgan's hair, cut by his own hand, and the half-dozen letters he got from him when they separated – the whole episode and the figures peopling it would seem too inconsequential for anything but dreamland.
>
> (TP, 414–15)

They learned to know their Pairs, which was useful, for they came
back another year for a longer stay, the general character of which
in Pemberton's memory to-day mixes pitiably and confusedly with
that of the first. He sees Morgan's shabby knickerbockers – the everlasting pair that didn't match his blouse and that as he grew longer
could only grow faded. He remembers the particular holes in his
three or four pairs of his coloured stockings.

(TP, 423)

The contents of the letters Pemberton has kept are explored more
fully in another passage:

From Morgan he heard half-a-dozen times: the boy wrote
charming young letters, a patchwork of tongues, with indignant
postscripts in the family Valapuk and, in little squares and
rounds and crannies of the text, the drollest illustrations – letters
that he was divided between the impulse to show his present
disciple, as a kind of wasted incentive, and the sense of something in them that was profanable by publicity.

(TP, 449–50)

The traditional romantic token of 'a lock of hair', which was cut
intimately by Pemberton's 'own hand', is at odds, in its physical
signification of a treasured remembrance, with what one would
expect to find at the heart of a tutor-pupil relationship. The 'half-a-
dozen letters' are another traditional romantic fictional device,
although the fact that there was 'something in them' that was
'profanable by publicity' is open to multiple interpretations. If they
contained, as is most likely, information about the Moreens' strait-
ened financial circumstances, or even revealed Morgan simply
being characteristically rude about his parents, the 'opulent youth'
might easily be given cause to question Pemberton's suitability as a
tutor. However, Morgan's self-indulgence and the informal nature
of the letters (which are, with their illustrations and 'indignant'
comments, more in the spirit of a letter to a friend than a tutor),
and the inevitable expression of affection which would at least
equal that expressed by Morgan to Pemberton's face, offers another
cause for their contents to be 'profane'. Finally, there is the matter
of Pemberton confusing in his mind two year-long trips to Paris, the

second of which mixed 'pitiably and confusedly with that of the first. He sees Morgan's shabby knickerbockers – the everlasting pair that didn't match his blouse and that as he grew longer could only grow faded. He remembers the particular holes in his three or four pairs of his coloured stockings . . .' It is not difficult to believe that these memories are deeper and more romantic than even the most acute sense of financial honour and duty could explain. It therefore appears obvious, given the extent of this retrospective obsessiveness, that Pemberton simply fell in love with the boy and is still finding it difficult to get over the fact. Like so many of James's male protagonists, he is locked on the past – on the adolescence of a boy, and his own time spent enjoying it.

The consequences on Morgan of the Moreens' financial distress, rather than the consequences on his own pocket, troubles Pemberton most throughout the story. Despite his treatment by Mrs Moreen, he sends her 60 francs from Oxford. What is principally at stake is a combination of his own distress at thinking Morgan unhappy and neglected, and Morgan's extreme sensitivity to his almost comically exaggerated pride:

> the strangest thing in the boy's large little composition [was] a temper, a sensibility, even a sort of ideal, which made him privately resent the general quality of his kinsfolk . . . It was as if he had been a little gentleman and had paid the penalty by discovering that he was the only such person in the family.
>
> (TP, 426)

> What came out of it most was the soreness of [Morgan's] characteristic pride. He had plenty of that, Pemberton felt – so much that it was perhaps well it should have had to take some early bruises. He would have liked his people to be gallant, and he had waked up too soon to the sense that they were perpetually swallowing humble-pie.
>
> (TP, 441)

> He had walked, from his infancy, among difficulties and dangers, but he had never seen a public exposure. Pemberton noticed, in a second glance at him, that the tears had rushed to his eyes and that they were the tears of bitter shame.
>
> (TP, 458)

The final quotation is from the end of the final chapter, when it is clear that the Moreen family have outspent their resources and are therefore no longer able to keep up the appearance of leading lives of immense leisure. It is largely because Pemberton, despite everything over the years, *has* behaved with dignity and respect that Morgan grew to idealise him. But Morgan's 'theory', that he can rid himself of the dreadful associations of 'public exposure' and 'bitter shame' by escaping with Pemberton, turns out to be tragic and ironic. What Pemberton immediately senses as a consequence is his own risk – to do with the possible exposure of his relationship with the boy – to be confronted with 'public exposure' and 'bitter shame'. He is left to face the prospect that he might actually have to live on equal terms in England with Morgan, and his failure ultimately to accept this challenge is what results in Morgan's symbolic death. So the relationship between Morgan's hurt pride and his close friendship with Pemberton is, throughout 'The Pupil', linked to the idea of their 'escape'; and in this way the difficulties surrounding money are inexorably linked to the question of Pemberton's feelings for Morgan, and how their relationship could never progress into the wider social world once Morgan comes of age. He wishes to adopt the boy and to take him away, but ultimately fails to live up to that ideal.

Tracing the reasons for this reversal brings to the fore the homosexual, or more precisely homosocial, subtext of 'The Pupil', and reveals the underlying thematic progression of the story. Morgan first hints about his knowledge that Pemberton will not be paid at the beginning of chapter 3. Pemberton reassures the boy that he believes his parents are 'charming', and Morgan 'unexpectedly, familiarly, but at the same time affectionately [remarked]: "You're a jolly old humbug!"':

> For a particular reason the words made Pemberton change colour. The boy noticed in an instant that he had turned red, whereupon he turned red himself and the pupil and the master exchanged a longish glance in which there was a consciousness of many more things than are usually touched upon, even tacitly, in such a relation.

(TP, 420)

The 'particular reason' for Pemberton's change of colour is to do with Morgan spontaneous and familiar display of affection. The general context is Morgan hinting that Pemberton does not understand the reality of his parents' motivation in having hired him, and Pemberton's reluctance to enter into this sort of intercourse (which has principally to do with money) with his pupil. But there is surely another, subtler subtext suggested by the 'long exchange of glances', the mutual embarrassment, and the solicitous authorial comment about the consciousness of there being 'many more things than are usually touched upon, even tacitly, in such a relation'. After all, what they actually end up secretly plotting to do is nothing less than run away together. This exchange marks the emergence of the dual theme that dominates the story. Pemberton grows more intimate with Morgan, where the question of money is concerned, than is normally allowed; and he likewise grows more intimate with him in general than is normal in such a relation. In the same paragraph the narrator says: 'Later, when he found himself talking with this small boy in a way in which few small boys could ever have been talked with, he thought of that clumsy moment on the bench at Nice as the dawn of an understanding that had broadened' (TP, 420). And the link between money and affection is at last made explicit by Pemberton when he admits to Mrs Moreen, after she has told of her inability to pay him: 'I'll stay a little longer. Your calculation is just – I do hate immensely to give [Morgan] up; I'm fond of him and he interests me deeply, in spite of the inconvenience I suffer' (TP, 433).

The most absorbing element of 'The Pupil' is that it is Pemberton who introduces the idea an 'escape', on the same page that Morgan twice calls Pemberton a 'hero':

'We ought to go off and live somewhere together,' said the young man.

'I'll go like a shot if you'll take me.'

'I'd get some work that would keep us both afloat,' Pemberton continued.

'So would I. Why shouldn't *I* work? I ain't such a *crétin*!'

'The difficulty is that your parents wouldn't hear of it,' said Pemberton.

(TP, 435–6)

This conversation defines the two contrary responses of Pemberton and Morgan to the question of spending their lives together, and they both become more entrenched in their opposing viewpoints as the question of their 'escape' increases as a realistic possibility. Morgan sees it as a 'boy's book' (TP, 454) that has been told by an heroic author, which miraculously will come true and provide him with a happy ending; Pemberton, though, is acutely aware of his social position and the restrictions of the real world. He has made the suggestion impulsively and will live, as Morgan will die, to regret it.

When Morgan reaches 15, the narrator remarks that:

> This fact was intensely interesting to him – it was the basis of a private theory (which, however, he had imparted to his tutor) that in a little while he should stand on his own feet. He considered that the situation would change – that, in short, he should be 'finished', grown up, producible in the world of affairs and ready to prove himself of sterling ability. Sharply as he was capable, at times, of questioning his circumstances, there were happy hours when he was as superficial as a child; the proof of which was his fundamental assumption that he should presently go to Oxford, to Pemberton's college, and, aided and abetted by Pemberton, to do the most wonderful things. It vexed Pemberton to see how little, in such a project, he took account of ways and means: on other matters he was sceptical about them ... How could he live there without an allowance, and where was the allowance to come from? He (Pemberton) might live on Morgan; but how could Morgan live on him? What was to become of him anyhow? Somehow, the fact that he was a bog boy now, with better prospects of health, made the question of his future more difficult... [Morgan] himself, at any rate, was in a period of natural, boyish rosiness about all this, so that the beating of the tempest seemed to him only the voices of life and the challenges of fate.

> (TP, 445)

The contrast between Pemberton's earlier enthusiastic outburst and his grim assessment of the situation in this passage is extraordinary. It is difficult to believe, indeed, that Pemberton even remembers that it was he himself who first suggested the idea of an 'escape'. 'It vexed Pemberton to see how little, in such a project, he took account of ways and means: on other matters he was sceptical about them ...' As it might have sufficiently vexed Morgan, if he had been given access to these thoughts, to ask Pemberton why in that case he had put the idea into his head. Another contrast is contained within the passage itself: between Morgan as an adult, with the horrible epithet 'producible' hanging over him, and his present 'natural, boyish state of rosiness'.

When at last Morgan begs Pemberton to take him away, immediately after he has greeted his return from Oxford, his words are as impatient as, literally, Pemberton's response is heartbreaking: 'Do it – do it, for pity's sake; that's just what I want,' Morgan begs, 'I can't stand this – and such scenes.' On the same page he again pleads: 'Take me away – take me away ...' and is said to be 'smiling at Pemberton from his white face' (TP, 451). Pemberton's initial reason for not carrying through his idea of their living together was that 'the difficulty is that your parents wouldn't hear of it'. Now it is he who will not consider positively the prospect, though it is actually being proposed by Mrs Moreen. He later explains his change of mind, or rather reveals his *changed mind*, since his actual reasoning on this matter is not articulated anywhere in the story: 'It was all very well for Morgan to consider that he would make up to him for all the inconveniences by settling on him permanently – there was an irritating flaw in such a view ... the poor friend didn't desire the gift – what could he do with Morgan's life?' (TP, 456).

The context of their relationship was the socially sanctioned intimacy of tutor and pupil, defined by Pemberton's attraction to Morgan's adolescent qualities. Pemberton has turned out to be that most fashionable of Victorian Oxford types: the boy enthusiast. Earlier, in response to Pemberton's desperate plead of 'What will become of *you*, what will you do?', Morgan had unwittingly encapsulated the reason for his eventual rejection with the simple, charmless response: 'I shall turn into a man' (TP, 448). Bell writes: 'Morgan has now arrived at an age when, at any moment, his own masculinity will reach a new level of sexual awareness, and – to speak in contemporary terms quite alien to James's way of thinking – he can become a "consenting adult."'[31] This is the sort of 'misrepresentation' of childhood Pemberton has been made to challenge.

The idea that a boy suddenly, 'at any moment', can become sexual is absurd. But though the term may have been unfamiliar to James, the concept of a 'consenting adult' was perhaps what was on his mind at the end of this story – but not in the way that Bell thinks. Pemberton no longer desires the gift of Morgan's life, for two main reasons: because there is no way that they could live together openly as two 'consenting' men in Oxford, as Morgan desires things should turn out; and because Pemberton no longer finds Morgan interesting because he has become, alas, that most uninteresting of things: a man, an adult; just like himself.

The ending presents Morgan's symbolic death as Pemberton finally, fatally hesitates at his crucial decision when both Mr and Mrs Moreen tell him, in front of Morgan, that he can take the boy away, wherever he likes and for as long as it suits him. 'For ever and ever?' Morgan asks:

> Morgan had turned away from his father – he stood looking at Pemberton with a light in his face. His blush had died out and something had come that was brighter and more vivid. He had a moment of boyish joy, scarcely mitigated by the fact that, with his unexpected consecration of his hope – too sudden and too violent; the thing was a good deal less like a boy's book – the 'escape' was left on their hands. The boyish joy was there for an instant, and Pemberton was almost frightened at the revelation of gratitude and affection that shone through his humiliation. When Morgan stammered 'My dear fellow, what do you say to that?' he felt that he should say something enthusiastic. But he was still more frightened at something else that immediately followed and that made the lad sit down quickly on the nearest chair.
>
> (TP, 459)

Morgan dies with his boyhood: 'The boyish joy was there for an instant'; 'He had a moment of boyish joy.' Pemberton acknowledges that he is now 'frightened' by Morgan's affection, that he can but feel he 'should' be enthusiastic about their escape. There is the important question of money, of how Pemberton could support Morgan, but as Mildred E. Hartsock long ago noted, there is 'a depth of feeling involved which makes irrelevant the mere matter of money'.[32] The death is a symbolic illustration of the divide between a private, ideal pederastic yearning and a public denial of its legitimacy now it threatens to leave the sanctuary of a teacher-pupil context, all of which is complicated by Pemberton's rejection of Morgan as he comes of age, gains his independence and becomes, as Morgan had so innocently put it, 'a man'.

6
The Uses of Obscurity

Allon White has examined James's movement towards modernism and obscurity by relating it to trends in publishing, psychology and education. His thesis spans the period also covered by Weeks in his analysis of the emergence of homosexuality in the late Victorian period, and so it can be extended to take account of the homosexual aspects of James's life and writing, and in particular his reactions to the Victorian gay subculture.

White analysed the fiction as being in equivocal relation to various social and publishing transformations, the most important of which was the emergence of an élite readership which set itself against the new mass literary market:

> There is evidence to show that, by the late 1880s, the fiction-reading public had begun to split into two different groups ... With the end of the three-decker the market for the 'respectable' novel seems to have split internally into an 'élite' or reviewers' public. Again and again... we meet the same distinction between an élite and popular audience.[1]

There was a related shift in reading habits, towards seeing novels, not as autonomous entities, but as representations of their author's psychology – the result of a new insistence that artistic ability should closely be related to various forms of abnormality:

> Within a few years in the 1880s, under the influence of proto-psychology, literary texts were transformed into primary

evidence of the inner private fantasies of the author. The sincerity of the relationship between author and middle-class reader ...[,] their mutual interest in the honest transcription of the emotional life, was supplemented by a new kind of relationship which made the old contract extremely difficult to keep. The author was suddenly placed at a disadvantage by the sophistication in reader response, he became vulnerable to a certain kind of knowing smile which found in his words the insufficiently disguised evidence of his most intimate preoccupations. As more and more intellectual readers began to regard fiction as a transformation of fantasy by various quasi-defensive devices, the notion of the 'truth' of the text, and the relations between text, author and reader, swiftly changed.[2]

The first specific negative mention in James's fiction of the 'vulgarity' of the new mass-circulation newspapers is in 'The Author of *Beltraffio*', where, as we have seen, they are said to have always been 'abnormally vulgar' about homosexual Ambient. In the same story, James had drawn the new distinction between 'mass' and the 'élite', by having Ambient announce: 'There's a hatred of art; there's a hatred of literature – I mean of the genuine kind. Oh the shams – *those* they'll swallow by the bucket!' The new mass readership and journalism, and the broader movement White associated with it, was famously observed by James in other stories and novels.[3] Examples include 'The Lesson of the Master' (1888) and 'The Figure in the Carpet' (1896), which deal with the relationship between a well-known but obscure male author and his prying, persistent, idolising young male critic. In 'The Aspern Papers' (1888) the widow of the eponymous author is said to have escaped the intrusiveness of her dead husband's obsessive critics, and the surprise is that 'self-effacement on such a scale had been possible in the latter half of the nineteenth century – the age of newspapers and telegrams and photographs and interviewers' (AP, 279). As well as observing the rise of a mass readership, James also became associated with the 'élite' group of English decadents grouped around *The Yellow Book*, the 'most dramatic casualties of the crisis in masculinity at the *fin de siècle*'.[4] Its editor, Henry Harland, himself idolised James to the point of appearing absurd.[5] James's short story 'The Death of the Lion' (1894) was published in its first issue, and 'The Coxon Fund' (1894) and 'The Next Time' (1895) subsequently appeared in *The Yellow Book*'s pages. While not 'decadent' like much of what appeared there, 'The Death of the Lion' in particular was concerned with questions of gender and 'notorious' authorship. The protagonist – a young reporter – remarks that 'in the age we live in one gets lost among the genders and the pronouns' (DL, 111); the story poses a question similar to that in 'The Aspern Papers': is not 'an immediate exposure of everything just what the public wanted?' (DL, 79).

James, however, would never have allowed himself to be viewed as so exclusive or decadent as to provoke the wrath of prying critics who had so eagerly condemned Wilde's *The Picture of Dorian Gray* for its homosexual insinuations and ambience,[6] and he had cause for erring on the side of caution. In the 1890s a number of American magazines commented negatively about his appearance in *The Yellow Book*. A writer in *Munsey's* stated that 'of late ... Mr. James has been in bad company ... He has become one of *The Yellow Book* clique', and called on James to return home to the comfortable moral certainties of America. *The Atlantic* noted that a 'super-subtlety of theme, for which no form of expression can be too carefully wrought ... place[s] Mr. James inextricably in the decadent ranks'.[7] If 'homosexual' is read for 'decadent', as many Victorians would have read it after Wilde,[8] and the context of a new emphasis on interpreting texts as representations of their author's private world that White outlined is remembered, then it becomes clear that the broader publishing and psychological context White examined can be made to relate to the emergence of the concept of the homosexual – and, in turn, to James's equivocal relationship to it.

The situation is complicated by the fact that James's desire to discover a new audience and his readiness to become associated with what was considered subversive never resulted in his giving up on the ideal of earning a decent living from his writing.[9] And he suffered a real-life battle with other readers who in fact found nothing at all in his plays and novels to appreciate. After the unsuccessful first night of *Guy Domville* he remarked that, though at least *some* of the audience clapped, they were less expressive than those who let out 'hoots and jeers and catcalls', whose roars were 'like those of a cage of beasts at some infernal zoo', and who, for James, represented 'the forces of civilisation' (HJL: 3, 508). A few days afterwards, he reflected: 'I have fallen upon evil days – every sign and symbol of one's being in the least *wanted*, anywhere or by any one, having so utterly failed. A new generation, that I know not, & mainly prize not, had taken universal possession. The sense of being utterly out of it weighed me down, & I asked myself what the future wd. be' (HJLL, 277). The conclusion James arrived at was that the way out of this quagmire was 'to *be* one of the few'. He would renounce, he said, 'the childishness of publics', and no longer seek to win over a large audience. Henceforth he would not care if 'scarce a human being will understand a word, or an intention, or an artistic element of any sort' in what he wrote (HJL: 3, 511). Michael Anesko has observed of this period that 'James shrewdly sensed that being *un*popular, unsalable at any price, had a cachet of its own – one that publishers, curiously, might bid for',[10] and one way James found to create for himself a new, intimate bond with more accommodating readers than those who had jeered his play and ignored his fiction was to write tales and novels which, while typically not explicitly or exclusively homosexual, would be recognised as dealing with *risqué* themes by the initiated. There is a revealing sentence in James's *Notebook* entry for 'The Figure in the Carpet' – a tale in which, incidentally, the famous author's directly inexpressible preoccupation with a unifying theme beginning with the letter P might have something to do with James's use of a capitalised P in his letter to Gosse about how direct discussion of Symonds's pederastic outpourings would be beyond him, despite his almost obsessive interest in it. James notes that tale will involve an 'author of certain books who is known to hold ... that his writings contains a beautiful and valuable, very interesting and remunerative *secret*, or latent intention, for those who read them with a right intelligence'.[11] James, too, was setting himself up as 'one of the few'.

The tension between James's wanting to be a part of the mainstream and realising that his only chance of finding a loyal, sustaining readership was by becoming more exclusive, and between writing stories and novels that expressed in a covert way homosexuality while remaining himself publicly and professionally distanced from all obvious manifestations of it, characterises a letter James wrote to his brother William about the appearance of 'The Death of the Lion' in *The Yellow Book* inaugural issue:

I haven't sent you 'The Yellow Book' – on purpose; and indeed I have been weeks and weeks receiving a copy of it myself. I say on purpose because although my little tale which ushers it in ('The Death of the Lion') appears to have had, for a thing of mine, an unusual success, I hate too much the horrid aspect of the whole publication. And yet I am again to be intimately – conspicuously – associated with the second number.

(HJL: 3, 482)

The movement in this letter – towards revelation and then finally back again to teasing concealment – is that also apparent in the letters James wrote to Gosse about Symonds. There is the same wish to be intimate with that which simultaneously James is eager to distance himself from. The story, he cannot help but note, is 'an unusual success'; and yet he finds unacceptable the notoriety that comes from an association with a publication that had such a particular kind of circulation. He claims to 'hate too much' publishing there; but in the same breath he reveals that he is once again – 'intimately, conspicuously' – to publish in its pages. This suggests that, far from hating it all too much, he could not actually bring himself to hate appearing there nearly as much as the public, self-protective side of his personality would have preferred. The same kind of ambiguity is evident in a famous letter James wrote to Gosse about the trial of Wilde:

Yes, too, it has been, it is, hideously, atrociously dramatic and really interesting – as far as one can say that of a thing of which the interest is qualified by such a quickening horribility. It is the squalid gratuitousness of it all – of the mere exposure - that blurs the spectacle. But the fall – from 20 years of a really unique kind of 'brilliant' conspicuity (wit, 'art', conversations – 'one of our 2 or 3 dramatists etc.') to that sordid prison-cell and this gulf of obscenity over which the ghoulish public hangs and gloats - it is beyond any utterance of irony or pang of compassion! He was never in the smallest degree interesting to me – but this hideous human history has made him so – in a manner.

(HJG, 126)

There is a careful balance between 'hideously dramatic' and 'really interesting', which is qualified by a sense of 'quickening horribility'.

James's 'interest' resurfaces in the final sentence, but again this is qualified by a mild disclaimer: 'in a manner'. The comment that 'it is beyond any utterance of irony or pang of compassion' should not necessarily be taken as signifying a lack of sympathy: Wilde's situation was simply so tragic, James appears to be saying, that it warrants a greater degree of complexity and careful contemplation than either response would have allowed for. It is clearly 'the mere exposure', in any case, that so shocked James, in typical Victorian bourgeois fashion, rather than what Wilde had actually got up to: he is most self-conscious about the ease with which one could fall into a 'gulf of obscenity', out of which one could look only to see 'the ghoulish public' gloating. That James had so recently suffered the wrath of an angry public, on the first night of *Guy Domville*, and that he had afterwards complained of falling 'upon evil days' and consequently of being made to ask himself 'what the future would hold', gives an added dimension to his response to Wilde. James must have recognised how his own low spirits after the rejection by a small section of English society in the relative safety of the theatre paled into insignificance when compared to the 'gulf of obscenity' into which Wilde had fallen, and that 'the ghoulish public' was now a much greater physical threat to Wilde than they had been to himself. There was sufficient similarity for James to have felt for Wilde in a very personal way, especially considering the manner in which homosexuality – and indeed Wilde himself – had been prominent in James's fiction during the past few years. Richard Salmon has written, in another context, of how James's response to the 'uproar' at the theatre invoked a vision of 'a conflict in which the cultivated author is threatened, almost bodily, by the insurrection of the "mass"'.[12]

Wilde's famous defence of same-sex attraction in his trial drew on classical and Renaissance examples of male love: 'The "Love that dare not speak its name" in this century is such a great affection of an elder for a younger man as there was between David and Jonathan, such as Plato made the very basis of his philosophy, and such as you find in the sonnets of Michaelangelo and Shakespeare.'[13] The points of reference are those that had previously been selected by Pater and Symonds, in the wake of Winckelmann, and to a lesser degree by James; but since the context was a trial for gross indecency involving rent boys, Wilde unwittingly made crudely explicit the hitherto largely denied or overlooked relationship between illegal sexual acts between men and boys and the classical inheritance apologists drew on to promote an image of the pederast as respectable, noble and pure. Many Englishmen had even begun to regard the homosexual scandals of the 1880s and 1890s as certain signs of the immorality that had toppled Greece and Rome,[14] and by the time of Wilde's conviction the evocation of the gay classical world had certainly lost its veneer of respectability.

An example of how an emphasis on manliness, refinement and classicism had become tainted with pederastic scandal is the publication in 1895 of an essay, 'The New Chivalry', by Charles Kains-Jackson, editor of the principal literary meeting place for pederastic enthusiasts entitled *The Artist,* in which a focus on the classical depiction of the adolescent male had long been the objectifying justification for the magazine's homo-erotic content.[15] Kains-Jackson argued that by adapting the relics of a mediaeval courtly convention, and evoking the 'mainly comradeship' of the classical world, the romantic exigencies of homosexuals in his own age might better be understood. But by the time 'The New Chivalry' was published, that comfortable sense of an educated acceptance of Hellenism (and therefore homosexuality) being tolerated by an indifferent mass had been replaced by the exposure of the social reality of homosexual desire and the resulting hostility of the public to it, and as a consequence of the negative response the essay received (including an indignant sermon directed against the author) Kains-Jackson was forced to retire as editor – this from a magazine which, under his editorship, had built up a large circulation during the previous decade by helping to define the Hellenistic foundations of Victorian gay discourse.[16]

Linda Dowling has written that Wilde's defence of homosexuality during his second trial, which received a spontaneous round of applause from the public gallery, marked the 'emergence into the public sphere of a modern discourse of male love formulated in the late Victorian period' by such writers as Pater, Symonds and Wilde himself. It was 'a new language of moral legitimacy pointing forward to Anglo-American decriminalisation and, ultimately, a fully developed assertion of homosexual rights'.[17] Ellmann similarly writes that it is in large part thanks to Wilde, 'both in his books and in his gaol testimony, that the taboo against writing about homosexual behaviour or other forms of sexuality began to be lifted in England'.[18] Equally true, however, is that, as an *immediate* consequence of Wilde's conviction, homosexuality was more easily categorised and therefore better controlled, stigmatised and condemned than it had previously been, and that paranoia amongst homosexuals dramatically increased, even to the extent that many elected to leave the country.[19] James found himself at odds with homosexual rights advocates as well as with those responsible for the persecution of homosexuals. Those who like him nevertheless remained in England, and who had in the past resisted social categorisation as 'homosexuals' but had been happy to associate privately with what we would now call expressions of homosexuality, would find it increasingly difficult to lead superficially conventional lives – particularly if they enjoyed a degree of literary fame and had to be mindful of the new demand for gossip about the private lives of authors.[20] It was surely this new sense of restrictivness that determined James to return his copy of *Modern Ethics* on such extraordinarily self-conscious grounds. It was, after all, merely a book sitting on a bookshelf in his private library. Any opportunity to 'veil' his sexual propensity from the public was, it seems, to be welcomed.

Symonds had died in 1893, Pater in 1894; they were not made to suffer the spectacle of Wilde's downfall. James, though, was left to face the consequences. What is extraordinary is that he neither fell silent nor became a hypocrite, but continued to write about homosexuality, to accept at least emotionally the legitimacy of his own homosexual desires, and to read the new publications dealing with homosexuality.[21] The discovery of Pater's gay-inflected essays in *The Renaissance* had influenced *Roderick Hudson* in 1875; the scandal of Symonds's private life had led to 'The Author of *Beltraffio*' in 1884; the increasing prominence of a gay aesthetic subculture in the late 1880s had filtered into *The Tragic Muse* and 'The Pupil'; and now, in the wake of the Wilde trial, there was a new gay social reality that would be reflected in James's fiction.

The story 'In the Cage' (1898) can be taken as an example of an indirect, perhaps even unconscious influence of the Wilde trial on James's writing.[22] Its emphasis is on scandal, blackmail, telegrams and unnameable sexual 'crimes', and an observer who leads a 'double life' in relation to it all inside and outside of a cage, and it is primarily concerned with heterosexual infidelity and the general question of gaining knowledge about other people's lives through inference and suggestion. It could also, however, be seen as creating a heterosexual world which creatively drew on the world of homosexual scandal – its telegraph boys, secret rendezvous, extra-marital affairs – which so intrigued James. It might be exploring the obsessiveness of men who, like James, were reluctant to be associated with that homosexual world but who nevertheless self-consciously took it all in from the shadows. In the story, Mr Mudge's comment about not understanding 'people's hating what they liked or liking what they hated' (IC, 171) accurately articulates what many readers have felt about James's treatment of his and others' homosexuality, and the treatment of that theme in James's fiction is also usefully summed up by another remark in the story about how through silence and 'everything they had so definitely not named, the whole presence around which they had been circling, became part of their reference' (IC, 198). The Catholic (and before his conversion openly homosexual) Marc André Raffalovich related how he remembered 'teasing James with a friend to know what the Olympian young man in *In The Cage* had done wrong', but that James 'swore he did not know, he would rather not know'.[23] It will be remembered that James would insist on not knowing about Symonds's homosexuality or homosexuality in society more generally, would deny ever having met Symonds and would distance himself, even in his private correspondence with trusted friends, from his private fascination with the Wilde trial.

It was James's misfortune that he began to find contentment in a series of intimate friendships with men at precisely the historical moment when English society moved, legally and socially, against homosexuality. As we have seen, in 1898 – the year James moved to Rye – the law was changed in England to make even homosexual soliciting a criminal offence. But in both his personal and literary capacity, James remained determined to explore his homosexual feelings in his private life and to be sincere to his wish to write about them in his parallel fictional worlds. Hugh Stevens has written that if in the 1890s James resisted 'the clarion call of decadence, and toes no particular party line in his public persona as a writer, the subtlety with which he supposedly remains "above suspicion" is impressive', and notes that if Wilde represented the 'public face' of 'queerness', James should conversely be seen as exploring the 'queer interiority' of those who remained, by comparison with Wilde, relatively closeted.[24] This idea can be taken much further in the context of James's movement towards establishing in his late novels and stories meanings and values by way of obscurity and implication and evasion and subtle suggestion.

James wrote to A.C. Benson that Lamb House was 'really good enough to be a kind of little becoming, high door'd, brass knockered *façade* to one's life,' and Edel comments that this indeed 'is what Lamb House became'.[25] James's style could be said to have become in a comparable way his literary façade. The year he moved to Rye, for example, he published 'The Turn of the Screw', in which Miles and Quint, unlike in their predecessors Pemberton and Morgan in 'The Pupil', are relegated to the realm of (what might perhaps be) make-believe, by way of being presented through the neurotic visions and suspicions of an untrustworthy governess. At the same time, James, by emphasising the unnameable, paradoxically made more explicit the connotations of social scandal than he had with the relatively open love of 'The Pupil'. Miles has been expelled from school, and the cause is said by the governess to have been 'revoltingly ... against nature' (TOS, 127), which would have indicated to the average Victorian reader that Miles had been expelled for homosexual activity: the 'spectacular expansion of single-sex public schools' in the late Victorian period 'produced a rich crop of sexual scandals'.[26] Most interestingly, Symonds's biographer claims that the volumes by Symonds that James returned to Gosse at the height of the Wilde scandal – the time he first conceived the idea for 'The Turn of the Screw' – were in fact Symonds's *Memoirs*, which were privately circulating at the time, rather than – as Edel and others have claimed – his *Modern Ethics*.[27] If this was the case, James would have read the following passage about Symonds's time at Harrow:

> One thing at Harrow very soon arrested my attention. It was the moral state of the school. Every boy of good looks had a female name, and was recognized either as a public prostitute or as some bigger fellow's 'bitch'. Bitch was the word in common usage to indicate a boy who yielded his person to a lover. The talk in the

dormitories and the studies was incredibly obscene. Here and there one could not avoid seeing acts of onanism, mutual masturbation, the sport of naked boys in bed together.[28]

If James did not read this, it serves anyway as a useful way of placing 'The Turn of the Screw' in an historical context, and when Forrest Reid complained that in his preface James refused 'to accept responsibility for what deliberately has been suggested'[29] he presumably meant this schoolboy homosexuality, and the related pederastic coupling of Miles and Quint. What Reid failed to see – and what critics now are only beginning to discover – was what was most absorbing and important, namely that James's manner, his refusal actually to name what is there or even to give confirmation that it is not merely imagined to be there, contained a new kind of responsibility and ambiguity, one that relied on a gap between his and his narrator's awareness of events, and thus allowed for a way of bypassing – or, looked at another way, creatively drawing on – the harsh homophobic climate of the late 1890s.[30] In this sense 'The Turn of the Screw', and the novels and tales that followed it that to a significant extent dealt with homosexuality, benefited from the fact that the subject had become directly unmentionable and that the classical allusions adopted by James in earlier, naturalistic novels such as *Roderick Hudson* had become obsolete. The need to find equally deep but superficially untraceable ways of representing same-sex attraction would prove to be a major influence on James's stylistic and thematic movement away from the moral absolutes of the Victorian world to a relativistic and pragmatic view of reality, as presented in the late phase. Between the truth of what Miles got up to at school and the admission of that truth stood the ghosts who screened it and discredited it (who can believe in ghosts?) and the added suspicion deflected onto the possibly hallucinating governess. In a sense homosexuality is both there and not there in that tale; it is inferred but unprovable. It is just this kind of intense subjectivity that would define James's late fiction. As *The Tragic Muse* had incorporated new ideas about the leading of 'double lives' and the positive self-definition by certain brave homosexuals, so in the later work the emergence of a gay 'consciousness' – reflected in the 1898 change to the law, which focused on soliciting and recognised that men could 'be' homosexual, even if their behaviour took place *only in the mind* – transforms James's fictional treatment of the subject once again, and in turn the stylistic, dramatic and narrative movement of his general fictional output. James, that is to say, enters into the consciousness of his male homosexual protagonists, as is best illustrated by way of reference to *The Ambassadors* and 'The Beast in the Jungle'.

Though published in 1903, the outline for *The Ambassadors* was written in 1899, the year James met and fell in love with Hendrik Anderson.[31] It is this biographical context, ignored by Jamesians, that should be kept in mind when reading the novel. Edel writes that James 'looked at Anderson as an inward vision of his own youth, his distant Roman days';[32] in the novel, Strether finds in Chad's Parisian life echoes of his own youth, and his own distant Parisian days. 'It was as if,' Edel continues, 'Anderson had been fashioned out of James's old memories and old passions';[33] just as Strether's overriding emotion when in the company of Chad is the sense of once again being young, of living through the younger man's youth. He is another of James's 'permanent adolescents', for whom Chad is 'a kind of link for hopeless fancy, an implication of possibilities' (A, 139). Most significantly, Edel remarks that James and Anderson 'spoke of intimate things, family, friends, affections. So Roderick and Rowland had talked years ago'.[34] But the homo-erotic comradeship of Roderick and Rowland was, as we have seen, contextualised by references to classical homosexuality and art. In the later decade during which *The Ambassadors* was written even such refined allusiveness had become too risky, and so when Strether begins to admire the 'happy young Pagan, handsome and hard' (A, 166), and his 'massive young manhood' (A, 110), the narrative obscures rather than elaborates. Shortly afterwards, Strether asks Chad:

'Have I your word of honour that if I surrender myself to Madame de Vionnet you'll surrender yourself to *me*?'

Chad laid his hand firmly on his friend's. 'My dear man, you have it.'

There was finally something in his felicity almost embarrassing and oppressive – Strether had begun to fidget under it for the open air and the erect posture. He had signed to the waiter that he wished to pay, and this transaction took some moments, during which he thoroughly felt, while he put down money and pretended – it was quite hollow – to estimate change, that Chad's higher spirit, his youth, his paganism, his felicity, his assurance, his impudence, whatever it might be, had consciously scored a success. Well, that was right as far as it went; his sense of the thing in question covered our friend for a minute like a veil through which – as if he had been muffled – he heard his inter-locutor ask him if he mightn't take him over about five.

(A, 167–8)

By allowing the legitimacy of Chad's friendship with Madame de Vionnet, Strether will increase his intimacy with Chad, and a wilful self-deception regarding the nature of that 'virtuous attachment' best explains the psychological motivation of Strether's otherwise absurdly innocent and for many tedious New England naiveté.[35] The 'thing in question' in the above passage is both the nature of the 'virtuous attachment' and Strether's homo-erotic but undeclared relation to Chad in relation to that attachment. When the matter threatens to become explicit, Strether is 'muffled' by a 'veil'. James had written to Gosse at the height of the Wilde scandal that 'these are days in which one's modesty is, in every direction, much exposed, and one should be thankful for every veil that one can hastily snatch up or that a friendly hand precipately [*sic*] muffles one withal'. The homo-eroticism in *The Ambassadors* is thus muffled.

James revealingly wrote in 1912 to Hugh Walpole about *The Ambassadors* in a way that combined discussion of the idea of permanent adolescence in the story with a summary of the need he had felt for obscurity when dealing with Strether's feelings for Chad. The point James is making has to do primarily with artistic principles, but can also be seen as bringing to the fore tensions and considerations which in the novel itself are only hinted at:

The whole thing is of course, to intensity, a picture of relations – & among them is, thought not on the first line, the lelation of Strether to Chad. The relation of Chad to Strether is a limited & according to my method only implied & indicated thing, suffi-ciently there; but Strether's to Chad consists above all in a charmed & yearning & wondering sense, a dimly envious sense, of all Chad's young living & easily-taken *other* relations; other not only than the one to him, but than the one to Mme de Vionnet & whoever else: this very sense, & the sense of Chad, generally, is a part, a large part, of poor dear Strether's discipline, development, adventure & general history. All of it that is of my subject seems to give me – given by dramatic projection, as all the rest is given: how can you say I'd anything so foul & adject as to 'state'?

(HJLL, 515)

In 'The Beast in the Jungle' the protagonist John Marcher lets his confidant May Bartram into a secret, and again the metaphor of the veil is employed: 'The rest of the world of course thought him queer, but she, she only, knew how, and above all why, queer; which was precisely what enabled her to dispose the concealing veil in the right folds' (BJ, 367). When Marcher later contemplates 'lifting the veil of his image at some moment from the past', he once more reflects: '(what had he done, after all, if not lift it to *her*)' [BJ, 394]. The story is primarily about how Marcher has been unable to see that May Bartram had loved him – 'The mistake would have been to love her; then, *then* he would have lived' (BJ, 401) – because of his introspective obsession with a belief that he has been singled out for something momentous, and his fear that he is not simply another anonymous figure in the great crowd of mundane humanity. The moral subtext – that one can find contentment and a sense of self-worth by focusing on the kind of small events and passions of daily life that make every individual unique – would have been familiar to anyone who had read *Middlemarch*. But questions remain. *Why* did Marcher not recognise that he was loved? What is it that he 'feels' that is so unnameable and subjective, and so potentially catastrophic if it were to become known socially? It is surely not simply a wish to be great and distinguished. He defines himself in the way that Gabriel Nash in *The Tragic Muse* and George Dane in *The Great Good Place* had: as deviant and abnormal, but only in terms of convention:

> 'The thing itself will appear natural.'
> 'Then how will it appear strange?'
> Marcher bethought himself. 'It won't – to *me*.'
> 'To whom then?'
> 'Well,' he replied, smiling at last, 'say to you.'
>
> (BJ, 361)

In *Roderick Hudson*, Rowland's love for Roderick had been contrasted with his superficial but unconvincing love for Mary Garland; that had provided his cover. In the same way, May Bartram is said by herself to act in 'The Beast on the Jungle' as Marcher's cover, but the kind of explicitness James had employed in *Roderick Hudson* in the conceptually innocent 1870s had become dangerous for James to be associated with after the turn of the century and it is the woman who takes centre stage at the expense of the homo-erotic passion. In the following passage, for example, it is May who combines the superficial heterosexual scenario provided by Mary Garland and the sympathetic ear of Cecilia, Rowland's cousin, who first introduced Rowland to the 'pretty boy' Roderick and had a great sympathy for Rowland's need to 'fall in love' with him. May says:

> 'Our habit saves you, at least, don't you see? because it makes you, after all, for the vulgar, indistinguishable from other men. What's the most inveterate mark of men in general? Why, the capacity to spend endless time with dull women – to spend it, I won't say without being bored, but without minding that they are ... That covers your tracks more than anything.'
>
> (BJ, 369)

The irony is that in this late tale James's inability to name Marcher's homosexuality led to the more explicit presentation of the narcissistic, homo-erotic pattern of homosexuality that had been implicit in his gay fiction for decades. Marcher's 'identity' is given by May because she allowed him to wander, lover-like, around her, arm-in-arm, with his younger self:

> The open page was the tomb of his friend, and *there* were the facts of the past, there the truth of his life, there the backward reaches in which he could lose himself. He did this, from time to time, with such effect that he seemed to wander through the old years with his hand in the arm of a companion who was, in the most extraordinary manner, his other, younger self; and to wander, which was more extraordinary yet, round and round a third presence – not wandering she, but stationary, still, whose eyes, turning with his revolution, never ceased to follow him,

and whose seat was his point, so to speak, of orientation. Thus in short he settled to live – feeding only on the sense that he once had lived, and dependent on it not only for a support but for an identity.

(BJ, 398)

Marcher could not have loved May because he wanted her so that he could love another younger man in the form of his own younger self. The passage serves as a summing-up of the theme of 'permanent adolescence' I have traced in so much of James's earlier fiction.

Notes

Chapter 1

1. Henry James, 'Gabriel D'Annunzio', in *Notes on Novelists* (New York: Charles Scribner's Sons, 1914), 231.
2. Leon Edel, *Henry James: A Life* (London: Collins, 1985), 512, for a discussion of Beerbohm's cartoon.
3. Max Beerbohm, 'Mr Henry James's Play', *Around Theatres* (New York: Knopf, 1930), 701–2.
4. M. Denneny et al. (eds), *The View from Christopher Street* (London and New York: Cassell, 1984), 295; Gore Vidal, *United States: Selected Essays: 1952–1992* (London: André Deutsch, 1992), 218.
5. Sheldon M. Novick, *Henry James: The Young Master* (New York: Random House, 1996), 109. The passage by James is from Leon Edel and Lyal H. Powers (eds.), *The Complete Notebooks of Henry James* (Oxford: Oxford University Press, 1987), 238.
6. *Times Literary Supplement*, 6 December 1996, 3–4.
7. *Times Literary Supplement*, 27 December 1996, 17.
8. Eve Kosofsky Sedgwick's essay 'The Beast in the Closet: James and the Writing of Homosexual Panic', in Sedgwick, *Epistemology of the Closet* (Berkeley and Los Angeles: University of California Press, 1990), 182–212, has become about as famous as it is possible for an academic essay to become, and is widely recognised as having initiated recent critical debates about the extent to which James sublimated his homosexual sensibility into his fiction. Critics who have written about James's homosexuality subsequently and have explicitly acknowledged a debt to Sedgwick's work include Wendy Graham, Michael Moon, John Carlos Rowe, Eric Savoy, Hugh Stevens and Linda Zwinger (see entries under these names in the bibliography). However, essays on James and homosexuality have been appearing since the 1960s, long before the emergence of 'queer theory', the most important of which are: Mildred E. Harstock, 'Henry James and the Cities of the Plain', *Modern Language Quarterly*, No. 29 (1968), 297–311; Robert K. Martin, 'The "High Felicity" of Comradeship: A New Reading of *Roderick Hudson*', *American Literary Realism*, No. 11 (Spring, 1978), 100–8; Richard Hall, 'Henry James: Interpreting an Obsessive Memory', *Journal of Homosexuality*, Vol. 8, Nos 3/4 (1983), 83–97; Melissa Knox, '*Beltraffio*: Henry James's Secrecy', *American Imago*, Vol. 3, No. 3 (Fall, 1986), 221–7; Adeline R. Tintner, 'A Gay Sacred Fount: the Reader as Detective', *Twentieth-Century Literature*, Vol. 41, No. 2 (Summer, 1995), 224–40. It is in this broader tradition that I am writing. Hugh Stevens, *Henry James and Sexuality* (Cambridge: Cambridge University Press, 1998), has presented

a wide-ranging, thorough and highly theoretical reappraisal of James's career by charting his complex reactions to the emergence of homosexuality and other *fin de siècle* sexual dilemmas. By way of a happy coincidence, Stevens discusses in detail only one novel I also discuss – *Roderick Hudson* – which we moreover have a significantly different take on. It is worth mentioning incidentally that the fact that our studies complement one another (rather than overlap) demonstrates how the subject of James's homosexuality may provide fertile ground for numerous interpretations, just as heterosexual subjects have.

9. Philip Horne, 'Henry James: the Master and the "Queer Affair" of "The Pupil"', *Critical Quarterly*, Vol. 37, No. 3 (Autumn 1995), 75–92. The quotation is from p. 80.

10. Lyndall Gordon, *A Private Life of Henry James: Two Women and his Art* (London: Chatto & Windus, 1998), 434.

11. John R. Bradley, 'Henry James's Permanent Adolescence', in Bradley (ed.), *Henry James and Homo-Erotic Desire* (Basingstoke: Macmillan, 1999), 51–3.

12. David Van Leer, *The Queening of America: Gay Culture in Straight Society* (London and New York: Routledge, 1995), Ch. 4, 'The Beast of the Closet: Sedgwick and the Knowledge of Homosexuality'.

13. Gordon, *Private Life of James*, 5.

14. Ibid.

15. Ibid., 391.

16. See Sheldon M. Novick, 'Introduction', in Bradley (ed.), *James and Homo-Erotic Desire*, 18.

17. Ibid., 1–2

18. See note 8, above.

19. Novick, 'Introduction', 8.

20. Gordon, *Private Life of James*, 74–5.

21. Ibid., 10.

22. See Jeffrey Weeks, *Coming Out: Homosexual Politics in Britain, from the Nineteenth Century to the Present* (London: Quartet, 1977), 14–15.

23. For a discussion of James's reactions to the Wilde trial, see pp. 130ff below.

24. Lee Siegel, 'The Gay Science: Queer Theory, Literature, and the Sexualization of Everything', *The New Republic*, (9 November 1998), 30–42.

25. See, for example, John Carlos Rowe, 'Hawthrone's Ghost in Henry James's Italy: Sculptural Form, Romantic Narrative, and the Function of Sexuality', *The Henry James Review* 20 (1999), 107–34, especially 129–30.

26. Siegel, 'The Gay Science', 41–2.

Chapter 2

1. Edmund Gosse, 'Henry James', *The London Mercury*, No. 7 (1920), 33.

2. Hugh Walpole, 'Henry James: A Reminiscence', *Horizon*, Vol. 1, No. 2

(1940), 76.

3. Edel, *James: A Life*, 652.
4. Ibid.
5. Ibid., 511.
6. Theodora Bosanquet, *Henry James at Work* (London: The Hogarth Press, 1924), 81.
7. Peter Ackroyd, *T.S. Eliot* (London: Hamish Hamilton, 1984), 13.
8. Edel, *James: A Life*, 663.
9. Eve Kosofsky Sedgwick, 'Shame and Performativity: Henry James's New York Edition Prefaces', in David McWhirter (ed.), *Henry James's New York Edition: The Construction of Authorship* (Stanford and London: Stanford University Press, 1995). The quotation is from pp. 215–16.
10. For the definition of narcissistic homosexuality, see Sigmund Freud, *The Standard Works of the Complete Psychological Works of Sigmund Freud*, trans. James Strachey (London: The Hogarth Press, 1973–4), 24 Vols, Vol. 14, 297–8.
11. Novick, *Young Master*, 36, 154.
12. Ibid., 33, 69, 84.
13. John Carlos Rowe, *The Other Henry James* (North Carolina, and London: Duke University Press, 1998), 223. Rowe was responding to the original publication in *Essays in Criticism* of my essay 'Henry James's Permanent Adolescence'.
14. For a critique of Freud's attitude to homosexuality from a post-gay liberation perspective, see Jonathan Dollimore, *Sexual Dissidence: Augustine to Wilde, Freud to Foucault* (New York and Oxford: Oxford University Press, 1991), 196–7, and Kaja Silverman, *Male Subjectivity at the Margins* (London and New York: Routledge, 1992), 161–2.
15. Jonathan Freedman, *Professions of Taste: Henry James, British Aestheticism, and Commodity Culture* (Stanford and London: Stanford University Press, 1990), 275–6.
16. Richard Dellamora, *Masculine Desire: The Sexual Politics of Victorian Aestheticism* (Chapel Hill, NC and London: University of North Carolina Press, 1990), 45.
17. For a general discussion of the related themes of nostalgia, narcissism and pederasty in western literature, from Virgil to contemporary gay fiction, see John R. Bradley, 'Disciples of St. Narcissus: In Praise of Alan Hollinghurst', *The Critical Review*, No. 36 (1996), 3–18.
18. Forrest Reid, *Peter Waring* (London: Faber and Faber, 1937), 238.
19. Peter Swaab, 'Hopkins and the Pushed Peach', *Critical Quarterly*, Vol. 37, No. 3 (Autumn 1995), 43–60. The quotation is from p. 51.
20. Of course, James is not alone in the nineteenth and twentieth centuries in exploring homosexuality in his fiction and relating to it in his life in terms of an adolescent fixation. Alan Hollinghurst, 'The Creative Uses of Homosexuality in the Novels of E.M. Forster, Ronald Firbank and L.P. Hartley', unpublished M.Litt. thesis (Bodleian Library, Oxford, 1980), explores the way in which these three writers have a 'sense of determinism about the life of the emotions endorsed by [an] incessant

exhausting repetition of the *idée fixe* of each psyche', and remarks that in the 'hands of a good artist such an idea can solidify into the structure of a work of art, or of a whole series of works of art' (5). Reading Hollinghurst's eloquent and incisive thesis was the initial inspiration for this study of James (a writer not discussed in detail by Hollinghurst). Other examples include A.E. Housman, about whom Hollinghurst has subsequently written in *The Guardian* (1 March 1996): 'Housman's poems gain force from the incessant backward glances they cast on youth from a later discontent. Housman thus appears adolescent and old before his time: a pattern not uncommon in very repressed personalities ... [A] sense of the physical and emotional separation seems to have spurred Housman into writing poetry ... and into creating his metaphorical world of sundered friendships, irreversible change and exile from a sense of happiness. Amorous and sexual emotions are clouded by regret and fear ... The book aches and sighs with loneliness, with the sleepless solitary dusks and dawns of the depressive's calendar.' Valentine Cunningham, *British Writers of the Thirties* (Oxford: Oxford University Press, 1988), 148–53, argues that W.H. Auden, Christopher Isherwood, Stephen Spender and other writers of the 1930s remained, because of their intense homosexual initiations and experiences at prep and public school, essentially adolescent in their outlook, and were to a significant extent driven afterwards by the pursuit of youths in similar situations (Auden, for instance, striking up an affair with a prep school boy). Sebastian Flyte, the protagonist of Evelyn Waugh's *Brideshead Revisited* (1945), is also fixated on his childhood and his later time at Oxford – where the bells are said to exhale 'the soft airs of centuries of youth', and where he himself cultivated a close and dependent friendship with Charles Ryder which later in the novel is explicitly said to have been defined by their love for one another. The homosexual writer Denton Welch, associated in his lesser capacity as an artist with Cyril Connolly's *Horizon* magazine, was knocked from his bicycle in 1935 when he was 23 years of age, an event described in his memoir *A Voice Through a Cloud* (1948). Welch's work has as its recurring, unifying theme adolescence, both his own and that of the virile and active boys to whom he frequently refers. The accident that crippled Welch was a real one; but it can also be seen (at the risk, admittedly, of seeming a little insensitive to his very real suffering) as bringing into play a sort of symbolic crippling, one that represents a failure to come to terms with the feeling of being (to paraphrase another pederast, Jean Genet) resentfully alive inside a rotting adult corpse. (For a discussion of this theme in Genet, see Jean-Paul Sartre, *Saint Genet: Actor and Martyr* [London: Routledge & Kegan Paul, 1952], Ch. 3.) It is also worth mentioning Hollinghurst's novels *The Swimming-Pool Library* (London: Hamish Hamilton, 1988) and *The Folding Star* (London: Chatto & Windus, 1994), themselves variations on the theme of the impact of adulthood on a particular kind of adolescent gay psyche. The protagonist of *The Swimming-Pool Library* defines the 'whole gay thing' as 'the unvoiced longing, the cloistered heart' (144), and, although his fixation on other younger boys who resemble his younger self is emotionally crippling, it is hardly so sexually: the novel is one of the most remarkable celebrations of gay sexual activity yet published. This last point is made in anticipation of a reaction to my take on James that would see it as homophobic – in the same way, for instance, that Gregory Woods, in *A History of Gay Literature: A World Survey* (New Haven and London: Yale University Press, 1998), unjustly criticised in a similar context John Sutherland's interpretation of Wilde's *The Picture of Dorian Gray* in the latter's study *Is Heathcliff a Murderer?: Puzzles in 19th-Century Fiction* (Oxford and New York: Oxford University Press, 1996). Sutherland wrote: 'one of the endeavours of homosexual love, with its cult of the marvellous boy, is to abolish sequence ... *The Picture of Dorian Gray* fantasises a world where middle-aged hedonists can be forever boys, equated in a timeless plane composed half out of lust, half out of the wish-fulfilling visions of the fairy story. Dorian Gray is, to play with the word, two kinds of fairy – the Faustian hero who sells his soul for youth, and the middle-aged, mutton-dressed-as-lamb gay, who will sell his soul to look young again' (198). Woods retorted that this was the 'unembarrassed rambling' of a 'homophobic critic', and asked: 'Does Sutherland seriously believe that heterosexual men have not constructed their equivalent cult of the marvellous girl? ... Literary critics are publishing this kind of complacent drivel all the time' (15–16). Woods is being naive, and the resort to personal insult is all the more unbecomingly because as a critic he is usually stylistically enchanting. As I remark in the main body of my text, there is – despite the existence perhaps of the 'marvellous girl' for heterosexual men – an obvious reason why narcissism can more easily be associated with homosexuality than heterosexuality, in that gay men were once boys and younger boys can therefore resemble – indeed mirror – the remembered image an older gay man may treasure of his younger, idealised self. This idea goes back as far as the Narcissus myth, and Wood himself refers to that myth in a gay context repeatedly in his study (see the entry in the index). It could not work in the same way for straight men for the obvious reason that they were not once girls.

21. Cyril Connolly, *Enemies of Promise* (London: Routledge, 1938), 271.
22. Edel, *James: A Life*, 511.
23. Susan E. Gunter and Steven H. Jobe (eds), *Dearly Beloved Friends: Henry James's Letters to Younger Men* (forthcoming, University of Michigan Press). An essay under the same title including extracts from a number of previously unpublished letters appears in Bradley (ed.), *James and Homo-Erotic Desire*, 120–130. Gunter and Jobe write that the letters to Jocelyn Persse 'are perhaps the most explicitly erotic James wrote'. Judging from the one they then go on to quote (129), that 'explicitly erotic' is profoundly qualified by the 'James ever wrote'.
24. Henry James to Hendrik Anderson, 8 December 1913. Quoted in Bradley (ed.), *James and Homo-Erotic Desire*, 128.

25. John Boswell, *Christianity, Social Tolerance, and Homosexuality* (Chicago and London: University of Chicago Press, 1980), 28–9.
26. Steven Seidman, *Romantic Longings: Love in America*, p. 23.
27. Novick, *Young Master*, 77.
28. John Addington Symonds, *Male Love: A Problem in Greek Ethics and Other Writings* (New York: Pagan Press, 1983), 96–7. Whitman wrote, in response to an inquiry by Symonds: 'About the questions on "Calamus", &c., they rightly daze me. "Leaves of Grass" is only to be rightly construed by and within its own atmosphere and essential character – all its pages and pieces so coming strictly together. That the Calamus part has ever allowed the possibility of such construction and quite at the time undreamed and unwished possibility of such morbid inferences – which are disavowed by me and seem damnable.'
29. For a discussion of the way in which James's attitude to Whitman changed between his review of 1865 and his later comments on Whitman in 1898 see Eric Savoy, 'Reading Gay America', in Robert K. Martin (ed.), *The Continuing Presence of Walt Whitman: The Life after the Life* (Iowa City: University of Iowa Press, 1992), 3–15.
30. Edel, *James: Treacherous Years*, 167.
31. Novick, *Young Master*, 370.
32. Linda Dowling, *Hellenism and Homosexuality in Victorian Oxford* (Ithaca, NY, and London: Cornell University Press, 1994), 36.
33. Richard Ellmann, 'James Amongst the Aesthetes', in Bradley (ed.), *James and Homo-Erotic Desire*, 27.
34. R.M. Seiler (ed.), *Walter Pater: The Critical Heritage* (London: Routledge & Kegan Paul, 1980) 293.
35. Ibid.
36. William E. Buckler (ed.), *Walter Pater: Three Major Texts* (New York and London: New York University Press, 1986), 191.
37. Phyllis Grosskurth, *The Woeful Victorian: A Biography of John Addington Symonds* (London: Longmans, Green & Co, 1964), 257–61.
38. Ibid., 253–4.
39. Weeks, *Coming Out*, 51.
40. John Addington Symonds, *Studies in the Greek Poets*, 2nd Series (London: Smith, 1876), 146. For a discussion of the homophobic conditions under which Symonds wrote his study of Greek poetry, see Dellamora, *Masculine Desire*, 160–4.
41. Adeline R. Tintner, *The Pop World of Henry James: From Fairy Tales to Science Fiction* (Ann Arbor: UMI Research Press, 1989), Ch. 2, 'James the Orientalist' and Ch. 3, 'Greek and Roman Legends: "Movements of the Classic Torch round Modern Objects"', has demonstrated that James's deep knowledge of both the Oriental and classical worlds provided him with a context in which he could contextualise his discussion of (amongst other things) homosexuality. Rowe, 'Hawthrorne's Ghost in James's Italy', 121–2, briefly argues that James self-consciously suggests homo-eroticism by use of classical allusion in his two early stories 'Adina' (1874) and 'The Last of the Valerri' (1874). In this and the

following chapter I have expanded on this theory. Regarding Whitman, in his autobiography James likened his own association with young men during the American Civil War with Whitman's famous (and now generally accepted homo-erotic) caring for them, which confirms that James himself drew parallels between his own early experience of America and 'dear old Walt's' (AUT, 424).

42. Quoted in F.O. Matthiessen, *The James Family: A Group Biography* (New York: Knopf, 1961), 494–5.

43. Edel, *James: A Life*, 438.

44. Symonds, *Male Love*, 101.

45. For a discussion of the falling out between Reid and James, see the introduction by Colin Cruise to *The Garden God* (London: Brilliance Books, 1986), iv.

46. Forrest Reid, *Private Road* (London: Faber and Faber, 1940), 64–75.

47. Edel, *James: A Life*, 724–5.

48. Horne, 'Henry James: the master and the "queer affair" of "The Pupil"', 91 (note 5), referred to this assessment by Menguin as 'extremely interesting' and incorporated it as evidence into his essay that attacked 'queer theorists' for their (to Horne erroneous) suggestion that James wrote about homosexuality and could be considered to have been in a meaningful way homosexual. Menguin suggests, Horne explains, 'an expressive emotional economy in which James's warm words and gestures of affection register precisely the absence of *sexual* possibility'.

49. Adeline R. Tintner, 'Henry James and Byron: A Victorian Romantic Friendship', *The Byron Journal*, No. 9 (1981), 52–64, and, by the same author, *The Book World of Henry James* (Ann Arbor: UMI Research Press, 1987), 95–102.

50. Jonathan Fryer, *André and Oscar: Gide, Wilde and the Art of Gay Living* (London: André Deutsch, 1997) offers an accessible account of Gide and Wilde's parallel homosexual adventures in southern Europe and North Africa. For an outline of reports on pederasty in the Classical and Oriental worlds during the nineteenth century, see Stephen O. Murray, 'Some Nineteenth-Century Reports of Islamic Homosexuality', in Stephen O. Murray and Will Roscoe (eds), *Islamic Homosexualities: Culture, History and Literature* (New York and London: New York University Press, 1997), 204–21, and Robert Aldrich, *The Seduction of the Mediterranean: Writing, Art and Homosexual Fantasy* (London and New York: Routledge, 1993), Ch. 3.

51. Wilfred Thesiger, *Arabian Sands* (London: Collins, 1959), 188.

52. Rana Kabbani, *Imperial Fictions* (Basingstoke: Macmillan, 1986; repr. by Pandora, with corrections, 1994), 121.

53. Henry James, *Italian Hours* (London: Charles Scribner's Sons, 1909), 56.

54. Mrs Humphry Ward, *A Writer's Recollections* (London: Macmillan, 1916), 328–9.

55. Leon Edel, *Henry James: The Treacherous Years* (Philadelphia: J.P. Lippincott, 1969), 297–8.

56. Aldrich, *Seduction of the Mediterranean*, 30, points out that the Antinous

myth was 'vaunted' by 19th-century homosexual writers.
57. 'Kismet', *The Nation*, No. 24 (1877), 341.

Chapter 3

1. Walter Pater, *Plato and Platonism* (London: Macmillan, 1893), 280–1.
2. Woods, *History of Gay Literature*, 168.
3. Ellmann, 'James Amongst the Aesthetes', 27.
4. Dellamora, *Masculine Desire*, Ch. 3, 'Hopkins, Swinburne, and the Whitmanian Signifier', has written about how both Hopkins and Swinburne also used Whitman's apparent (but not sexually explicit) homo-eroticism as a way of exploring their own various reactions to homosexuality in a 'manly' context. For a more detailed exploration of Hopkins's reactions to homosexuality in his life and his writings, which in certain interesting ways mirror James's own, see Ch. 2 of the same study, and Swaab, 'Hopkins and the Pushed Peach', 43–60.
5. Stevens, *James and Sexuality*, 70–2.
6. Leon Edel, *Henry James: The Untried Years* (New York: J.B. Lippincott, 1953), 250.
7. Ibid.
8. This passage from *The Portrait of a Lady* is quoted, in a different context, by Robert K. Martin, 'Failed Heterosexuality in *The Portrait of a Lady*', in Bradley (ed.), *James and Homo-Erotic Desire*, 91.
9. Wendy Graham, 'Henry James's Subterranean Blues: A Rereading of *The Princess Casamassima*', *Modern Fiction Studies*, Vol. 40, No. 1 (Spring 1994), 51–84, persuasively argues that in *The Princess Cassamassima* (1887) James may be alluding to both the classical world and the reputation of the Orient for pederasty to imply a homosexual undertone to the protagonist Hyacinth Robinson's relationship with Paul Muniment. See especially p. 52.
10. Henry James, *Watch and Ward* (New York: Grove Press, 1960; repr. 1979), 47.
11. Ellmann, 'James Amongst the Aesthetes', 27–8.
12. Pater, *Three Major Texts*, 191.
13. Martin, 'The "High Felicity" of Comradeship', 102–3.
14. In his introduction to *Roderick Hudson* (London: Rupert-Hart Davis, 1960), 16, Edel wrote: 'The chief interest in this novel focuses on Roderick and his patron, Rowland, and his aloof New England conscience.' In *Henry James and His Cult* (London: Chatto & Windus, 1964), 20, Maxwell Geismar defines the friendship between Rowland and Roderick as 'close, rather touching, wholly innocent [and] masculine'.
15. Precilla L. Walton, *The Description of the Feminine in Henry James*, 76.
16. Novick, *Young Master*, 497–8.
17. Ibid., 497.
18. He does, however, mention it in *The Tragic Muse*.
19. Winterbourne is said to be 'extremely devoted' to a 'foreign lady' in

Geneva who is older than himself, though nobody has ever seen her (DM, 155). At the end of the story, when Winterbourne again returns to Geneva, he is said once again to be 'much interested' in a 'very clever foreign lady' (DM, 202). Since he is presented as being naive about, and even afraid of, women in the story itself, the idea of the mysterious women – while thickening the plot in that her 'cleverness' provides a contrast to Daisy's 'shallowness' – has no meaningful significance to the main narrative. The narrator explains how in Geneva 'a young man wasn't at liberty to speak to an unmarried lady' who was young (DM, 157), and whatever Winterbourne could have experienced with the old lady has had no affect on his confused dealings with Daisy in Rome. Winterbourne, anyway, is said to be 'studying' that foreign lady 'hard', meaning that even if she does indeed exist Winterbourne's analytical, objective approach to women as a type has remained.

20. (E, 64).
21. See Jean Goodner's introduction to Henry James, *Daisy Miller and Other Tales* (Oxford: Oxford University Press, 1985), xvi.
22. Ibid., 8. In the original version, Winterbourne had 'decided that he must advance further, rather than retreat' (DM, 157).
23. Ibid., 57.
24. Ibid., 71.
25. Ibid., 74–5.
26. See Millicent Bell, *Meaning in Henry James* (Cambridge, Mass. and London: Harvard University Press, 1991), 65.

Chapter 4

1. Symonds, *Male Love*, vii.
2. Weeks, *Coming Out*, 21.
3. Ibid., 25.
4. Eric Haralson, 'The Elusive Queerness of Henry James's "Queer Comrade": Reading Gabriel Nash of *The Tragic Muse*', in Richard Dellamora (ed.), *Victorian Sexual Dissidence* (Chicago and London: University of Chicago Press), 191–210. The quotation is from p. 208 (note 22).
5. Ibid., 194.
6. Edel, *James: A Life*, 427.
7. Jane Turner (ed.), *The Dictionary of Art*, 35 Vols (London: Macmillan, 1996), Vol. 4, 284.
8. Symonds, *Male Love*, 72–3.
9. Ibid., 82–5.
10. Weeks, *Coming Out*, 19–20.
11. Symonds, *Male Love*, 82.
12. Ibid., 91.
13. Ibid., 43.
14. Haralson, 'The Elusive Queerness', 208.

15. Novick, *Young Master*, 370.
16. See Leland S. Person, 'Homo-Erotic Desire in the Tales of Writers and Artists', in Bradley (ed.), *James and Homo-Erotic Desire*, 115.
17. Edel, *James: A Life*, 438–9.

Chapter 5

1. Weeks, *Coming Out*, 19.
2. Ibid., 21.
3. Robert Peters, 'Foreword', in Symonds, *Male Love*, vii.
4. Ibid., ix.
5. Weeks, *Coming Out*, 37.
6. See, for example, Person, 'Homo-Erotic Desire in the Tales of Writers and Artists', in Bradley (ed.), *James and Homo-Erotic Desire*, and Rowe, *The Other Henry James*, Ch. 4, 'Textual Preference: James's Literary Defences against Sexuality in "The Middle Years" and "The Death of the Lion"'.
7. Dellamora, *Masculine Desire*, Ch. 9, 'Theorising Homophobia: Analysis of Myth in Pater'.
8. Woods, *History of Gay Literature*, 173–4.
9. Ibid., 175.
10. Richard Ellmann, *Oscar Wilde* (London and New York: Penguin, 1988), 128, 288.
11. Ellmann, 'James Amongst the Aesthetes', 37ff.
12. For a discussion of the influence of Wilde on the character Nash, and *The Tragic Muse* on Wilde's *The Picture of Dorian Gray*, see ibid.
13. Ibid., 37.
14. Rowe, *Other Henry James*, 76.
15. Elaine Showalter, *Sexual Anarchy: Gender and Culture at the Fin de Siècle* (London: Bloomsbury, 1991), 16.
16. See, for example, Philip Horne's introduction to *The Tragic Muse* (Harmondsworth: Penguin, 1985).
17. Michel Foucault, *The History of Sexuality*, trans. Robert Hurley (New York: Vintage, 1980), Vol. I, 43.
18. Brian Reade (ed.), *Sexual Heretics: Male Homosexuality in English Literature from 1850 to 1900* (London: Routledge & Kegan Paul, 1970), 31.
19. Ellmann, 'James Amongst the Aesthetes', 37.
20. Haralson, 'The Elusive Queerness', 201.
21. Woods, *History of Gay Literature*, 176.
22. Rowe, *Other Henry James*, 99.
23. Edel, *James: A Life*, 474.
24. Peter Gay, *The Bourgeois Experience: Victoria to Freud* (Oxford and New York: Oxford University Press, 1984), 288.
25. Helen Hoy, 'Homotextual Duplicity in Henry James's "The Pupil"', in *The Henry James Review*, Vol. 14, No. 1 (Winter, 1993), 34–42. There is an equally theoretical but much more absorbing reading of 'The Pupil'

in Linda Zwinger, 'Bodies that Don't Matter: The Queering of "Henry James", *Modern Fiction Studies*, Vol. 41, Nos 3–4 (Fall-Winter 1995), 657–80.

26. Horne, 'The Pupil', 85.
27. Ibid., 88.
28. See Reinhard Kuhn, *Corruption in Paradise: The Child in Western Literature* (Chicago and London: University of Chicago Press, 1982), for a discussion of the changing perceptions about and depictions of childhood and children in western literature from Rousseau to the present, including a very brief consideration of the 'enigmatic child' in James's fiction, 20–1.
29. A revision to the New York Edition of the story makes the 'love' explicit. At the most intimate moment between Pemberton and Morgan, when Pemberton accepts at Morgan's urging a position in Oxford to tutor another youth, the narrator comments in the original version that 'Pemberton held him, his hands on his shoulders' (TP, 96). In the New York Edition this is changed to: 'Pemberton held him fast, his hands on his shoulders – he had never loved him so' (*The New York Edition of the Novels and Tales of Henry James*, Vol. 11, 575).
30. Geismar, *James and His Cult*, 115.
31. Millicent Bell, 'The Pupil and the Unmentionable Subject', *Raritan*, Vol. 16, No. 3 (Winter 1997), 49–63. The quotation is from p. 60.
32. Hartsock, 'James and the Cities of the Plain', 305.

Chapter 6

1. Allon White, *The Uses of Obscurity: The Fiction of Early Modernism* (London: Routledge & Kegan Paul, 1981), 31–2.
2. Ibid., 45–6.
3. Richard Salmon, *Henry James and the Culture of Publicity* (Cambridge: Cambridge University Press, 1987), gives the most thorough analysis of this theme in James.
4. Showalter, *Sexual Anarchy*, 170.
5. Katherine Mix, *A Study in Yellow: The Yellow Book and its Contributors* (London: Macmillan, 1960), p. 169.
6. Ellmann, *Oscar Wilde*, 86, 128.
7. *Munsey's*, 13 June 1895, 310; *The Atlantic* (January 1897), p.169. Both of these references are pointed out in Freedman, *Professions of Taste*, 177.
8. Showalter, *Sexual Anarchy*, 171, argues that 'decadence' came to be seen as '*a fin-de siècle* euphemism for homosexuality' long before this remark in *The Atlantic* was published. For a more general discussion of the relationship between decadence and homosexuality, and James's relationship to both, see Wendy Graham, 'Henry James's Thwarted Love', in Carol Siegel and Ann Kibbey (eds.), *Eroticism and Containment: Notes from the Flood Plain*, Genders 20 (New York: New York University Press, 1994), 66–95, and Regenia Gagnier, *Idylls of the Marketplace: Oscar*

Wilde and the Victorian Public (Stanford and London: Stanford University Press, 1986).

9. Edel, *James: A Life*, 663.

10. Michael Anesko, *'Friction with the Market': Henry James and the Profession of Authorship* (New York and Oxford: Oxford University Press, 1986), 143.

11. Edel and Powers (eds.), *Notebooks*, 136.

12. Salmon, *James and the Culture of Publicity*, 64.

13. Ellmann, *Oscar Wilde*, 435.

14. Showalter, *Sexual Anarchy*, 3.

15. *The Artist* (July and October 1889).

16. For a discussion of this incident and of the influence more generally of *The Artist* magazine on late nineteenth-century gay discourse, see Timothy d'Arch Smith, *Love in Earnest: Some Notes on the Lives and Writings of the English 'Uranian' Poets from 1880 to 1910* (London: Routledge and Kegan Paul, 1970), 182–3, and Dellamora, *Masculine Desire*, 157.

17. Dowling, *Hellenism and Homosexuality*, 2.

18. Richard Ellmann, *a long the riverrun* (New York: Knopf, 1988), 10.

19. Reade, *Sexual Heretics*, 53.

20. Edel, *James: A Life*, 571–2, discusses James's irritation at the media interest in his private life after a Miss Grigsby had put it about that Henry James was interested in getting engaged to her. If the media thought this worthy of commentary, one can imagine how they would have reacted had a scandalous story about James and younger men been leaked. What is remarkable, of course, is James's insistence on pursuing his male love objects privately, even if he did so only in an epistolary context. Hugh Stevens, 'Queer Henry *In the Cage*', in Jonathan Freedman (ed.), *The Cambridge Companion to Henry James* (Cambridge: Cambridge University Press, 1998), 135 (note 16), remarks that the 'biographical construction of a sexually timid James should bear in mind that in the wake of the Wilde trials, such erotic *writing* [was] more daring and risky than illegal sexual activity conducted in private'.

21. See Gunter and Jobe, 'Dearly Beloved Friends', for a summary of James's relationships and correspondence with Anderson, Fullerton, Persse, Sturgis and Walpole. Fred Kaplan, *Henry James: The Imagination of Genius* (New York: William Morrow, 1992), 401, writes: 'Something extraordinary began happening to Henry James in the mid-1890s, and more frequently in the next decade. He fell in love a number of times. He established intimate relationships, beyond his usual friendships, that for the first time provided him with the feeling of being in love.' Meanwhile, Tintner, *Pop World of Henry James*, 90, notes that James read the chapters on homosexuality in Otto Weininger's *Sex and Character* (1898). James also read the two-volume biography of Symonds by Horatio F. Brown (1895), and it is extremely likely that he read Marc André Raffalovich's *Uranisme et Unisexualité* (1896), since he had been friends with the author for some considerable time by the time it was published.

22. For much fuller readings of 'In the Cage' in this context see Eric Savoy, '*In the Cage* and the Queer Effects of Gay History', *Novel*, No. 28 (1995), 284–307, and Stevens, 'Queer Henry *In the Cage*'.
23. Reid, *Private Road*, 70.
24. Stevens, 'Queer Henry *In the Cage*', 124–6.
25. Edel, *James: Life*, 462. The quotation from the letter to Benson is quoted by Edel on the same page.
26. Weeks, *Coming Out*, 35.
27. Grosskurth, *Symonds: A Biography*, 319.
28. Phyllis Grosskurth (ed.), *The Memoirs of John Addington Symonds* (London: Hutchinson, 1984), 94.
29. Reid, *Private Road*, 70.
30. Tintner, 'A Gay Sacred Fount', has convincingly argued that in *The Sacred Fount* (1901) – James's most infuriatingly indirect and elusive late novel – the covert lovers sought out by the unnamed narrator are homosexual, namely Gilbert Long and Guy Brissenden. The obscurity thus derives in large part from James's wish to incorporate this male–male coupling as the centre-piece of the novel but in a way that makes it not easily traceable. Again, this reflects the ironic situation of James in the late 1890s – of on the one hand finding homosexual content-ment in his life while on the other being barred from discussing, as he had done previously, the subject openly in his fiction.
31. Edel, *James: A Life*, 506.
32. Ibid., 495.
33. Ibid.
34. Ibid., 495–6.
35. Geismar, *James and his Cult*, 269, writes that if Strether is unable to guess at the truth of Chad's relationship with Madame de Vionnet then 'he is deliberately self-deceived'. When Strether later finds out that they are having a sexual relationship, the narrator states: 'He kept making of it that there had been simply a *lie* in the charming affair – a lie on which one could now, detached and deliberate, perfectly put one's finger' (A, 393). So it is when Strether becomes 'detached' from the events he has been witnessing that he finally admits the truth to himself, largely one supposes because he realises that his intimacy with Chad, now that the affair has been made explicit, cannot continue on the earlier stated terms (that Strether, by surrendering himself to a Madame de Vionnet he pretends to be virtuous, can rely on Chad surrendering in turn to himself).

Bibliography

Ackroyd, Peter, *T.S. Eliot* (London: Hamish Hamilton, 1984).

Aldrich, Robert, *The Seduction of the Mediterranean: Writing, Art and Homosexual Fantasy* (London and New York: Routledge, 1993).

Anesko, Michael, *'Friction with the Market': Henry James and the Profession of Authorship* (Oxford and New York: Oxford University Press, 1996).

Bell, Millicent, 'The Pupil and the Unmentionable Subject', *Raritan*, Vol. 16, No. 3 (Winter 1997).

Boswell, John, *Christianity, Social Tolerance, and Homosexuality* (Chicago and London: University of Chicago Press, 1980).

Bradley, John R., 'Henry James's Permanent Adolescence', in John R. Bradley, ed., *Henry James and Homo-Erotic Desire* (Basingstoke: Macmillan, 1999).

—— 'Disciples of St. Narcissus: In Praise of Alan Hollinghurst', *The Critical Review*, No. 36 (1996).

Brake, Laurel, *Subjugated Knowledges: Journalism, Gender and Literature in the Nineteenth Century* (Basingstoke: Macmillan, 1994).

Bristow, Joseph, *Effeminate England: Homoerotic Writing after 1885* (New York: Columbia University Press, 1995).

Bosanquet, Theodora, *Henry James at Work* (London: The Hogarth Press, 1924).

Connolly, Cyril, *Enemies of Promise* (London: Routledge, 1938).

Crompton, Louis, *Byron and Greek Love* (Berkeley: University of California Press, 1985; repr. London: GMP, 1997).

Cunningham, Valentine, *British Writers of the Thirties* (Oxford: Oxford University Press, 1988).

D'Arch Smith, Timothy, *Love in Earnest: Some Notes on the Lives and Writings of the English 'Uranian' Poets from 1880 to 1910* (London: Routledge and Kegan Paul, 1970).

Dellamora, Richard, *Masculine Desire: The Sexual Politics of Victorian Aestheticism* (Chapel Hill, NC and London: University of North Carolina Press, 1990).

Denneny, M., et al. (eds), *The View from Christopher Street* (London and NY: Cassell, 1984).

Dollimore, Jonathan, *Sexual Dissidence: Augustine to Wilde, Freud to Foucault* (New York and Oxford: Oxford University Press, 1991).

Dowling, Linda, *Hellenism and Homosexuality in Victorian Oxford* (Ithaca, NY and London: Cornell University Press, 1994).

Edel, Leon, *Henry James: A Life* (London: Collins, 1985).

—— *Henry James: The Untried Years* (New York: J.B. Lippincott, 1962).

—— *Henry James: The Conquest of London* (New York: J.B. Lippincott, 1962).

—— *Henry James: The Middle Years* (New York: J.B. Lippincott, 1962).
—— *Henry James: The Treacherous Years* (Philadelphia: J.P. Lippincott, 1969).
—— *Henry James: The Master* (New York: J.B. Lippincott, 1972).
Eifenbein, Andrew, *Byron and the Victorians* (Cambridge: Cambridge University Press, 1995).
Ellmann, Richard, *a long the riverrun* (New York: Knopf, 1984).
—— 'James amongst the Aesthetes', in John R. Bradley, ed., *Henry James and Homo-Erotic Desire* (Basingstoke: Macmillan, 1999).
—— *Oscar Wilde* (New York: Knopf, 1988).
Fielder, Leslie A., *Love and Death in the American Novel* (New York: Stein and Day, 1960; rev. edition 1966/1975).
Foucault, Michel, *The History of Sexuality*, trans. Robert Hurley (New York: Vintage, 1980).
Freedman, Jonathan, *Professions of Taste: Henry James, British Aestheticism, and Commodity Culture* (Stanford, Calif. and London: Stanford University Press, 1990).
Freud, Sigmund, *The Standard Works of the Complete Psychological Works of Sigmund Freud*, trans. James Strachey, 24 Vols (London: The Hogarth Press, 1973–4).
Fryer, Jonathan, *André and Oscar: Gide, Wilde and the Art of Gay Living* (London: André Deutsch, 1997).
Gagnier, Regenia, *Idylls of the Marketplace: Oscar Wilde and the Victorian Public* (Stanford, Calif. and London: Stanford University Press, 1986).
Gay, Peter, The *Bourgeois Experience: Victoria to Freud* (Oxford and New York: Oxford University Press, 1984).
Geismar, Maxwell, *Henry James and His Cult* (London: Chatto & Windus, 1964).
Graham, Wendy, 'Henry James's Thwarted Love', in Carol Siegel et al., eds, *Eroticism and Containment: Notes from the Flood Plain. Genders 20 (New York: New York University Press, 1994).*
—— 'Henry James's Subterranean Blues: A Rereading of *The Princess Casamassima*', *Modern Fiction Studies*, Vol. 40, No. 1 (Spring 1994).
Gordon, Lyndall, *A Private Life of Henry James: Two Women and his Art* (London: Chatto & Windus, 1998).
Gosse, Edmund, 'Henry James', *The London Mercury*, No. 7 (1920).
Grosskurth, Phyllis, *The Woeful Victorian: A Biography of John Addington Symonds* (London: Longmans, Green & Co, 1964).
Gunter, Susan E. and Jobe, Steven H. (eds.), *Dearly Beloved Friends: Henry James's Letters to Younger Men,* in John R. Bradley, ed., *Henry James and Homo-Erotic Desire* (Basingstoke: Macmillan, 1999).
Hall, Richard, 'Henry James: Interpreting an Obsessive Memory', *Journal of Homosexuality*, Vol. 8, Nos 3/4 (1983).
Haralson, Eric, 'The Elusive Queerness of Henry James's "Queer Comrade": Reading Gabriel Nash of *The Tragic Muse*', in Richard Dellamora, ed., *Victorian Sexual Dissidence* (Chicago and London: University of Chicago Press, 1999).
—— 'Lambert Strether's Excellent Adventure', in Jonathan Freedman, ed.,

The Cambridge Companion to Henry James (Cambridge: Cambridge University Press, 1998).

Harstock, Mildred E., 'Henry James and the Cities of the Plain', *Modern Language Quarterly*, No. 29 (1968).

Hollinghurst, Alan, 'The Creative Uses of Homosexuality in the Novels of E.M. Forster, Ronald Firbank and L.P. Hartley', unpublished M.Litt. thesis (Bodleian Library, Oxford, 1980).

Horne, Philip, 'Henry James: the Master and the "Queer Affair" of "The Pupil"', *Critical Quarterly*, Vol. 37, No. 3 (Autumn 1995).

Hoy, Helen, 'Homotextual Duplicity in Henry James's "The Pupil"', *The Henry James Review*, Vol. 14, No. 1 (Winter 1994).

James, Henry, 'The Aspern Papers', 'The Author of *Beltraffio*', 'The Beast in the Jungle', 'The Death of the Lion', 'In the Cage', 'The Pupil', and 'The Turn of the Screw', in Leon Edel, ed., *The Complete Tales of Henry James*, 12 Vols (London: Rupert Hart Davis, 1962–4).

—— *The Ambassadors*, ed. Christopher Butler (Oxford: Oxford University Press, 1985).

—— *The American*, ed. William Spengemann (Harmondsworth: Penguin, 1981).

—— *The Art of Criticism: Henry James on the Theory and Practice of Fiction*, eds. William Veeder and Susan M. Griffin (Chicago and London: Chicago University Press, 1986).

—— 'The Author of *Beltraffio*', in Frank Kermode, ed., *The Figure in the Carpet and Other Stories* (Harmondsworth: Penguin, 1986).

—— *Autobiography*, ed. F.W. Dupee (New York: Criterion Books, 1956).

—— *The Complete Notebooks of Henry James*, eds. Leon Edel and Lyall H. Powers (Oxford and New York: Oxford University Press, 1987).

—— *The Complete Plays of Henry James*, ed. Leon Edel (London: Rupert Hart Davis, 1949).

—— *Confidence*, in *Henry James: Novels: 1871–1880* (New York: Library of America, 1983).

—— *Henry James: A Life in Letters*, ed. Philip Horne (London: Allen Lane, 1999).

—— *Henry James Letters*, 4 Vols, ed. Leon Edel (Cambridge, Mass: Harvard University Press, 1974–84).

—— *Italian Hours* (New York: Charles Scribner's Sons, 1909).

—— '*Kismet*', *The Nation*, No. 24 (1877), p. 341.

—— 'A Light Man', in Maqbool Aziz, ed., *The Tales of Henry James, Vol 1: 1864–1869* (Oxford: Oxford University Press, 1973).

—— *Notes on Novelists and Some Other Notes* (New York: Charles Scribner's Sons, 1914).

—— *The Portrait of a Lady*, ed. Robert D. Bamberg (New York: W.H. Norton, 1975).

—— *Roderick Hudson*, ed. Geoffrey Moore (Harmondsworth: Penguin, 1986).

—— *The Sacred Fount*, ed. John Lyon (Harmondsworth: Penguin, 1994).

—— *Selected Letters of Henry James to Edmund Gosse, 1882–1915: A Literary Friendship*, ed. Rayburn S. Moore (Baton Rouge and London: Louisiana

State University Press, 1988).

—— *The Tragic Muse*, ed., R.P. Blackmur (New York: Dell Publishing, 1961).

—— *Watch and Ward* (New York: Grove Press, 1960; repr. 1979).

Kabbani, Rana, *Imperial Fictions: Europe's Myths of Orient* (Basingstoke: Macmillan, 1986; repr. by Pandora, with corrections, 1994).

Kaplan, Fred, *Henry James: The Imagination of Genius* (New York: William Morrow, 1992).

Knox, Melissa, '*Beltraffio*: Henry James's Secrecy', *American Imago*, Vol. 3, No. 3 (Fall 1986).

Kuhn, Reinhard, *Corruption in Paradise: The Child in Western Literature* (Chicago and London: University of Chicago Press, 1982).

Martin, Robert K., 'The "High Felicity" of Comradeship: A New Reading of *Roderick Hudson*', *American Literary Realism*, No. 11 (Spring 1978).

Matthiessen, F.O., *The James Family: A Group Biography* (New York: Knopf, 1948).

Mix, Katherine, *A Study in Yellow: The Yellow Book and its Contributors* (London: Macmillan, 1960).

Murray, Stephen O., 'Some Nineteenth-Century Reports of Islamic Homosexuality', in Stephen O. Murray and Will Roscoe, eds, *Islamic Homosexualities: Culture, History and Literature* (New York and London: New York University Press, 1997).

Novick, Sheldon M., *Henry James: The Young Master* (New York: Random House, 1996)

—— 'Introduction', in John R. Bradley, ed., *Henry James and Homo-Erotic Desire* (Basingstoke: Macmillan, 1999).

Pater, Walter, *Plato and Platonism* (London: Macmillan, 1893).

—— *Three Major Texts*, ed. William E. Buckler (New York and London: New York University Press, 1986).

Person, Leland S., 'Homo-Erotic Desire in the Tales of Writers and Artists', in John R. Bradley, ed., *Henry James and Homo-Erotic Desire* (Basingstoke: Macmillan, 1999).

Reade, Brian (ed.), *Sexual Heretics: Male Homosexuality in English Literature from 1850 to 1900* (London: Routledge & Kegan Paul, 1970).

Reid, Forrest, *The Garden God* (London: Brilliance Books, 1986).

—— *Peter Waring* (London: Faber and Faber, 1937).

—— *Private Road* (London: Faber and Faber, 1940).

Rowe, John Carlos, *The Other Henry James* (North Carolina, and London: Duke University Press, 1998).

—— 'Hawthorne's Ghost in Henry James's Italy: Sculptural Form, Romantic Narrative, and the Function of Sexuality', *The Henry James Review* 20 (1999).

Salmon, Richard, *Henry James and the Culture of Publicity* (Cambridge: Cambridge University Press, 1997).

Sarotte, George-Michelle, *Like a Brother/Like a Lover: Male Homosexuality in the American Novel and Theatre from Herman Melville to James Baldwin* (Garden City, NY: Doubleday, 1978).

Savoy, Eric, 'Reading Gay America', in Robert K. Martin, ed., *The Continuing*

Presence of Walt Whitman: The Life After the Life (Iowa City: University of Iowa Press, 1992).

—— '*In the Cage* and the Queer Effects of History', *Novel*, No. 28 (1995).

Sedgwick, Eve Kosofsky, 'Shame and Performativity: Henry James's New York Edition Prefaces', in David McWhirter, ed., *Henry James's New York Edition: The Construction of Authorship* (Stanford, Calif. and London: Stanford University Press, 1995).

—— *Epistemology of the Closet* (Berkeley and Los Angeles: University of California Press, 1990).

Seidman, Steven, *Romantic Longings: Love in America, 1830–1980* (New York and London: Routledge, 1991).

Seiler, R. M. (ed.), *Walter Pater: The Critical Heritage* (London: Routledge & Kegan Paul, 1980).

Siegel, Lee, '*Literary License*: How "Queer Theory" Mindlessly Sexualizes Henry James, William Shakespeare, and Just about Everything Else', *The New Republic* (9 November 1998).

Silverman, Kaja, *Male Subjectivity at the Margins* (London and New York: Routledge, 1992).

Sinfield, Alan, *The Wilde Century: Effeminacy, Oscar Wilde and the Queer Movement* (London and New York: Cassell, 1994).

Showalter, Elaine, *Sexual Anarchy: Gender and Culture at the Fin de Siècle* (London: Bloomsbury, 1991).

Stevens, Hugh, *Henry James and Sexuality* (Cambridge: Cambridge University Press, 1998).

—— 'Queer Henry *In the Cage*', in Jonathan Freedman, ed., *The Cambridge Companion to Henry James* (Cambridge: Cambridge University Press, 1998).

Swaab, Peter, 'Hopkins and the Pushed Peach', *Critical Quarterly*, Vol. 37, No. 3 (Autumn 1995).

Symonds, John Addington, *Studies in the Greek Poets*, 2nd Series (London: Smith, 1876).

—— *A Problem in Greek Ethics and Other Essays*, ed. John Lauristen (New York: The Pagan Press, 1993).

—— *The Memoirs of John Addington Symonds*, ed. Phyllis Grosskurth (London: Hutchinson, 1984).

Thesiger, Wilfred, *Arabian Sands* (London: Collins, 1959).

Tintner, Adeline R., *The Book World of Henry James* (Ann Arbor: UMI Research Press, 1987).

—— 'A Gay Sacred Fount: the Reader as Detective', *Twentieth-Century Literature*, Vol. 41, No. 2 (Summer 1995).

—— 'Henry James and Byron: A Victorian Romantic Friendship', *The Byron Journal*, No. 9 (1981).

—— *The Pop World of Henry James: From Fairy Tales to Science Fiction* (Ann Arbor: UMI Research Press, 1989).

Turner, Jane (ed.), *The Dictionary of Art*, 35 Vols (London: Macmillan, 1996).

Van Leer, David, *The Queening of America: Gay Culture in Straight Society* (London and New York: Routledge, 1995).

Vidal, Gore, *United States: Selected Essays: 1952–1992* (London: André

Deutsch, 1992).

Walpole, Hugh, 'Henry James: A Reminiscence', *Horizon*, Vol. 1, No. 2 (1940).

Walton, Priscilla L., *The Disruption of the Feminine in Henry James* (Toronto: University of Toronto Press, 1992).

Ward, Mrs Humphry, *A Writer's Recollections* (London: Macmillan, 1916).

Weeks, Jeffrey, *Coming Out: Homosexual Politics in Britain from the Nineteenth-century to the Present* (London: Quartet, 1977).

White, Allon, *The Uses of Obscurity: The Fiction of Early Modernism* (London: Routledge & Kegan Paul, 1981).

Woods, Gregory, *A History of Gay Literature: A World Survey* (New Haven and London: Yale University Press, 1998).

Zwinger, Linda, 'Bodies that Don't Matter: The Queering of "Henry James"', *Modern Fiction Studies*, Vol. 41, Nos 3–4 (Fall–Winter 1995).

Index